A COMMONPLACE KILLING

A COMMONPLACE KILLING

SIÂN BUSBY

ISIS

LARGE PRINT

Oxford

First published in Great Britain 2013
by
Short Books

Published in Large Print 2014 by ISIS Publishing Ltd.,
7 Centremead, Osney Mead, Oxford OX2 0ES
by arrangement with
Short Books

CIP data is available for this title from the British Library

ISBN 978–1–4450–9938–5 (hb)
ISBN 978–1–4450–9939–2 (pb)

Printed and bound in Great Britain by
T. J. International Ltd., Padstow, Cornwall

An Introduction by Robert Peston

Siân Elizabeth Busby died on September 4 2012 after a long illness. A few days later I transcribed her handwritten manuscript for the end of *A Commonplace Killing,* her final novel. My motive was selfish: I wanted to keep talking to her. I still do. The tears could not be staunched as I read, deciphered and typed. Foggy-brained, the transcription was spoiled by spelling mistakes and typographical errors. All mine. Siân's prose was as pellucid and accurate as ever. And brave. Here she was, all hope lost of reprieve from the lethal cancer, reflecting on what it is like to know that death awaits on the morrow.

What caught me off guard is that the work is complete, and — for me at least — more or less perfect. Siân worked on it until the illness became excruciating and wholly incapacitating. I did not know, until reading handwriting as familiar as my own and hearing her voice in my head, that she had finished this exquisite work. I should have guessed. When Siân put her formidable mind to a project, whether it was teaching herself to read as an infant, years before going to school, or curating a museum on the history of Judaism (a non-Jew, she could hold her own in a scholarly spat with the rabbis, and inevitably knew far more about my inherited faith than me), or directing a 19-hour Chinese opera, she always triumphed. And as if to accentuate my own vanity, she was never smug, always dissatisfied with her own efforts, routinely critical of her achievements.

Given more time, she would have embellished the final handwritten section of *A Commonplace Killing,* which you can find in this edition from page 259 onward. It is not quite as rich in detail and description as the earlier part of the book. But I am not sure that matters. A lost world still pulsates in the slightly more spare and sparse narrative. If anything, I found the starker prose more moving, although I cannot claim to be a detached reader.

It is a difficult question whether the circumstances in which a book is written, or any work of art forged, are relevant to our appreciation of it. I am clear that Siân would not have wished you to make any allowances for her debilitated state during the act of creation. But you do not need to indulge her. *A Commonplace Killing* is a jewel. Even so, for the proud spouse, if not for Siân, it matters that she finished the book after she had received her death sentence. On August 3 2012, the consultant oncologist at the Royal Marsden, Sanjay Popat, a compassionate, assiduous and expert physician whom we came to think of as a friend during the years he was in charge of Siân's treatment, gave us the latest in a succession of scan results. Medical science could no longer help Siân, except — perhaps — to take the edge off acute and constant pain. "This is where I say goodbye," he said.

It was almost exactly five years to the day after Siân — who is probably the only person I know who has never smoked a cigarette — was diagnosed with lung cancer.

In the ensuing years, she never despaired or resorted to self-pity, even as the cancer spread, on a couple of occasions to the brain, later to the liver and spine. The cycle of surgery, body-racking chemicals and radiation was relentless. Life became punctuated by terrible shocks and emergencies. Yet those who met her at pretty much any point in this ordeal encountered the Siân they had always known: solicitous, supportive, witty, insightful, unselfish. Through the sheer force of her will, Siân remained poised and beautiful. She eschewed drama. Most of our friends had no idea how ill she really was. Siân did not wish to be seen by others as someone who was suffering from a lethal cancer. She did not want to be classified as infirm and she did not need maudlin sympathy. The priority was that our boys, Max and Simon, should not be constantly bothered and worried by friends and neighbours asking for the latest prognosis on her health. Siân just got on with living.

Her huge magnificent novel, *McNaughten* — which for me is the last great Victorian novel, a symphony of fantastical stories, rich in disquisitions on the absurdity of life — was written when Siân's illness had become for us just one of those things. I know this may seem odd, but these were wonderful years for Siân, Max, Simon and me. The cancer did not haunt us. If anything, it helped us to understand what matters in life: family, first and foremost; work that fulfils; friends, beauty and fun.

By the time Siân was completing *A Commonplace Killing,* the cancer could no longer be confined to the background. It was a monster laying waste to our family. Siân was being turned into an invalid, in almost unimaginable pain most of the time. For her, what was perhaps worse, was that she was being robbed of her ability to take care of those she loved. Even so, Siân somehow put what I might euphemistically describe as her personal cares to one side, and got down to finishing the book you have in your hands. This probably seems slightly bonkers, given the overwhelming and unstoppable facts of her mortal illness. But she (and I) had an important if not wholly rational conviction that where there is life there is hope, that there is no point living in constant fear, and that there is an almost moral imperative not to be ground down by circumstances, even if those circumstances are an express train thundering in our direction.

Writing for Siân was not work but part of who she was. I kept letters that she wrote to me when we were at university more than 30 years ago and when we were too briefly a couple in our very early twenties (we were then apart for a dozen years). Here is funny, beautiful and fizzing 18-year-old Siân, not long out of the local comp (like me), writing to me at Balliol from Sussex University:

"I've been concentrating on a new theory of political power and ideology, a bit outside my scope of course, although I do have 'O' Level Sociology. The crux of my theory is that the ruling class maintain power because they are 'softies', not exactly homosexuals or anything, but — you know — they read books and newspapers like *The Times* and listen to classical music, etc, all of which the average oppressed individual, because of ingrained social attitudes, regards as a bit 'wet', thus preventing him from ever attaining any position of power. His own undeveloped tastes are of course amply catered for by the media (weapon of the ruling class by which they perpetrate the ideology suited to the status quo), which tells them (by stereotypical representations) that those attributes which are conducive to political power are 'a bit wet'.

"I gleaned this theory from compulsive reading of the Beano, which portrays the class struggle in such terms, especially in the characterisation of Dennis the Menace (proletarian) and Walter 'the Softie' (surely a future member of the elite — en route for a university career and possibly a political career afterwards). Walter is seen as the butt of all Dennis's pranks — mystifying the real area of oppression represented only in the slippering Dennis receives from his father at the end of each strip: implying that it is wrong to make fun of the elite, at the same time as putting Dennis the Menace over as a real 'working class hero' — but (ironically) not in the revolutionary sense, for Dennis is oppressed by his behaviour to Walter, which is symptomatic of the attitude that the elite are 'soft' and the working classes want nothing to do with them or their means of power.

"I hope all this is of some use to you PPE students at Oxford."

Siân's own family background was more Menace than Softie. On one side, they had been tenant dairy

ix

farmers in West Wales for hundreds of years, never wealthy although respectable and respectful. Others of her forebears were more working class, from South Wales, and horse dealers from Essex. Her own childhood was 1960s bohemian: a mercurial and irascible actor father who bolted, no money to spare, stability provided by devoted and adored grandparents, Nanny and Bumby. To a large extent, Siân and her younger sister Nicole had to bring themselves up. From a pretty early age, as far as I can gather, Siân was clear that escape from the shackles of birth meant trying to emulate Walter the Softie: I have never met anyone as well read or brainy, nor with such enduring passion for self-improvement, as Siân.

What she made of herself was beyond the hopes and dreams of her antecedents. Her Bumby was a hatter, who latterly specialised in novelty fairground hats; she was told by her grandmother that a bright girl like her could do very well as secretary and Girl Friday to a City gent. Siân had just enough confidence, encouraged by friends such as my own parents (she was a school friend of my sister Juliet), to be more ambitious for herself, and she became the first of her line to go to university. But, to be clear, she was not interested in conventional power, or fame or glory, about which she was scathing. All she ever wanted to do was make things. She was an artist.

After university, Siân spent 20 years as a maker of arts films and television documentaries, interspersed with dancing in avant-garde cabaret, making learned exhibitions and creating ambitious "immersive" events long before that became fashionable (with a group of talented artists, collectively called 2Step, most of whom were strong, self-deprecating women like herself). It was not till 2000, when the BBC and Channel 4 were no longer commissioning enough serious arts programmes to sustain a full-time career in filming operas and ballets, that Siân discovered what I had always seen as her proper vocation: writing.

Although the style and content of her five books — *A Wonderful Little Girl*, *Boudicca*, *The Cruel Mother*, *McNaughten* and *A Commonplace Killing* — are dizzyingly diverse, they are a recognisable family. Madness, depression and the hard-to-fathom workings of the human mind are recurring themes. The history of her own forebears is explicit in one book, *The Cruel Mother*, and implicit in the rest. The places where she (and I) grew up and have lived are usually recognisable, if transplanted to an earlier age. Or to put it another way, the books are all conspicuously Siân.

In a way, *A Commonplace Killing* is the most Siân of all. The story was sparked by a sordid murder that happened in Holloway shortly after the end of the Second World War. She had been told about it by Nanny and Bumby. For several years, she had talked to me about how she felt there was a book to be made from her memory of a scandal that was still being discussed in her family when we were children in the 1960s. The north London she depicts is a London that she and I remember from our childhoods: when we were growing up, bomb-sites remained relatively commonplace; Holloway, Islington and Camden were places not of multi-million pound homes for investment bankers but of relative squalor and poverty; rationing may have long since disappeared, but our parents talked of the war as a comparatively recent event.

I think Siân was determined to finish this novel partly to prove her victory over her illness, and partly because she would have thought of it as honouring her past, especially Nanny and Bumby. It was in the second week of August that she tied up the loose ends. It was a characteristically blustery summer day in West Wales. Siân sat, feet tucked under her bottom — as neat, elegant and self-contained as ever — on the sofa of our small flat overlooking the Aberystwyth prom, alternating her gaze between the spume of glorious Cardigan Bay and her notebook.

Given the advanced state of her illness, it was remarkable that she had the energy to work for as long as she did. But it was not for another five weeks, till the weekend of September 15, that I was brave enough to read her manuscript and could marvel at her victory over devastating circumstance. Because as you will see, her final reflections, written without sentimentality, and not mawkish or maudlin in any way, are about the imminence of death and how so many of us waste our talents and our time on earth. And although there is the melancholy and shadows of the flickering flame, there is also a faith in a better life that has been tested but not broken.

Siân was neither ready for her own death nor reconciled to it. Very occasionally she grumbled against the palpable unfairness, but she was courageous and stoical to an extent that tested my credulity. Close to the end, after we had returned from Aberystwyth to the north London that shaped us, Siân endured a restless troubled night in the Marie Curie Hospice in Hampstead. I was with her all the time, sleeping on a mattress on the floor. She was never once hysterical; she was dignified and calm throughout the worsening nightmare. But having been pressed by the consultant who visited her one morning very close to the end, she conceded that she experienced night-time anxieties about never again waking up. Minutes after Dr Lodge left us, she turned to me. "Did I tell the doctor I was frightened of dying?" she asked, in a weak voice, eyes barely able to open. "He must think I am really stupid."

And there is the authentic voice of the woman I loved for most of my conscious life (we became friends as teenagers although it was not till we were in our mid-thirties that I finally did the one really inspired thing I have ever done, which was to ask her to live with me and then marry me). She was the most brilliant, caring, humane and loving person I have met. And funny. I miss her all the time. I hope you derive a sense of her rare qualities from *A Commonplace Killing*.

R.P.
December 29 2012

For my darling boys, with all my love

Author's Note

In constructing this story I have followed closely the police files on several murders committed in London in the immediate aftermath of World War Two, ensuring that details of detective procedure and police investigatory methods at that time are as accurate as possible. All the locations exist or existed at the time; anything else that is knowable has been reconstructed with as much attention to verisimilitude as possible. Everything else is the product of my imagination. Any resemblance to persons living or dead is purely coincidental.

"Won't it be wonderful — some day, one day —
when things are like they used to be?"

The Two Leslies, 1943

CHAPTER
ONE

That neglected triangle where the Camden, Holloway and Caledonian Roads intersect, long oppressed by soot and the continuous rumble of the railway, its bounds set by the gloomy bulk of the women's prison and the desolation of the empty Livestock Market, had been done for long before the Hitler War blasted every last vestige of respectability to smithereens. From the tops of buses you could see how, in other parts of town, the bomb-sites had been transformed by clumps of fireweed, willow-herb and ragwort; but in Holloway only fireplaces and doorframes, like overturned tombstones, protruded from rubble patches scattered with the broken bones of chimney pots. Within a few minutes' walk, you might find yourself passing Pentonville on hanging day, or the Crippen murder house; but for the most part Holloway languished in obscurity: a meagre landscape of peeling stucco and thwarted ambition unrolling in street after nondescript street of villas built in more aspirant times and gradually declined into bed-sitting rooms inhabited by prostitutes, Irish navvies, coloureds, army deserters. And then came the V-weapons, almost putting the whole lot out of its misery.

1

Most of that particular terrace was just about clinging on; which is to say that although a good portion of it was awaiting demolition, there was at that time only one house-sized space, marked off by a piece of rusting corrugated iron that guarded access to a bare stretch of emptiness, sparing passers-by one of those startling glimpses of the horizon, so unsettling to Londoners which, since the War, had become a common hazard of going out. We had come to refer to these vacant spaces as "bomb-sites"; this one, like all the others, was utterly devoid of life, history and anything else of value, with the exception of one unremarkable London plane. This tree was now all that stood between the street and the precipitous gully of the London and North Eastern Railway, since the Jerries, in aiming for the railway, had obliterated instead a cramped row of soot-blackened houses which had overlooked the track for the best part of a century. The bomb-site was now entirely at the mercy of regular wet suffusions of acridity; and every time a train shrieked along the tracks to and from King's Cross, the shattered houses on either side of it shuddered, silently relinquishing fragments of masonry.

A gang of kiddies spotted the leg sticking out from behind the plane tree. Through the smut-laden steamy shimmer, the heat of a midsummer morning, there was a woman's leg, stockinged and dressed in a high-heeled shoe, extending from a just-glimpsed skirt hem. The kiddies assumed it belonged to a shop-window dummy, dumped along with the pram skeleton, the chipped and overturned lavatory, the rubber johnnies and the lipstick-stained cigarette ends. They were going to throw stones at it when they realised that the leg belonged to the body of a woman. You could see nearly all of her chest. Her wide-open eyes stared past the plane tree leaves to the sky beyond. Her tongue stuck out of the corner of her mouth, swollen like a lump of raw liver. The blue and red stripes around her neck told at a glance how life had been wrung out of her by a pair of human hands.

Nobody — not even the kiddies — was all that surprised to find her there. These things happened: more and more these days. Holloway was a dump, peace not yet a way of life, and the war had laid waste to everything, leaving common decencies bereft and clinging on for dear life, shrapnel-pocked, shuddering in the aftermath of the great prolonged shriek as they let go of the old certainties.

CHAPTER
TWO

Her first thought upon waking was that bread would be going on the ration on Monday and she had better get up quickly and go down to Nag's Head in search of some. She checked her wristwatch. It was seven o'clock, which meant that there would already be a queue outside the baker's, even though he didn't open until eight. Some people had nothing better to do than stand in queues all day. She couldn't bear the thought that she might be one of them. She sighed and considered not getting up, not joining the queue, not buying bread. She wondered how much longer this was going to go on for. How much more she could take? Everything was somehow less than what it had been before — before the war had begun; before it had ended. The war had been over for more than a year, but it was still there, still deciding everything. The war this; the war that; before the war; during the war; and now, after the war. It got on her nerves.

She had been tired since 1939. It had been exhausting, wondering whether you were going to die in the next air-raid, worrying yourself sick about Douglas. Walter had only had a desk job, but he had still been sent overseas; she had lain awake at nights wondering what she would do if he was sent home a cripple. She hadn't given a great deal of thought to how they would carry on if he came home whole and entire, because hardly anyone thought that far ahead in the war. You told yourself that there would be a time when everything was like it had been before, but you didn't really believe it; hoping against hope, that was it, for six years. Even as she was taking down the blackout curtains she was wondering how long it would be before she would be putting them up again.

Walter, in the bed beside her, rolled over on to his side, snoring slightly; the bed-springs creaking. The whole house creaked. It was a pity that the Germans hadn't brought the whole lot down, then they might have got one of those Orlit homes, like she'd seen in a newsreel: fitted kitchens, indoor lavs and little bits of garden.

"Jerry-built rot," Wally had said. "Temporary homes for temporary lives."

But the pre-fabs were better than the bomb-site they lived in, which was falling to pieces around their ears. They couldn't even go in the front parlour because of the bombing.

It's the future, she thought. You had to move with the times. And the idea of staying put appalled her. It wasn't just the house — she had lived in plenty of dumps before — it was everything. It was Holloway; it was making do; it was standing in queues all day until your legs ached; it was Walter. It wasn't that she had wanted him to be dead; it was just that she hadn't wanted him to come back to her. The day he came home he had sat at the kitchen table in his uniform, with his kit-bag on the floor, eating a plate of fish-paste sandwiches.

"We shall have to give it a go, old girl," he declared, "be a proper family again — for the boy's sake." And the whole course of the rest of her life had been decided.

She should have told him there and then that the War had changed everything, but you felt obliged to pretend the past six years hadn't happened; that everything was still like it had been: it was what everyone was doing. And with his sad grin, looking so diminished, so battered and spent, she had felt sorry for him. She sighed and followed a crack across the width of the ceiling. If she was to have any chance of finding some bread, she would have to get up and commence the drudgery of her day. Bread was going on the ration on Monday. She sighed again. It all fell on her shoulders, always, and she was sick to death of it. She fantasised about putting her head in the oven, or swallowing a mouthful of bleach. The notion always made her feel a brief flicker of triumph. They would all be sorry then, she thought.

She left the bed and crossed to the dressing table. It was already bright and sunny outside; not that she bothered to look out of the window: she knew what was there, and it was nothing worth seeing. The sun's glare only made everything look worse, and no matter how warm it was outside, inside the house it was always damp. She listened to the familiar sound of something falling between the walls, and thought about running away. Why shouldn't she have the sort of life where you dressed for dinner and met people for cocktails? This line of thinking always brought her down, and she was soon telling herself not to be such a bloody fool. Men were not going to fall like ninepins any more: she would end up desiccated and lonely, working as a waitress in a nasty little café and living in dingy lodgings somewhere awful, somewhere just as bad as Holloway. Kentish Town. Brecknock. A good smack in the eye that would be.

It was usual, at this point in the habitual train of thought, that she would gratify herself by asking how they would all get by without her doing everything; imagine Walter finally realising how much she did for him. She didn't think much about Douglas: he was nearly eighteen, courting and working in an office; she doubted that he would miss her all that much. Her sister Mavis would have to come up from Jaywick to take care of Mother, which would serve Mavis right. She had treated them all like dirt when they went to her in the war: people who'd been billeted on strangers were treated better. She had hardly bothered with Mother for the past three years, and no doubt wouldn't bother with her now. She had no doubt that Mavis would have Mother put away, and there was no way she wanted that on her conscience. It often came to this impasse; or sometimes she would persuade herself that Douglas was at that difficult age when a son needed his mother. If she was able to assure herself that both Douglas and Mother would get along without her, then she would work herself into indignation asking why she should be the one to leave when she was the one who

7

had worked her fingers to the bone keeping everything together all through the war. And besides, it was her house — or rather it was Mother's house — so why should she be the one to go and live in a bed-sitting room? Surely, Walter ought to be the one to leave. She generally sat at the dressing table for some time, as she did on this particular morning, turning all of this over and over in her mind before acknowledging that she was stuck with her rotten life.

She reached across for her pigskin handbag, rummaging inside it for her cigarette case and lighter. It was a filthy habit that she had picked up during the war, partly on account of her nerves, and partly because when you were out with a gang they all smoked, and the men liked to offer you one so that they could reach across to light it for you. There was something really rather marvellous about steadying a man's hand as he lit you; looking deep in his eyes. Being a mother, she had not had to take a factory job or join the services; she had chosen instead to do her bit for married servicemen on leave, GIs looking for a little fun before they went off to the front: all those wonderful men, so handsome in their uniforms. During the war any reasonably good-looking girl could have had the time of her life; and even though she had been touching forty, she had been more than a little good-looking. She supposed that now that the war was over there really was no reason any longer to smoke. She supposed that she ought really to give it up. Cigarettes were so expensive these days, and decent ones difficult to come by; but she only ever had two at the most: one in the morning and one on a Saturday evening when she went out to the pictures or the variety hall. She didn't go mad when the shops ran out, not like Evelyn did.

She was inspecting her features in the mirror for signs of aging; the smoke softening the blow. She pulled the skin of her cheekbones taut and told herself that nobody would ever guess that she was forty-three with a grown-up son. Then she irritably stubbed out her half-smoked cigarette in the ashtray. Her frayed nerves showed on her unmade-up face: six years of sirens and bomb blasts and red tape and shortages. She pulled out her hair rollers one by one, releasing dyed, but not brassy, blonde curls; she brushed them out bitterly. She supposed the back must look a frightful mess; she would ask Evelyn to help her with it later on: she liked to look nice when she went to the pictures. It was all she had to look forward to these days.

She tied her dressing gown around her and crossed back to the bed. Wally stirred slightly, muttering to himself as she picked up the chamber pot from underneath his side of the bed. She went out on to the landing, pausing at the top of the stairs.

"Evelyn," she called up to the attic, "I say, Evelyn, I've got to go out and buy some bread."

She stood in the drab wall-papered silence, listening to the pattern of her breathing, following the line of another deep crack along the length of the banister.

"Evvie, dear," she repeated, a little louder this time. "Would you mind getting Walter and Douglas their breakfast while I'm up at the shops?"

There was a low murmur of assent from the attic; the creak of bed-springs. She went downstairs and emptied the chamber pot in the outside lav.

The kitchen was also the parlour, since a V-weapon, which had taken out a fair bit of the street, had rendered the front part of the house unsuitable for occupation. The parlour ceiling had fallen down with the impact, which had also taken out the windows, which were still boarded up. At meal-times four of them crammed around the drop-leaf table in the kitchen with the wireless in the middle, getting on one another's nerves, until Douglas and Evelyn went to their own rooms, leaving her alone with Walter and their accumulation of weariness, regret and resentment. She threw a couple of pieces of coke and some rubbish from the scraps pail into the boiler and fanned the fire by opening and closing the door. The boiler took a while to get going, and Wally insisted on its being turned off by ten o'clock every morning in order to conserve fuel. How fortunate it was for the rest of them that she was always up in time to ensure that there would be enough hot water. She stabbed at the fire for a few moments, then banged the poker on the grate and went to look inside the bread crock. There was almost half a loaf, enough to do for breakfast. She ran it under the tap until it was almost saturated, crossed to the range, lit the gas and popped the sodden loaf in the oven. Then she filled the kettle and waited for it to boil.

Mother's tray consisted of a cup of milky tea and one or two digestive biscuits, and laying it and taking it up to the old lady was the sort of task which Evelyn could easily have offered to take care of each day; but Evelyn hardly ever did anything without being asked, and most of the time it was easier to do it yourself. She had only herself to blame for allowing this situation to develop, and perhaps because of this, it played badly on her nerves.

Evelyn was a nice kid, if a bit common; and although there were plenty of things about her that drove her potty, in the main they got along pretty well. They had met at a dance in the last year of the war. She had felt sorry for the girl. Both her parents had been killed in the same incident, leaving the kid on her own and only seventeen. When Evelyn had been bombed out of her lodgings, she hadn't thought twice about asking her if she wanted to rent the attic room; the extra money had come in useful, and they had been company for one another, sharing ups and downs, confidences. It was better to go out on the town with another woman, even if people did assume that Evelyn was her daughter. When the war ended, Evelyn lost her job in the factory and had been living in the attic — rent-free! — ever since. Lately it had seemed that liberties were being taken. Rooms were hard to come by and they could easily have asked fifteen bob a week for the attic: the exact sum on numerous "To Let" postcards in the tobacconist's window. If the kid had ever once offered to help out around the house instead of paying rent the situation would have been a little more acceptable, but the offer was never made. Perhaps this was just as well: she could clean the whole house from top to bottom in the time it took Evelyn to put on her stockings; and once the kid had put the best part of a cabbage in the pig-bin. It got on her nerves, but she could never have put Evelyn out on the streets. The kid was flighty and none too bright: left to her own devices she would almost certainly end up in trouble or in Holloway prison, or both.

She swallowed a few mouthfuls of tea and ate half of one of Mother's digestives before taking the tray upstairs. There was no point depending on other people. Only the selfish, like Walter and Evelyn and Mavis, seemed to be able to do that. Her problem was, she was not selfish, which meant she was put upon. She had stayed out of pity for them all. It felt better to think about it that way; better than acknowledging that you stayed because you were afraid to leave.

Mother's room was curtain-heavy, thick with dust and chamber-pot odours. Apart from during air-raids, when they used to shove her underneath it, the only time Mother had ever left her bed in the past couple of years was to be sat on the commode. She leaned over the tiny white head that was poking out from the top of the candlewick bedspread and checked it for signs of life, and when she was sure that Mother had not passed away in the night, briskly pulled back the bedclothes. The waft of ammonia smarted her eyes.

"Mother," she said, "wake up, dear. It's time for you to go." The old lady blinked dazedly as the sodden nightdress was pulled over her fragile bones. "Let's get you on the po, dear. One. Two. Three . . ."

With the poor old thing drooped on the commode in naked and bewildered silence, she checked the bed. The frayed towel that Mother had been lying on was sopping wet, but the bedspread was only a little bit damp, and only needed airing. She opened the window and put it on the ledge. The towel and the nightdress would all need washing, but unless she could persuade Evelyn to take care of it, that would have to wait.

"I'm going up to Nag's Head," she said as she wiped down the rubber undersheet, Mother gazing at her in wonder. "I've got to try and get some bread. It's going on the ration on Monday." She fetched another threadbare towel from a pile at the end of the bed and spread it over the rubber sheet.

Before putting Mother back into bed, she inspected the worst of her bedsores, sprinkling Fuller's Earth on them; then she slipped a clean nightdress over the frail bones. She lifted the old lady off the commode, amazed, as she always was, that someone could be so diminished and yet still be here.

"You haven't the foggiest what I'm on about, have you, Mum?" she said. "Never mind, dear: you're better off out of it. You really are."

The commode was full, which was good because it meant that the fresh towel would stay dry for a while. The amount of washing she did was terrible. She closed the seat. She would offer Evelyn a bob or two to deal with it. There was no time now to make another trip to the backyard, and it wasn't as if Mother would know one way or another. If she'd had more time she might have wiped the poor old thing's face and brushed her hair so that she looked a little less senile, but as far as anyone could tell, Mother didn't mind about that either.

She always used to look smart as a bandbox, she thought. Then she broke up the digestive biscuit into a saucer of lukewarm tea which she placed on the night-table. She knew that it would still be there the next time she checked.

CHAPTER
THREE

Divisional Detective Inspector Jim Cooper had been asleep in his armchair for no more than a few hours, perhaps three or four, when the telephone woke him on what was supposed to be his first day off in three months. Nodding off had not been a simple matter: it had taken a large glass of whisky and almost the whole of the Stokowski recording of the St John Passion — *It is done; such comfort for suffering human souls! I can see the end of the night of sorrow* — which was the last thing he could remember before the jangling of the telephone roused him.

His first thought was that it would be something bad. His second, as he stumbled to the hallway to pick up the receiver, was that he had been a damn fool to drink a tumbler of whisky on a pretty much empty stomach, especially when he ordinarily touched nothing more rigorous than a half-pint of Bass, and that only very infrequently. His third thought was that, with whisky at twenty-five bob a bottle (always supposing you could lay your hands on the stuff), the blasted jigger had cost him the best part of one and threepence.

He snatched up the receiver.

"Got a woman here who's been strangled, sir."

Unless discussing Arsenal FC or the post-war decline in goalkeeping, Detective Inspector Frank Lucas, the senior CID officer on duty at Caledonian Road over the weekend, was a man of very few words — all of them spoken with a weary inflection guaranteed to induce enervation in even the most ebullient of listeners.

"She's on a bomb-site, sir," Lucas continued, not waiting to be asked, "just off the Cally Road. Next to the railway line."

Cooper cursed. Tucking the receiver under his chin, he hunted among the accumulation of grubby scraps of paper on the hall table for a pencil and, having found one, attempted to scribble on the wall the address that Lucas was giving him. He cursed again when the lead snapped.

"I'll send a car, sir," said the detective inspector with an audible sigh; then there was a click and everything went dead.

Cooper dropped the receiver on to the rest, ran his hands through his hair and cursed again.

He had known it would be something bad, but this was terrible. A random sex killing is every detective's worst nightmare: they have the tendency to shatter the precarious routine of your life, eighteen hours a day for the foreseeable future; then there are the newspaper reporters; the misguided and the lunatic coming forward with their false leads and confessions, all of which must be checked out; and let us not forget Upstairs applying the thumbscrews. But worse than any of this is that every detective knows — even before he embarks on the investigation — that the chances of ever resolving a random sex killing are about as good as your chances of marrying Ingrid Bergman.

Caledonian Road. Cooper mused upon the rotten blasted luck of that. A few streets to the west or south and his opposite numbers in neighbouring "G" or "Y" Divisions would be thumping the wall in frustration. There was no comradeship: the Metropolitan Police Force was in the middle of an unprecedented crime boom; the number of offences committed since VE Day was more than twice that of 1939 and, despite numerous enticements, the force was still seven thousand men short. Scotland Yard could be depended upon to supply fingerprint experts, photographic boys and the boffins in the lab at Hendon, but the only way HQ would concern itself any further with such a commonplace matter as the murder of a tart in a bad area was if the DDI buggered up. And Jim Cooper was unlikely to do that.

He had not a single blemish on his conduct record; it had taken him just five years to make CID; and he had been the youngest ever DDI in London when he took over "N" Division at thirty-nine. No doubt they'd have preferred a family man, but it was war-time and most of the family men had joined up. He had not joined up, a despicable fact which in his more self-pitying moments made him want to grind his fists into his temples. His reasons for not joining up were lamentable, pathetic even. He had no wife and family to think of, and other men who did had thought nothing of making the gesture. He had done his bit in the last lot, drowning a thousand times a day in Passchendaele mud; but so had plenty of others who hadn't thought twice about joining up again. It was hard not to hate yourself for that. All through the war, every day, he must have asked himself a hundred times: "Am I a coward?" Of course, policing was a reserved occupation — some poor bloody idiot had to ensure that law and order were enforced after all — but this did not excuse him in his own mind. It counted for nothing when you walked into a pub and a chap in uniform looked you and your lounge suit up and down and muttered, "Some people!" as he pushed past you on his way out. The disgust conveyed in those two words . . .

And so, it didn't matter to Cooper that his appointment as DDI was as solid as they come; that everybody reckoned that he was among the very best when it came to the delicate tasks of tailing spivs and extracting information from narks; that even the most determined crooks had a sneaking regard for him. London was doubtless lucky that he had stayed behind and helped to see her through her darkest hour, but he took no personal pride in the fact. He knew every dismal inch of his manor from St Ann's Road to Highbury Vale, thousands of villainous faces were etched into his memory, he had sent many deserving souls to prison, recovered hundreds of thousands of pounds' worth of stolen property, but as far as he was concerned none of it counted one jot.

He ran an appraising hand across his stubble and wondered how bad it would look for a divisional detective inspector to attend a murder scene unshaven;

then he made his grudging way to the bathroom, where he took down his razor and shaving mug from the shelf above the sink and inspected his bloated and sagging features in the mirror. He was a little stouter than was ideal and well worn to the point of shabby, but his keen blue eyes could usually be depended upon to give a surprisingly youthful beam to the rest of him. Marjorie had once told him that he looked like the film star Joel McCrea. They'd been to see *Wells Fargo* at the Savoy on Holloway Road. He was trying to remember whether it was the first time they'd been to the pictures together, or the only time. He glanced at his watch and was pleased by what it told him. It had taken, what, fifteen, maybe twenty minutes: usually he was thinking about Marjorie as soon as he opened his eyes of a morning. Perhaps I am finally forgetting her, he thought; then he caught his reflection in the mirror. Who was he trying to kid? He had been miserable as sin every day since she had left him; and he knew damn well he would never forget how happy he had been. For a moment he wondered if he might cry. Come along, old man, he urged: it was a long time ago; almost another world. Before the war; before everything changed for ever. He certainly didn't look like a film star today. He grimaced at the bleary visage in the mirror. As a matter of fact, he looked even more battered than usual, if such a thing were possible. The youthful eyes were bloodshot and had retreated into the grey puffiness that surrounded them; and somewhere in the course of the previous evening's rough-housing he had collected a nice shiner on his right cheekbone. He stroked it. Nothing like the glint of a brass knuckleduster coming towards you to keep you in your place. He sighed. It was no more than he deserved.

He whipped up a meagre, rationed lather in his shaving mug, slapped it over his cheeks and chin and then scraped it off, painfully, ineffectually, resentfully, with a blunt safety razor. He had always held that not shaving on a Sunday was one of the few benefits to be derived from bachelorhood, which is in so many ways a wretched condition for a man to find himself in at forty-four; but Sundays were no longer any different from any other day. Weekend leave was a thing of the past; nights routinely broken by urgent summonses to derelict buildings, damp canal sides, desolate railway depots and all the other dismal settings which the most dispiriting areas of north London had to offer. Lorry-loads of tea, butter, cigarettes, whisky, even typewriters, were disappearing all over "N" Division, and the streets of Tottenham and Stamford Hill and Holloway were awash with stolen and forged coupons. There were opportunities for crime in every public house, variety hall, café and shopping street the length and breadth of the manor. And it was all, all of it, his problem.

He'd spent the night just past lying on a flat roof in Tottenham Hale, overlooking an alley reeking with other men's piss, watching the comings and goings from an "abandoned" warehouse. When he had given the order to his men, they'd come under a hail of bricks, bottles, blackjacks and armoured fists, but no razor-studded spuds. A pity, he thought ruefully; I could have done with a decent shave and a nice baked potato. They'd made two arrests and taken a haul of several thousands of pounds' worth of black-market sugar, though they had been looking for eggs — people can just about survive without stockings and cigarettes, but they need to eat — and he reckoned this success ought to keep Upstairs out of his hair for a couple of days while he dealt with the blasted sex murder. A couple of days would have to do it: Upstairs had a notoriously short memory. It was barely a fortnight since, after two whole days and nights spent cramped in an Austin 7, he'd secured a thousand pounds' worth of chocolate bars; a week before that it had been ladies' shoes, yet neither of these successes had kept the super off his back for more than a day or two. And then there was the blasted paperwork. He was always behind with his paperwork. This is not to mention the unedifying meditation upon the greed and the numerous lusts and jealousies of others; the welter of human despair that confronted him; the hour upon hour of tooth-combing through evidence — most of it spurious; the hour after hour spent interviewing cocky spivs who were better dressed, better fed, and in every way more gratified than he was. He could have measured out his life in the cups of cold, grey tea he had shared with weasel-featured informants, or in the ten-bob notes he could ill afford, shelled out to the same. A couple of days ago one of his narks had told him that he had it all wrong: "It ain't the crooks you oughter be watchin' out for, Mr Cooper," he'd said; "it's the general public what's the real villains. If they didn't want things they can't 'ave there'd be no black market. It's all down to them, see. Them and the government."

He had to admit that there was something in that. Looking for a little bit extra from under the counter or off the back of a lorry had become a national pastime. Counterfeiting, swindling, short-changing, stealing: the desperate pursuit of nylons, tea, whisky, sausages and cigarettes had made criminals of everyone. Except, that is, Jim Cooper. For in these morally etiolated times, when most people would have happily sold their own mothers for twenty Players, DDI Cooper would have nothing whatsoever to do with blacketeering. He sensed that to relent on this one point of principle would have made a mockery of everything: and there was more than enough bathos to his life already.

Done with eviscerating his face, he wiped off the residual soap on a tea-towel and (styptic pencils having gone the way of button boots and tinned salmon) dabbed a little bit of tooth powder on the more painful of the grazes. He supposed that the red weals did, at least, assure onlookers that he had shaved, since there was precious little other evidence of the same elsewhere on his raspy chin. What he would give for a packet of safety blades.

He went into the kitchen and refixed yesterday's collar to yesterday's shirt and looped yesterday's still-knotted tie over his head. Then he collected his jacket from its home on the back of the kitchen chair, patting it for his pipe and tobacco pouch. The Welsh rarebit he had attempted to make for his supper the night before was mocking him from the dresser table, and as he watched it slide off the plate into the scraps pail, he made a mental note never again to grill Canadian powdered cheese. He had been driven to such drastic action by extreme want: he had been hungry ever since the day war broke out.

The parp of a motor horn from the street below was his cue to collect his ancient Homburg and crumpled mackintosh from the coat-stand in the hall; and as he closed the front door and ran down the stairs he entertained thoughts of a nice little café he knew on the Seven Sisters Road, wondering if there would be time to stop off for a cheese roll and a quick cup of tea on his way to the murder site. But then he remembered that it was Sunday and the café, along with everything else, would be shut.

CHAPTER
FOUR

It got on her nerves, the way Walter peered at the mirror as he cut his ridiculous little 'tache with such exaggerated care; the way he stood in front of the fireplace in his collarless and cuffless shirt, his braces dangling either side of his legs. He'd always been vain, but he was no longer a good-looking man, and it irritated her that he still behaved as though he was. She could not abide the way his chin, never strong, had by now almost completely vanished; his straw-coloured hair was thinning; his icy blue eyes were now slush. Everything about him reminded her of all that they had once been; of all that they might have been. She suppressed the urge to sweep away his shaving things, lined up on the mantelpiece along with the clock and their wedding photograph, just as she suppressed the need to sweep away Walter.

He appeared to be listening to the wireless, but Walter never listened to anything; like all men painfully unaware of their own limitations, he preferred the sound of his own voice.

"Fancy them wanting communism," he was saying, in a voice flecked with incredulity and indignation.

"Who wants communism?" She hated the way he always had to put in his tuppence-worth, engaging with the BBC as if he was an equal.

"The Jews," he said, as if only a moron would have failed to follow his line of thinking.

She scalded the teapot with water from the kettle. Evelyn and she often had a good laugh at his expense. "Oooh Walter," the kid would say, wickedly, "you ought to be on *The Brains Trust*, really you should." And Walter, being so vain and so lacking in humour, had no idea that he was being mocked, and would preen, unbearably smug.

"Fancy them wanting communism," he continued, "when they're the biggest capitalists of all."

She spooned tea from the caddy into the pot.

"You have to feel sorry for them, though, don't you?" she said. "They've had a rotten time of it, poor sods. It's no wonder they want a revolution."

Walter did not respond. He was concentrating all of his efforts on attaching his collar and cuffs. In the mirror she could see where his pale hair was thinning in two neat lines either side of his head.

"I didn't know you were going in early," she said. "I'd have got you up if you'd told me. I've been up since before seven." She poured him a cup of tea and set it down on the table, alongside a plate of toast and marge scrapings. "I'm going to Nag's Head to try for some bread. It's going on the ration on Monday."

Walter gave a sardonic little laugh.

"More of our food going to feed fat Germans," he said.

25

"I don't know about that." She found a perverse pleasure in contradicting him. "They're living on liver sausage made out of sawdust."

"They deserve to," he said. "They deserve to starve."

"What, even the kiddies?"

Walter spat on the palms of his hands and slicked back his hair. She congratulated herself. Twice in one morning: it was childish, she knew, but she enjoyed shutting him up.

"Have you got half a crown I could have?"

"That depends. What do you want it for?"

"I want it to treat my fancy man to tea at Lyons. What do you think I want it for? I've hardly got a penny left to spend on the necessaries. There's a pile of washing in Mother's room that needs doing, and I was going to give Evelyn a couple of bob . . ."

He put his hand in his trouser pocket and jangled his change, searching through the coins on his open palm, before selecting a half-crown, which he tossed on to the table.

"She won't do a damn thing without payment," she said. "Can't you say something to her? She just ignores me and you know how much I hate a scene. Why should I have to shriek up the stairs like a fishwife every time the floors need mopping?"

Walter was chewing on his toast, his jaw clacking as it moved from side to side in a sort of circular motion. His teeth didn't fit him properly.

"We could get fifteen bob for that room if she wasn't here," she said.

"Don't know who you'd get, though, do you, old girl?" He took a slurp of tea. "Wouldn't do to have a stranger in my own home. Don't think I could stand for that."

She was going to say that it wasn't his home; it was her mother's home; and if it was left to him they'd still be living in two rooms over a stationer's up at Archway. A fine start to married life that was.

He wiped his 'tache with the edge of his finger, first one side then the other.

"Utter tosh!" he declared to the wireless. "Atom bombs are over in a flash. Never even know what's hit 'em. Not like the tortures those little yellow beasts inflicted on the poor ruddy POWs. If the Hun had dropped an atom bomb on us we'd be getting over it by now."

You silly sod, she thought; we'd all be dead. Perhaps that's what he had meant: the dead were out of it, weren't they? It's the rest of us who have to suffer it all.

"Do we have to talk about the war," she said. "It gets on my nerves."

"Well, you had better get used to it, old girl." He put on his doorman's overcoat and checked in the mirror that the gold braid epaulettes where lying straight on his shoulders. "I'm afraid that this is the world we live in. Two world wars have given it to us, and we shall just have to get on with it."

Walter swept his coat sleeve across the peak of his cap before placing it on his head, tugging it into position fore and aft. He was presently engaged as a doorman — he preferred commissionaire — at

Gamages, the department store. It was all he could get. Before the war he had been in insurance, but they were all Freemasons and his old firm hadn't been prepared to take him back when the war ended. Or so he said. He'd never advanced much in all the years he was there, and she doubted that that was all down to the Freemasons. She wished he would find something in the insurance line: they were in arrears with the Provident. She could let it lapse, but it seemed terrible to do that.

"I'll tell you what, old girl," he said, "it isn't how I imagined my life going." What did he expect, she thought bitterly, with his modest talents, his ill-formed opinions on everything, his fading Deb's Delight looks?

Walter put his foot up on the fender and bent forward to polish his shoe, furiously rubbing a cloth back and forth. She drank a cup of tea. It's not his fault, she thought; he couldn't help it that he wasn't any longer the handsome boy in the immaculate blazer who'd laid himself out on the grass with his head in her lap. Canvey Island; the summer of 1925. It wasn't his fault, but she blamed him all the same. They were both browned off, and disappointment was all they shared these days. It isn't really anybody's fault, she told herself. It's everything. It's the memory of before the war and during the war; and now they were after the war and instead of looking forward, she was looking back and she could not bear the mockery, the reproachfulness of memory.

Walter had finished polishing one shoe and was putting his other foot on the fender, and she wondered if he felt the same as she did; whether he longed for all the things they could not have: hope, passion, tinned peaches, Pond's Cold Cream.

He kissed her on the top of her head.

"Goodbye, old girl," he said. Then he tilted his head to one side and said, in an exaggerated stage Cockney: "Now be-hiyive!" It was their little joke; a joke which, like Walter's hair, had grown thin over the years. He wagged his finger at her in mock admonition. "Behive wifie — else I shall have to spank you!"

She heaved a sigh of relief when she heard him close the front door behind him, releasing an immense knot of tension which she had been holding in her stomach without realising.

Oh God, she thought. Could I possibly be any more miserable without him?

CHAPTER
FIVE

It was dazzling and hot as he walked from the flats towards the car, where his driver was leaning against the bonnet. She stood smartly to attention the instant she saw him, her wide attractive mouth forming a smile. She was an A4 Branch girl: pretty, well shaped, with a slight look of the actress Wendy Hiller about her. She had reddish hair that was tucked under her cap; her fresh complexion had a healthy smattering of freckles. When he was closer to her he could see that she had very fetching green eyes. He had more or less given up the habit of looking at girls' figures, but even he could see that she had a jolly good one, beneath the shapeless bulk of the A4 Branch uniform. His detective's sense for such things led him to conclude that she was about twenty-five, twenty-six: too young for him. But then all the A4 Branch women were too young for him, apart from those who were the same age as him, and so resolutely unattractive that it was no mystery to anyone why they had never married.

She held open the door for him.

"Policewoman Tring," she said. "I've been assigned to drive you around today, sir."

She possessed all the attributes of fresh air, common sense and decency. He liked her.

He tossed his hat and mackintosh on to the back seat and settled into the motor; she shut the passenger door, walked around to the driver's side and got in next to him.

"And how are you this morning, sir?" she asked as she started the motor.

He felt a little like a young charge being taught manners by Nanny, but he didn't mind.

"Well, a nice kipper wouldn't have gone amiss," he said. "And I don't mean one of those creosote-dipped frights they try and pass off on you these days either. Of course, you're too young to remember the delights of the pre-War kipper."

She was manoeuvring skilfully out of the parking space.

"Oh, I don't really care for fish, sir," she said, "and you have to queue such a long time for it, don't you?"

"I wouldn't know."

"Oh no, I don't suppose you would, sir. I meant your wife, of course."

"Afraid I'm not married."

He had no idea what made him tell her that. He hoped to God it didn't sound like a pass.

"Me neither," she said.

"Well, no — of course not . . ."

She was laughing now.

"Why? Am I really that frightful?"

"Oh no, no — not at all." He really was a damn fool.

She glanced down at her uniform.

"Actually," she said, "they're going to relax the marriage bar."

"Are they really? I hadn't heard."

"Do you approve?"

"We need all the chaps we can find at the moment."

"Even lady chaps?"

He smiled and turned to look out of the window. She indicated left and headed towards Clissold Park.

"Isn't it a lovely day?" she said, after a little while had elapsed. "Not a cloud in the sky!"

The park was dotted with dogs, skipping children, courting couples: all the usual evincements of hope. Everyone was supposed to believe now that there was a change in the air: a spirit of fairness and justice; an end to the inequities of the old pre-war world. All of that. Otherwise, everyone said, what had it all been for? He despised this popular notion almost as much as he despised the one that held that somehow everything had declined after six years of death and destruction. He, for one, did not miss the acridity, the brick dust clogging your lungs, the broken glass crunching underfoot, the flames blistering the sky, the bucket loads of decomposing flesh. And nor did he feel any nostalgia for Hitler and the obscenity of the horror camps; the reducing of human beings to scorch marks in a matter of seconds. He had no time for either point of view: as far as he was concerned war changed nothing. It didn't last time and it won't this time. He was certain of that. Everything will just keep ticking on until the next one.

"Yes," he said, "lovely day. Pity we have to spend it on a murder."

"Did you have plans, sir?"

No, he had not had plans: even if he had genuinely believed this was to be his first day off in Lord knows how long, he would not have had plans. As it was he was probably relieved that work had spared him the guilt and misery of spending a lovely day alone in the flat, with a pipe and the gramophone.

"I was planning to go into HQ at some point," he said. "We nabbed a couple of wide boys last night."

"No peace for the wicked."

"No. Not really." He thought for a moment. "I suppose I might have gone into town for a spot of lunch." This was partly true, in so far as he had to eat and there was nothing in the flat, not now he had flagrantly wasted his last slice of bread and an entire ration of powdered cheese. He hadn't even had a cup of tea since some time the previous evening: he had run out of milk and he couldn't abide tea without milk; not that this mattered very much as he had run out of tea as well. "I'm absolutely famished; can't stop thinking about hot buttered toast."

"Oh dear!" she said, with what sounded like genuine dismay.

"It's entirely my own fault; I'm as useless as a sign in an Aberdeen shop that asks customers to count their change before leaving."

It was a feeble joke, hardly Max Miller, but he laughed in spite of himself for the first, and last, time that day. Her legs were only a few inches from his and

33

pretty enticing, even in the thick black stockings and the flat black shoes of the A4 Branch. He angled himself away from temptation.

"I don't suppose you're useless at all, sir," she was saying, sounding rather like a nanny giving encouragement to a backward child. He drummed his fingers on the dashboard and looked out of the window. "I might go to the flicks if we finish in time," she said.

"Unlikely," he said. He scarcely went to the cinema these days, only to see the news if he had time; pictures were awful rubbish for the most part, and it was depressing walking home alone afterwards. "Too warm for the pictures today, anyway," he said.

"Yes. I suppose it is." They fell silent for a few moments; she turned up the Blackstock Road. "All this frightful crime," she said. "It seems hardly a day goes past without some awful murder or other." He sighed. "Look at that awful man they caught in Eastbourne the other day."

"Bournemouth," he corrected.

"The one who murdered those poor girls in the boarding house."

"Neville Heath."

"He was an officer!"

She shuddered.

"Actually, I think he just posed as one."

"And then there was that poor little Welsh girl who was shot dead. And a week later another poor little mite — strangled — in Kent of all places! Ten years old! And that woman strangled in Piccadilly. I heard they'd questioned three Yanks about that!"

34

He did not want to discuss sex murders with her.

"Maniacs have been with us since the days of Jack the Ripper," he said. She paid him no heed.

"It's something to do with the post-war psychology," she averred. "Thousands of men — trained killers — let loose on the world. They've seen terrible things; they've suffered and they're scarred. And of course a good many of them are deserters."

He loathed the pseudo-psychiatric drivel that had become part of common parlance since the war. Thanks to *John Bull* magazine and the Home Service, everyone was now a blasted Freudian; just the other day he'd heard some fellow on a bus talking about how the Germans had a "persecution complex", whatever the dickens that was. Not uncommonly for a detective, he had no interest whatsoever in why men do bad things.

"All crooks have their reasons," he said, "which they will give if asked and sometimes even if not asked: poverty; drink; absent fathers; absent mothers; a bump on the head . . . It's all absolute tosh to my mind." He had heard it all at one time or another and the self-pity of a certain type of criminal nauseated him. As far as he was concerned using war as some sort of justification for misbehaviour was simply more of the same. He'd been through another war before the last one, and he had suffered and seen terrible things — along with millions of other men, most of them, like him, schoolboys. Were they all irrevocably scarred, too? He pondered for a moment before deciding, with no particular ill-feeling, that he probably was.

"But aren't you curious, sir? Don't you want to understand what motivates them?"

"Not really. To be curious about a thing you have to find something surprising in it, and I'm afraid that nothing surprises me any more."

"I see." She appeared to be pondering this. "So you don't think that there's anything about the current situation . . ."

"There's certainly a good deal of crime at the moment, if that's what you mean," he said, "but most of it is of the hum-drum sort. To my mind very little is fundamentally different from what went before; there's just more of it. People break the law in the first place because they want to; and in the second, because they can. War-time. Peacetime. That's really all there is to it." She seemed dubious. "There certainly are a lot of young men who have been thrown out of the services and are unable to find a situation. They've spent all the money they received selling their demob suits and they think they might as well turn to crime. But the sort of crime which the majority of them turn to has nothing to do with murdering schoolgirls, or strangling good-time girls, or chopping up their wives and burying them in the cellar. For the most part, it simply has to do with one racket or another. The dibs, the gelt, the mazuma, the moolah: that's the only motive any of them require. The war — rationing, shortages and so forth — has supplied a capital opportunity. You might say that the current crop of villains are merely supplying a demand."

They were passing the dreary expanse of Finsbury Park, where every blade of grass had been turned brown by the hot summer sun; or maybe by the war, which had limned the whole world in a sepia wash. Everything had looked just as drab when he had come back from France in 1918. He was young then, of course; a boy who could still recall the sharp colours of childhood, and the contrast had hit him with the force of a blow. Perhaps the colour had never returned in all that time and he simply hadn't noticed, becoming gradually accustomed to the dun, muted tones.

The desolate railway arches of Finsbury Park Station were looming before them, and he was thinking tormenting thoughts of fried egg and bacon when he spied a familiar figure a short distance away, making its limping progress towards the Astoria picture-house. Cooper did not believe in a criminal type, not as such; but he could always tell a villain by the way he dressed. The fellow he had just spotted was wearing a suit of profligate cut and a ten-guinea hat set at such a cheap angle it looked no better on him than a costermonger's cheese-cutter cap would have done. He knew precisely who it was by the unbalanced gait, a legacy of the Ardennes offensive.

"Hello," he murmured. "That's exactly what I'm talking about."

"Do you know him, sir?"

"Know him? I've known him since he was six years old with his backside hanging out of his trousers and his father's old boots tied on to his feet. He used to stuff the toes with newspaper so they wouldn't fall off when he was running away from the police." Cooper smiled at the recollection. "He grew up over there in the Bunk, on one of the worst streets in London."

The crime-ridden area adjacent to Finsbury Park Station had almost been bombed clean away, but its traces were still apparent in every villain in north London, and no doubt would be for generations to come.

"Pull over, will you?"

She stopped the car in front of the Clarence Hotel, and Cooper wound down the window.

"On your way to church are you, Johnny?"

Johnny Bristow, one-time juvenile delinquent turned spiv, stopped in his tracks. He wasn't the sort who stood around on street corners trying to sell half a pound of black-market butter; Bristow planned big jobs and made contact with big buyers, and every detective in the Metropolitan Police Force was after him. Cooper automatically checked for a blackjack that might well have been protruding from the waistband of the boy's trousers, but was not: a pity as he could have had him for that.

"What do you want, you flat-footed bastard?"

Cooper was not troubled by the newer sort of wide boys. Most of his colleagues saw trouble everywhere in these post-war days, but he knew criminals as a class, and understood that they were all the same when it came down to it: mostly pretty stupid. The current crop of third-rate spivs were kids who had grown up fast on the streets during the air war, burgling bombed premises from the age of ten; little sods who deserved a damned good hiding from fathers whom they never knew, or who were away on active service or dead. Some of them, like Johnny, had grown into violent thugs armed with razor-studded potatoes and bottles of acid, but they were still kids. That was what war did: it blighted youth, one way or another; it extinguished innocence at a stroke; it made contentment and happiness an impossibility: it made boys grow up too fast; or rather it made them think they had grown up. They all cried for their mothers when a judge sentenced them to be flogged, or hanged.

"Now, now, Johnny," Cooper said. "That's no way to greet an old friend."

"I ain't done nothing, so you ought to leave me alone. Go and catch some crooks, why don't you. I'm a respectable businessman. Your wages come out of my rates, copper."

"I didn't realise that they were letting blacketeers and slum landlords into the Rotary Club these days."

The boy snorted.

"Trying to impress your girl are you, Mr Cooper?"

Cooper had to admit that there was probably an element of truth in that.

"Picked up a couple of your chums last night, Johnny. Quiet Sid and 'Little' Jimmy Dashett. They've been very naughty boys. Just thought you'd like to know that they shan't be joining you for tea and crumpets for a while."

"They ain't no friends of mine, Mr Cooper."

"Really? We'll see what they have to say about that." Cooper turned to look at the scowling kid, fixing him with a penetrating gaze for as long as Johnny met it. "Well," he said, as the spiv looked away first, "I shan't keep you any longer, Johnny. I know how busy you tycoons are."

He motioned to Policewoman Tring to move on.

"It makes me sick, spivs like that getting away with it," she said, as she changed gear and sped a little faster along the empty road towards Nag's Head.

"I suppose you've never had a pair of stockings or a lipstick from a blacketeer?"

He felt a little caddish, but moral indignation always made him tetchy.

She was quiet for a few moments.

"The world's in a pretty bad way, isn't it, sir?" she said.

"Yes. Yes it is."

He watched the dusty misery of Seven Sisters Road slip past the window, marking the back alleys, the pubs with their grimy saloon bars, the cafés with their fly-blown sugar bowls: he knew it all with an unseemly intimacy and it had touched him, insidious, infecting. He sighed. It was too late now for insight. The fact of it was he was tired of it all, and the future was not any longer his problem.

CHAPTER
SIX

Making herself presentable for the baker took some considerable amount of time; for, although she enjoyed catching the attention of men, she was always careful to avoid being seen as the sort of woman whom men regard as a "possible". In any case the baker was a respectable married man whose daughter helped in the shop: she just wanted to look her best for him, so that he would be inclined to be good to her, in an under-the-counter sort of way. She wasn't going to give herself for a loaf of bread, like those German housewives selling themselves on the streets.

Her girdle was on its way out and the suspenders were unreliable, so she slipped a tatty old garter over her leg. There was nothing worse than having your stockings hanging down. A wave of despair washed over her. People shouldn't have to live like this, she thought. And for a moment she wondered if she might actually cry. If she started she might never stop, so she pulled herself together and put on her skirt and jacket and inspected herself in the mirror. Motherhood had not ruined her figure, like it did for so many other women; when she was dressed — ideally with a good foundation garment — she still had the semblance of a good figure.

She tied a patterned scarf around her hair in a sort of artistically arranged turban. It was hard to believe that there had ever been a time when she would no more dream of going out without a hat on than she would of flying to the moon and back; the war had caused so many standards to slip. She checked that her seams were straight and slipped on a pair of high-heeled black and white calf shoes; a pair of white lace gloves and the pigskin handbag completed the look. She checked the whole ensemble in the mirror. Coo, what it is to have sex appeal, she thought as she went downstairs.

The hall was damp and gloomy: brown linoleum worn at the edges, ochre wallpaper. The whole house was hideous, dingy, a dead or dying thing, breathing a redolence of shellshock, abandonment, neglect.

"I'm off!" she cried. Her voice resounded in the indifferent silence. She stood there for a moment, at the top of the stairs, acknowledging the turmoil of her nerves, her frustration; the injustice of her situation. She closed her eyes telling herself that she could scream. Curiously, the thought settled her.

Outside was bright and warm, the breezeless air thick with gasometers and railway smuts. In the heat there was the smell of something decaying. As she walked along the road, she thought how there was a terrible loneliness about the abandoned houses; how it was impossible to believe that things might ever be nice again. As she prepared to cross towards Nag's Head, she could see that the line of badly dressed women formed outside the baker's shop already extended past the tobacconist's and the draper's. Some people have nothing better to do than to stand in a queue all day, she thought. A few of the women, the narrow-minded ones, were looking her up and down as she took her place at the back of the queue. They were thinking how there was nothing austerity about her: how the powdered nose and the slick of black-market vermillion marked her out as one of those women who had had "a lovely war". How she pitied them, with their headscarves tied under their chins like Russian peasant women and their patched and darned stockings kept up with threepenny bits. A bus passed by on the other side of the road, a flash of red breaking the monotony of the greyness of everything else. Muswell Hill, it said on the front, and briefly she wondered what it would be like to cross the street and board it; she was picturing herself alighting somewhere that had been largely untouched by the war, somewhere green and airy: somewhere nice. She could find a nice little room somewhere and a job in a hat-shop. On Saturdays she would go to the pictures. She would have lunches in nice places. She would meet gentlemen for cocktails. Nice men; handsome men, who were looking for a little harmless diversion. It would be just like the war again, only without the bombs and the filth.

She snatched an admiring glimpse of herself in the draper's window, the pigskin handbag swinging from her arm with elegant insouciance. Why shouldn't she have those things? Other people did, so why not her? She dwelt gloomily on the drabness of her life, wishing Mother dead, Walter gone. Why were there always so many obstacles in her life? Why did nothing ever go

CHAPTER
SEVEN

They had crossed the Holloway Road and now they were turning down a depleted side street over which hung a thick cloud of engine steam, through which, as it dispersed, Cooper could see DI Lucas. He was standing on the pavement in front of a house-sized gap, smoking a cigarette, with the perpetual air of dismay he always exuded. The poor chap ought by rights to have been pruning the roses in his bungalow garden, and it was a great misfortune to him that he was that rare commodity: a hard-working and dependable copper in a time of national emergency. A short distance from Lucas, a group of head-scarved women and scruffy kids marked the arrival of the patrol car with a slight stirring of interest. Lucas ground his gasper underfoot and removed his hat — not as a sign of respect, but because he needed to fan his beetroot face.

It was immediately apparent to Cooper, as they pulled up alongside, that the murder scene was in the grip of a deep torpor: the uniform on sentry duty was stifling a yawn; a detective sergeant was standing idle in the shade of a shrapnel-scarred tree; and a couple of other flatfoots were poking a rubble-strewn area in front of a sort of makeshift doorway constructed out of corrugated iron, in what could only be described as a desultory fashion. It was uncommonly hot for the time of day, but this alone did not account for the general apathy. Fact was, there was none of the excitement that attends a crime scene when it is replete with evidence.

Cooper pinched the corners of his eyes between a thumb and forefinger. He was already out of his depth and he hadn't even left the car.

Lucas leaned in at the passenger window.

"The pathologist is already here, sir," he said, "and I took the liberty of summoning someone from the fingerprint department."

Cooper made a little moue of disapproval. He was as fastidious in his work as he was careless with his appearance, and always preferred a scene of crime to be as unharried as possible. They never were, of course — what in life is? You must always adjust to the precedents set by others.

"Run along and fetch a cup of tea for the guv'nor," Lucas instructed Policewoman Tring, who had come round to open the passenger door. "There's a good girl."

"Milk, please. No sugar," Cooper said.

"I'll try and dig up a sandwich for you as well, sir," she said.

He glanced up at her, meeting her crystal-clear green eyes. He was surprised to see that she was smiling at him, and shaking her head.

"Whoever is supposed to be looking after you," she said, "is doing a rotten job."

He stepped on to the pavement, self-consciously smoothing back a slick of hair. He was thinking, I must look positively distempered. He was long overdue a haircut and it was easier to find a piece of the True Cross than a jar of ruddy Brylcream.

"Thanks," he said. "A sandwich would be just the ticket."

He glanced back at her as he followed Lucas towards the relative safety of the murder scene. She had retrieved his mackintosh from the back seat of the motor and was shaking it out. He watched her fold it neatly and place it on the passenger seat. The action made him feel momentarily benign, then he remembered that he was about to visit a murder scene. He sighed, and braced himself against the inevitable proliferation of doubt and disappointment.

You could say that the first visit to a crime scene was a sort of fresh start: a prelude of calm, organisation and procedure, before the descent into the chaos of human entanglement. For the next few hours all he would have to do was scrutinise the surface for physical evidence, finding sanctuary in the forensic analysis of telling details. Murder is, of course, an all-too-human matter, but on the first visit to the scene of a murder a detective is obliged to detach himself from the muck and confusion of feelings. And nobody appreciated more than Jim Cooper how a detective flourishes best in a solitude that is uncontaminated by the traces of others.

They pressed through the piece of corrugated iron, lighting upon a stretch of wilderness where brambles and nettle patches vied for space with shattered masonry. A few yards from where they stopped he could see a plane tree with a piece of old door propped against its trunk. There was a tarpaulin draped over the whole structure.

"What the dickens is that?" he demanded.

Lucas rocked on the toes of his shoes.

"Ah yes," he said. "I'm afraid that one of the witnesses is responsible for that, sir. He was anxious to preserve the victim's modesty."

"Good grief! You mean the body's in there?" It beggared belief. "Who else has been tramping over my murder scene? The Arsenal first eleven?"

Lucas brought his lips together shrewdly.

"It's rather hot today, sir," he said, "and the body's been out all night."

Cooper sighed.

"Who was the first on the spot?"

The first on the spot always interfered; always left some blasted trace, fouling up the whole of the investigation.

"Some kids found her."

"Kids, eh? Did they touch anything?"

Lucas shrugged.

"Take them down to the station and get a statement. Tell their mothers to expect a home visit some time in the next couple of days." He sighed again. "Thought I could rely on you to keep us out of trouble, old man," he said.

A couple of hundred yards from where they were standing, from deep beneath a steep bank, a train screeched past, filling up the vacant space with the pungency of burning coal in a heavy goût of damp, sooty debris. As it cleared, Cooper could see the pathologist emerge from behind the tented structure. He stood next to the plane tree, addressing an attractive girl assistant who made a note of everything he said. Cooper watched him enviously, kicking over a patch of dust with the toe of his shoe. Must be nice to deal in scientific certainties, he thought.

"Any idea who she is?"

Lucas shook his head.

"No handbag?"

Lucas shook his head again.

"There would have been a handbag." Cooper was as sure of that as he could be of anything. The victim would have acquired the Blitz habit of keeping everything of any value or importance in her handbag, which she would have kept close by her, ready to be grabbed at a moment's notice. During the Blitz he had instructed countless officers to find the handbags before they did anything else when attending a bomb-site. It helped with identification, of course, but also prevented all those coupons and identity papers falling into the wrong hands.

Lucas had removed his hat and was mopping the sweat from his forehead with a large damp handkerchief.

"I should say it's fairly obvious what we're looking at here, sir," he said.

"Always beware of the obvious," said Cooper.

"We were on this street just a few days ago," the DI continued. "There's a house just along the road there — very badly bombed. The landlord called us in to clear out squatters." He stuffed the handkerchief back into his pocket. "Deserters." He paused to allow the significance of this to sink in. "Of course, the buggers moved back in again as soon as we'd gone."

Cooper appreciated his DI's line of thinking, and considered ordering a raid on the property. The landlord was sure to oblige. They could bring in anyone who failed to give a good account. They might find the handbag, or the victim's papers; but even if they didn't, it wouldn't take a lot to make it stick.

"This is murder, Frank," he said.

Lucas shrugged.

"They're deserters, sir," he said. "Bloody deserters."

Cooper let the implication hang in the air between them, and looked about him at what remained of the street. He remembered the night — eighteen months ago — when the V-weapon had fallen there, killing eight people. One of his men had found a human head on top of a shed roof. If he remembered correctly, two elderly spinster ladies had lived in the house that had occupied the murder site. They dug out one, dead, from the rubble. The other one was never found. There was that faint odour of sewage that hung over everywhere that had been badly bombed; those houses that remained were mostly Class "B"s awaiting demolishment.

"If I had just murdered someone," he reasoned, "and had all the advantages a stolen handbag might afford, this is the last place I would stay."

Lucas nodded shrewdly.

"I would have headed for the nearest main road — Caledonian Road — less than half a mile away that way, Holloway Road the same that way. A tuppenny bus ride and you have the whole of London at your disposal; within twenty minutes it would be as if you had never been here." Cooper took out his pipe and began to clean it with a matchstick.

He would have liked to have put in motion a dragnet of sixty men, strung out at two-yard gaps, slowly moving forward, eyes locked to the ground. He could hear the gales of laughter from Upstairs. Sixty coppers! If they could muster sixty coppers in the whole of London it would be a blasted miracle.

"Organise a search of every front garden and dustbin between here and the main bus routes," he said.

"Are we looking for anything in particular, sir?"

"Clues, Detective Inspector."

"Like a handbag?"

"Well, that would do for a start." He sucked on the empty pipe a couple of times until it squeaked. "And have someone get on to the missing persons bureau at the Yard."

A short distance away a fingerprint chap was delicately twirling a brush over the surface of a wall. He felt almost as jealous of him as he did of the pathologist. The chances of either of them telling him a thing of any use that he couldn't have figured out for himself were, he reckoned, pretty remote. The infallible was nearly always the least part of it.

"I say! DDI Cooper, isn't it?" The pathologist was coming towards him, with his Harley Street drawl. He dusted off his pin-striped knees with an immaculate handkerchief which he handed to the girl assistant, then peeled off and handed her his rubber gloves. "Well, well! Haven't seen you in a dog's age, old man," he said. He made a half-turn towards the body and gestured elegantly in its direction. "Death probably occurred eight to twelve hours ago — not more than fourteen, but I would hate to stake my reputation on that. It was quite warm last night which always buggers up the readings. Should be able to tell you a bit more when I've got her on the slab, old man; but at first glance I'd say it's a classic case of right-handed strangulation. There's a fair bit of bruising on the knuckles of her right hand. Would have left a nice shiner on the receiving end," he said. "Bit like the one you're sporting, Cooper, old bean."

Cooper stroked his cheek. He'd almost forgotten about the bruise he'd sustained the previous night.

"So there was some sort of a fight then," said Lucas.

The pathologist gave them both his bedside smile.

"Ah! That's for you fellows to deduce," he said.

Cooper filled his pipe.

"Nothing unusual about a tart getting into a fight with a customer who refuses to pay her," said Lucas. "It happens most Saturday nights. Sometimes, every so often, it goes too far."

The girl assistant handed the pathologist his hat and helped him into his beautifully cut jacket. She brushed specks of soot from the shoulders with the flat of her hand.

"Well, I had better get back to my Sunday lunch," the pathologist was saying, "else the good lady wife shan't be too happy with me!" He made his way towards his shiny motor with the girl assistant. "See you in the cold-store tomorrow, old man," he said.

Cooper struck a match and puffed on his pipe until it was alight. Unless the prof found her name and telephone number tattooed upon her backside, the post-mortem was probably an irrelevance. The woman had been strangled after some sort of fight and sexual assault. That much was obvious to all but a blind fool. He turned his attention back to the murder site. Everything he needed to know was there, somewhere; it was simply a question of knowing where to look. The problem was, it all took time and time was the one thing he did not have.

Lucas handed him the murder bag and the pair of them made their way towards the makeshift tent. Cooper had a pretty good idea what he would find there. He looked at the body as dispassionately as possible, but, as always, a wave of ineffable sadness lapped over him. No matter how many times you came upon it, death was always what it was: pointless and unedifying. All through the war, bodies found beneath piles of rubble with their legs blown off; once a sleeved arm found in a street shelter. He'd seen a prostitute strangled with her own stocking on a seedy divan (sex murderers had feeble imaginations) and a respectable mother of three children dumped in a filthy alley following an abortion gone wrong. He might have supposed that it would all be different now that the world was at peace, but the people of Holloway were still dying stupid, unnecessary deaths: they were still committing suicide; they were still being run over; they were still burning in fires, and they were still being stabbed, battered and strangled.

He enumerated the tell-tale signs, every one of them a cliché. Blouse open; breast exposed; skirt pulled up over the thigh; legs spread apart, left one at a right angle to the other where it had fallen away; tongue distended, emerging from the corner of the mouth; tell-tale specks of blood discolouring the eyes, which were wide open. This one had a cut on her chin just as the pathologist had said. And her drawers were lying on the grass next to her.

"That's odd," he said. The drawers of sex murder victims were usually found torn to ribbons and wrapped around one or other ankle. "And look at the blouse: unbuttoned, not ripped apart."

"According to the neighbours," Lucas said, "this yard is regularly used as some sort of a lovers' lane." He sniffed. "People behave these days like they were in the back row of the pictures. Everyone knows what went on in the blackout."

Cooper knelt on the ground beside the body.

"She's lying on her mackintosh," he noted.

"Protecting her clothes while they did the business."

"Yes, I suppose so." He was thinking that taking the time to spread out a mackintosh on the ground was hardly compatible with violent assault.

He took out a magnifying glass from the murder bag and bent over the woman's body, running the glass slowly back and forth across the dark bruising on her neck. When he'd seen enough he stood up and composed a detailed mental picture of the prostrate figure at his feet. Then he lit his pipe and took a few ponderous draughts.

"I want a complete set of photographs showing the location of the body," he said, "and the position of the paths and roads around the site. There's a fair bit of undergrowth which we shall need to search."

"Are we looking for anything in particular, sir?" asked Lucas, wiping a line of sweat from his upper lip with the back of his hand.

"I don't suppose we shall know until we find it, Detective Inspector. Have someone make a scale drawing of the scene."

It was occurring to him that she didn't look like a tart. She was — had been — a good-looking woman of about forty, and tarts of forty did not in general look all that good. He noted the peroxided and carefully waved hair, the lacquered nails, the smart well-fitted skirt and jacket, the neatly laundered blouse, the undarned nylons, the high-heeled shoes. This was a woman who had evidently taken good care of herself.

Somebody somewhere will be missing her, he thought.

He looked back towards the piece of corrugated iron marking the entrance to the murder scene and tried to visualise her coming in there with her murderer. He walked towards the entrance and, stopping halfway, crouched down to inspect the ground. It was hard and dry. There was no evidence that he could see of anyone having been dragged through the scrub and the dust.

"Looks like she came in here of her own accord."

Lucas nodded in agreement.

"There's hardly a woman in London who doesn't have a secret. Bastard kids and VD — that's the real legacy of the war for you."

Cooper puffed on his pipe in a non-committal way and looked about him once more, mentally tracing the route they might have taken towards the tree. Spotting something, he stooped to inspect a patch of ground a few yards in front of the body, two or three feet square, beside a pile of stones. The vegetation beneath the shelter of the tree was well trodden.

"I'd say they came to a stop here," he said. The grass and plants were only just beginning to wilt, and among the pile of stones scattered about here and there was a large piece of limestone, part of the foundations of the bombed house, he assumed. Squinting against the plume of smoke from his pipe, he squatted beside it. "Probably stood here for a while before lying down on the ground."

"And doing the business," said Lucas.

There were a couple of blades of grass on the surface of the stone, most likely transferred from the ground. Without being asked, Lucas handed him a pair of tweezers, then unrolled a leather strip from the murder bag and selected a glass test tube. He held it out towards Cooper and received a blade of grass from the tweezers.

56

Cooper now shifted his focus to two cigarette stubs that were lying in close proximity to a couple of used prophylactics, beneath the thicket that had grown up around the base of the tree. He picked up one with the tweezers and examined it closely. The end was coated in dark red lipstick.

"That looks like the same shade she's painted her nails to me," he observed. "What do you think?" Lucas nodded, unconcerned one way or the other, and deposited the stubs into another test tube. Cooper was examining the soles of the dead woman's shoes, from where he had retrieved another blade of grass.

"So," said Lucas, "they came in over there and walked up to the tree; stood here for a while; shared a fag. She removes her drawers, they spread out the mackintosh; she asks him for the money; he tells her she must be joking; they have a bit of a fight; he forces himself upon her and strangles her. And then he took her handbag."

Cooper pondered this scenario.

"Something about it doesn't seem right," he said.

"I don't know; seems routine to me, sir."

Cooper leaned back on his heels and fanned himself with his hat, looking about him all the while for anything else that might supply a clue, the significance of which he had yet to, might never, discern. He stood up and crossed to the remains of wall on either side of the corrugated iron, scratching at the pointing, scraping particles of brick dust with the blunt end of the tweezers into yet another glass phial.

The little things are the most important, he told himself. Sherlock Holmes. Sherlock Holmes had not seen the things he had seen, but that did not detract from the truth of the observation. A blade of grass, a scraping of brick dust, might be all it took to hang a man. It never failed to astonish him.

Dejection came upon him suddenly. Who was he fooling? Not himself. He was gathering these fragments of information not because he was some sort of latter-day genius of detection, but because he did not know what else to do. That was the unpalatable truth of it.

"The trouble is," Lucas said as if reading his thoughts, "a detective needs information, and you know as well as I do, sir, there's never any information in a case like this. Know thine enemy — that's what it says in the Bible, isn't it?"

"Actually, I think it's Sun Tzu — *The Art of War*."

"Know thine enemy. That could have been written by a detective. Trouble is, I'm not sure I want to get to know the sort of blighter who strangles a woman with his bare hands. That's why we're not up at Scotland Yard, you and I. We're not cut out for homicide. Our skills lie in other directions — but you're hardly likely to find out who a murderer is from a friendly nark in exchange for a ten-bob straightener, are you?"

Of course, Lucas was quite right in all of this. And as is often said, murder is an intimate act: only two people know for sure what took place between them, and one of them is dead.

Cooper gripped the stem of his pipe between his teeth.

"All we can do, old chap," he said, "is follow the procedures and hope to God we don't miss anything."

He called over the fingerprint specialist and watched him collect a set of prints from the dead woman. If she was a tart chances were that her dabs would be on file and then at least they'd have a name.

Lucas lit a cigarette and took a deep draught, releasing clouds of obscuring smoke from his nostrils.

"I don't suppose there's any chance of Upstairs sending one of their murder experts over, is there, sir?"

Both tacitly acknowledged the absurd unlikelihood of that. Lucas drew again on the cigarette, coughed, removed it, and contemplated the glowing tip between his thumb and forefinger. Cooper spent a few moments fussing with his pipe, relighting it and puffing away until he was satisfied he would be able to respond in as mild a tone as was possible. Policemen live at the edge of frustration and resentment and it can wear you down, if you let it.

"I'm afraid we can't pick and choose which cases we investigate, Frank."

"It makes no difference to me, sir, my twenty-five years will be up this time next year, thank bloody Christ — but you're still young. You still have a career." Lucas attacked his cigarette: he was laconic in everything he did and said, but he smoked furiously, taking it out on the hapless fag. "You don't need to be Sherlock Holmes to know that this one can't be cracked, no matter how hard you try. Bet you a bob to a bootlace on that. You'd be better off sticking to the racketeers. That's the way to get Upstairs to notice you. They shan't thank you for wasting time and money on a commonplace killing — not in the middle of a blasted crime wave." He smoked the cigarette down to the bitter end, throwing the butt to the ground and grinding it underfoot as if to make sure that it really was dead.

Cooper bit irritably on the stem of his pipe.

"Murderers are generally in an agitated frame of mind," he said. "They do idiotic things — make mistakes."

Lucas lit another cigarette.

"I shall have to let DS Phillips go by six o'clock, sir," he said. "He's supposed to be on stake-out over in Enfield tonight."

"Keep him here until the light goes. And for God's sake, get those blasted uniforms out searching the dustbins."

CHAPTER
EIGHT

She had been standing in the queue for half an hour or more when the woman behind her jabbed her in the small of her back.

"Shift yourself, why don't you."

A gap had opened up in the line in front of her and she moved into it. She might have said something to the woman but didn't because she was never rude to people, even in these sparse times when manners and good behaviour seemed to have gone along with so much else. She might have said that, she supposed. She considered turning around, but the moment had passed.

She had become transfixed by a vast hoarding on the opposite side of the road, an advertisement for Snowfire Vanishing Cream affixed to an exposed end-wall where a cinema used to be. She was wondering whether the line drawing of a woman's head was supposed to be the actress Pat Kirkwood, and whether actresses were paid in jars of vanishing cream. She couldn't see the point of advertising things that you can't buy anywhere. Only available in strictly limited quantities. Ask your grocer to save you some from his next supply. This is produced in complete conformity with the authorised economy standards. It made you sick.

Her back was killing her, and so were her feet, and she longed to remove her girdle and high heels. She was still just outside of the shade of the baker's awning; it was still hot. Her blouse was irredeemably stained with perspiration under the arms and when she moved she could feel a cooling patch of damp between her skin and her girdle. She wished she could take off her jacket.

Queuing is simply not fair, she thought; she had said as much all through the war. Why couldn't the government introduce some sort of distribution system so that everybody got what they needed — all the same? People shouldn't have to stand about all day. The woman in front of her was saying: "I knew I should have gone to the ABC on Camden Road", and she wondered if she'd be better off going there now; then it came to her that the ABC had two women behind the counter and she was probably better off with the baker.

She couldn't understand why it was taking so long. A person could die in the time it takes to get served. It was impossible to see inside the shop because the windows had been boarded up since a V-weapon had taken every single pane of glass more than a year ago. A lot of the other shops in the row had been obliterated. She wished she hadn't remembered that, trying to push away the memory of the greengrocer and his wife scrabbling frantically in the ruins of their shop for the body of their little girl. Pat Kirkwood has such lovely skin, she thought: I wonder how much a pot of vanishing cream goes for on the black market? The advertisements mocked you with the lure of things you couldn't get hold of even if you had the money and the points. Vanishing cream, Heinz Tomato Soup, French girdles. The list was endless. She supposed that there must be people who had these things in abundance; people who knew other people. It was all luck when you came down to it.

Across the road another Number 43 came and went. Friern Barnet via Muswell Hill. The sight of it made her nervy. She was a bundle of nerves and in a bath of perspiration. She hoped it wasn't the Change. She didn't want any more kiddies — she'd almost died having Douglas — but she was not ready for the Change. Her sex appeal was the only thing keeping her from a shrivelled existence in a dingy bed-sitting room. When she thought of all the things other people got away with, all the things other people had, it made her feel ill. Pat Kirkwood and her bloody vanishing cream. She reckoned she had five years left before the Change aged her irrevocably, and after that no man would ever look at her again.

She rummaged in the pigskin handbag for a gold-coloured compact, dabbing at the line of perspiration on her top lip.

"Tut! Look at Lady Muck," said one of the women in the queue behind her, "making herself cheap."

She lingered unnecessarily over the blonde curls protruding artfully from beneath the front of her turban. The face-powder sat on her damp skin like a grotesque mask; the mingling of perspiration and rubber filled her nose. She felt queasy, as if she might faint. It was only the tiredness that was stopping her from crossing the road and starting over again. Somewhere nice; somewhere the war hadn't touched. Who could blame her for that? You had only to look at what her life had come to. Nobody would blame her. Nobody. Not even Mavis.

Another woman left the baker's and the whole line moved up one more space and she found herself, at long last, standing in the shade of the awning. She would buy the bread, she would take it home and then she would set about changing her life. Buying the bread would be the last thing she ever did for any of them.

The thought made her panic; then it made her sad.

The woman who had just left the baker's was holding out her basket.

"'Ere, look at that. Gorn. Look at that."

She was a big fat Cockney woman, the sort you used to see in the newsreels standing in front of their bombed-out slums, shaking their fat fists at Hitler as Bob Danvers-Walker said something meaningless about courage and guts. She was toothless, arms like raw sausages, immense bosom like an overstuffed bolster. She was probably only in her thirties but she had let herself go with years of drudgery relieved by hop-picking or whatever women like her did for amusement: stout-drinking, knees-upping.

"'Ave a look at that," she was demanding, thrusting out her basket indignantly.

There was a small split tin and half a dozen buns lying at the bottom.

"All stale," she spat. "Rock 'ard." She tossed her head back towards the baker's. "'E's taking fuckin' liberties." A few women gasped. The Cockney's face was blotchy with indignation. "Fobbin' us off with yesterday's unsolds! The lousy rotten sod!"

Muted, apathetic expressions of dismay came from the other women in the queue, but not one of them relinquished her place in the line. After a little while another woman left the shop, armed with, she told them all, half a cottage loaf, four sausage rolls and a few broken jam tarts.

"I queued over an hour for that," she said. "It's disgusting. They get better treated in Germany."

"They got better treated in Belsen," someone else averred.

She wondered why people talked such rot.

Once more, they all moved up a place until there were only four women standing between her and the baker's. The grimy reality of the coal-carts, the drays, the lorries rumbling past her on the Holloway Road played badly on her nerves; the brick dust weighing down the corner of the tattered awning depressing her terribly. Her eyes strayed once more to the other side of the road, the line of red buses standing out against the relentless grey of everything else. A tuppenny bus ride was all it took, but still it was more than she could ever hope for.

Oh, pull yourself together, do, she told herself. You're getting on my nerves. Things were getting better. She didn't expect men to fall like ninepins for her any more

— those days were gone — but she still had sex appeal. Nobody would ever believe that she was forty-three.

After a few more minutes there were only two women in front of her and she could see inside the shop; she could smell the rolls and loaves.

She smoothed her skirt and adjusted the hem of her jacket, glancing over her shoulders to check one turned calf and then the other. Her seams were perfectly straight. Everything was going to be alright.

CHAPTER
NINE

Cooper was scarcely aware of her coming to stand at his side. He had no idea how long she had been standing there, patiently holding out a tray bearing a plate of sandwiches and, amidst an assortment of dirty crockery, an untouched cup of tea.

"I do hope fish-paste is acceptable, sir," she said. "It was the nearest thing to a kipper I could find." He wondered if she was making fun of him. If so, he didn't mind. He tamped down his pipe with his thumb, slipped it back into his pocket and reached for a sandwich. A train passed below them, coating everything with thick grey smoke, softening the harsh glare of the sun. She coughed.

"This is hardly the place for a nice girl like you," he said over the engine rattle.

She smiled slightly, expertly.

"I'd drink the tea while it's still warm, sir, if I were you," she said. "It's been standing for a few minutes. You were terribly busy — I didn't want to disturb you." She was to be commended for her correctness, he supposed. He was long out of practice where women were concerned.

"You should have waited somewhere else," he said. "I could have come and found you, you know. A murder scene — it's — well, it's not pleasant."

He drank the tea down, washing away the sandwich, and when it was all gone he asked her if there was any chance of another.

"I'm sure there is," she said. "The next-door neighbours are very obliging."

He set down his cup on the tray, pleased when she didn't leave immediately. He wiped the crumbs from his mouth with his handkerchief. She was looking at the ground, pensive; her face was slightly flushed, her tawny eyebrows knitted in consternation.

"You know," she said at last, "I was in Nairobi with the ATS." Then without another word, she turned sharply and picked her way across the rubble and the weed patches with her tray of dirty tea things, leaving him wondering what on earth he had said to upset her.

Lucas had come to stand at his shoulder, fanning himself with his hat.

"I've arranged for a conference at Cally Road, sir, nine tomorrow morning."

Cooper thanked him. The DI ran the edge of his hand across his brow and shook a few drops of sweat on to the brown-tipped grass.

"Shall I let the body go now, sir?"

"Yes. Yes. I suppose we better had."

"Is everything alright, sir?"

"Yes. Quite alright." He sighed. "It's been a long weekend."

"You're telling me."

Cooper watched the stretcher-bearers lift the body, wrapped in a sheet, and carry it away. The next time he would see her would be in the morgue; the rest of the after-death routine was practical, tedious and best left to Lucas.

"Sir, I think you'd better take a look at this."

Lucas was indicating the spot where, until a few moments before, the woman's body had been lying, and pointing at the navy-blue raincoat that had been spread out upon the ground beneath her.

"If I'm not very much mistaken, that's a man's mackintosh," he said.

Cooper came across and crouched beside the garment.

"Bag it up," he said when he had seen enough to know. "I'll take it back to divisional HQ with me and give it a damn good going over."

For the first time that day there was a palpable energy to the murder scene. Lucas called across to Policewoman Tring, who was standing a short distance off bearing another tray laden with yet more cups of tea for the male officers.

"Girlie, get rid of that tray and take the guv'nor to Stoke Newington straightaway with the samples," he barked, "and when you've done that get yourself back here as quick as you can. I need you to support the men on door-to-door inquiries."

Cooper waved his hand dismissively.

"Oh no," he said. "I don't need a lift. Waste of petrol and manpower. I can make do with the Tube. Besides," he risked a quick glance at her, "Policewoman Tring would be much better used here."

Lucas brought his lips together shrewdly, the way he always did whenever he was about to countermand an order.

"Do you really think it's wise to entrust important evidence to the Piccadilly Line, sir?" he asked.

They didn't speak much on the drive back to Stoke Newington. The combination of heat and lack of sleep was beginning to get the better of him. He drooped against the side of the open window through which the warm air scarcely moved, thinking of sausages, mashed potatoes and fresh, not tinned, peas. When that became too tormenting he thought of Bach, St John Passion, of the night of sorrow measuring out its final hour, the woman lying in the morgue, the evil men do, the waste, the terrible bloody waste.

"DI Lucas and the other men are all saying that the chances of catching the killer are next to none," she said, "and it's a waste to put so much effort into the investigation." She swallowed hard. "One of them described it as a commonplace killing. What's commonplace about a man strangling a woman with his bare hands?"

He looked out of the window. We've just been through a war in which countless numbers perished, he thought; what's one more corpse on a bomb-site?

"There are around half a dozen murders committed in London every year that are never solved. An apparently random killing is the hardest case of all to crack. We shall all do our best, of course; but we must be realistic."

You had to keep reminding yourself that it mattered: the woman on the bomb-site mattered. They all mattered.

"I'm sorry, sir, but I think it's bloody awful." There was a pink tinge creeping up her neck. "You can't have men getting away with killing women, even if some women do deserve it."

He could not ignore the utter sincerity, the heart-rending quiver in her voice, the flush of genteel outrage.

"As a matter of fact," he said, allowing it all to touch him, "I agree with you."

She turned briefly from the road to glance at him, her green eyes shining with emotion.

This glorious creature, he thought, gazing upon her erect head, her purposeful expression now returned to the road ahead of them; and for a brief moment he was almost hopeful — almost — for the sort of future that she, and others like her, would strive to build with decency and hard work and a sense of justice. He hoped to God that they would not mess it up like his generation had done; and beyond the rattle of the motorcar, beyond the charred streets dusty in the brilliant sunlight, he began to discern the possibility of a world finally at peace.

Or rather, he corrected himself, a post-war world: not the same thing at all, old man. Not the same thing at all.

CHAPTER
TEN

The dream was always the same: it didn't seem to matter how much or how little he had had to drink. It always ended with him flying through the air with the feeling that the inside of his head had been blasted to smithereens and something, some vital part of him, was gone for ever. He never dreamed about hitting the water, floating for God knows how long in the frozen sea clinging to a hatch cover; he did not dream about drowning. He dreamed of flying, which to his mind was a strange thing for a sailor to do.

He had woken up late, still the worse for drink, and gone out to look for cigarettes. He had woken to the dream as he always did these days, and the memory of the dream had stayed with him, vivid, all the way along the Seven Sisters Road; more real to him than the rush and confusion of the street with its crowds of ugly, worn-out people; the bints wearing trousers and the skinny arses on them; the fumes and shrieks of the motor cars and buses.

He had no recollection of the night before, of how he had found his way back to his digs: none of it was as memorable to him as was the dream. The dream was so powerful, he often wondered if that was where he actually existed and it was everything else that was unreal. Of course he knew that this was crazy talk; and the navy doctor had thought so too: he'd tried to fob him off with nerve tonic, but he wasn't having any of that. One time he'd tried to talk to his pal about it, but it was kind of hard to put into words: he didn't want to look like a nut-case; better to keep that sort of thing to yourself. In the tobacconist's he wondered if he had died and was a ghost. He wondered how you could tell for sure.

Kensitas or Weights: that was all that was available under the counter, unless you didn't mind filthy Turkish which was all that you could get over the counter. He didn't like Kensitas, so he bought ten Weights, which cost him the best part of two bob. He had heard that Jerry POWs got twenty-five cigs a week, which made you wonder what it had all been about. He went into the café next door to smoke over a cup of tea and a cheese roll. The cheese roll cost him tuppence and tasted faintly of rubber, but he was hungry and needed something to sop up all the alcohol from the night before. He ate it all in one go and ordered another. The waitress was an alright piece, even though she was cock-eyed. He winked at her when she brought him the roll, and smiled slowly as she turned her nose up at him, the snooty little cow. He reckoned he'd have been better off staying down in Portsmouth; at least the bints there knew how to treat a fellow who'd spent four years fighting for his country.

He'd sort of come to the conclusion that the navy suited him; leastways he'd seen enough of how it went on the outside to know that civvy street was not for him. Funny thing: he'd been low priority for demob, seeing as he didn't have dependents and his injuries didn't seem to count, and he'd spent months marking off the days — a lot of them spent in the stockade — but now that he had been demobbed it seemed as if he spent all his time wondering whether he ought to join up again. There were times when he felt like leaving the navy had been a sort of betrayal, which was pretty funny when you thought about it.

He knocked the ash of his cigarette into his saucer and smoked without interruption until the rest of it had gone. Then he stuck another cigarette in the corner of his mouth and called over to the waitress for more tea. He wanted to see if she was going to look at him again as if he was dirt. The snooty little cow did not disappoint. He curled his top lip and struck a match on the table-top, his eyes watering against the whiff of sulphur as he held it up to the cig.

He wondered whether, if he was to go to another part of London, he might like it better. He sure hated Holloway, but a pal of his had a room in Finsbury Park and rooms were hard to come by, so he reckoned he'd been lucky there. The house was opposite the park in a crumbling terrace that was subsiding because of the bombing. The room smelled of damp, and was up a set of rickety stairs covered in a seasick-green carpet. It reminded him of being on a ship. There were three rooms to a landing and an outdoor lav, and it was twenty-two bob a week, which was a fucking liberty seeing as the place was such a dump. He and his pal split it, even though his pal was still in the navy and only there one weekend in three. Still, it suited them. They had a system if one of them got his hooks on a bint, not that this happened for him all that often.

He drank his tea and smoked. He caught the waitress looking at him a couple of times, but he wasn't bothered one way or the other. He could have had her if he put his mind to it; maybe he would. He was a good-looking fellah. He took trouble with his appearance. The jacket, in particular, he was very pleased with. He had a sweet little number going on, and as a matter of fact, he was thinking of pulling off another little caper that very afternoon. He was a bit short, and his pal had gone to Brighton with a girl. He had enough left over for a few cigs and drinks, but not much more. He had plans to take the Tube down to King's Cross so's he could pinch another suitcase. His system was simple: he simply waited for the porter to turn his back and then helped himself to whatever was on top of the trolley. The luggage was being forwarded, so nobody was keeping much of an eye on it. A few weeks before he'd picked up a brand-new grey pinhead suit which must have cost at least two guineas; another time he'd got a gold enamel powder compact and a pair of nylons. If the waitress played her cards right he might let her have them. He also had a set of silver egg spoons which he had plans for. There was a woman in his lodgings, a horrible fat old whore, who ran a coupon racket. She charged a couple of bob a piece for them, but he reckoned she'd let him have some in exchange for the egg spoons. He laughed lightly to himself at the thought of the fat old whore. The coppers thought all racketeers were the same and looked out for blokes with thin 'taches, long jackets, wide-cut trousers. The police were mugs. The fat old whore had worked more coupons than half the spivs in London put together. With a few of them coupons he could get the little cock-eyed waitress to go with him alright; not that he needed coupons to get a tart, but it all helped. You'd think that spending four years serving your country would entitle you, but it didn't seem to: matelots didn't get any more of anything — coupons, bints — than anyone else.

He finished his tea and asked for a coffee, and the waitress did that half-shrug thing girls do when they like the look of you but don't want you to know it. He yawned, bored with it already; bored with everything. He thought he might take himself up west so's he could buy one of those hats with Jimmy Cagney's autograph on the sweatband, but no sooner had he thought it than he knew it was unlikely that he would do it; he had already decided at some point that he'd end up sitting in the café, smoking, drinking tea and coffee, eating rubbery cheese rolls, until it was time to go back to the room and get ready for the pubs to open. The thing of it was this: since the war he had occupied a vacant space, going through each day and from one day to the next sitting about in cafés waiting for pubs to open; then sitting about in pubs getting lit up. His was a pointless bloody existence: a curse to him. A fucking curse. Maybe tomorrow, which was Sunday when the pubs and cafés were all shut, maybe then he'd go to

King's Cross and pinch a suitcase, but other than that he had no particular ambition. It had all been blown out of him when he was sent flying through the air.

He scowled at the cigarette he was smoking and told himself that it was fucking London that was doing this to him: its sordidness, mapped out in pubs and cafés all stinking of grease and toilets. He suffered an overwhelming confusion in the noise of the shopping streets, in the hell of the buses and the crowds of people. No sooner had he come off the train at Waterloo than he was sorry he'd listened to his pal; sorry he'd come. Sorry he hadn't stayed in Portsmouth. He was sorry for a lot of things. The bloke at the Resettlement Office had told him how he had to start planning for the rest of his life; how he'd come through a tremendous ordeal; how he needed to get some training so's he could get a job. Jobs were hard to come by. You needed skills. You needed certificates. It wasn't enough for you to have spent four bloody years fighting for your country and having parts blown out of you, parts of you that you needed. It all made him want to fucking spit. Not that he was one of those commies who spend their time on the wireless and in the newspapers going on about building a future where everyone was more equal. He didn't have any time for that. He imagined that to be a commie you had to care about the future, and he didn't give a shit: it had taken him four years to reckon he didn't have one, and now here he was waiting for the pubs to open and maybe tomorrow he'd take a train ride and pick out a nice piece of luggage for himself, and how was that for making the world a more equal place? He kept his sailor's uniform clean and pressed, ready for when he was needed again.

He stretched his legs out under the table, blowing smoke rings at the ceiling and wondering how it would have been for him if he'd never lost whatever it was, if he'd stayed like he'd been before. He had flown through the air. He had seen the sea on fire.

It made you think. It really did.

The waitress brought his coffee, and slopped it down on the table in front of him. He fixed her with a cool appraising look, up and down, the whole length of her body. She had a squint, but her figure wasn't half bad. Not bad at all. She looked back at him, their eyes locking briefly. It was enough. He leaned back in the chair until he had lifted the front legs clean off the ground, laughing lightly; smoking.

CHAPTER
ELEVEN

"Lil! Lil! Wait for me!" Evelyn was pink and breathless with the effort of catching her up. "I thought it was you. I saw you from the other side of the road!"

"Glory! If I'd known you were coming out, you could have saved me a job," she said. "Honestly, Evvie, you never think. Do you know, I had to queue nearly two hours for bread." She held up a string bag containing a small split tin loaf, a few buns, a slab of stale fruit cake and a parcel of chopped meat slices. "All morning, and look what it's got me. And the boy in Jolly's was very rude to me, just because I wasn't sure if I had enough points. 'Don't you know your entitlement after all this time, madam?' I ask you."

"Cheeky little sod," said Evelyn. She had linked arms with her and was steering them both through the crowds. "Got any cigs, Lil?"

"No, I haven't. And you shouldn't smoke in public. It looks very common. Didn't your mother teach you anything?" Evelyn smiled back at her blankly. There really was no point: the girl would not be told. "I was thinking of walking down to the coster at Finsbury Park Station. It's very rough down there, but I heard a woman in the greengrocer's say that you can get lettuces there for ninepence."

"No," Evelyn said.

"I wasn't going to pay a shilling for one the size of an orange."

"Ooh! Hold up a minute . . ." The girl had stopped in the middle of the pavement, forcing everyone else to go around her. She was turning over the side of one of her shoes. "Oh, I can't hardly walk in these, Lil. Innit awful? I feel like a tramp going out in them, honest I do."

She looked at the girl's long brown legs extending from her little white ankle socks. The legs were the product of hours spent sun-bathing in the backyard with her skirt hitched up. She really was very common.

"There's ever such a nice pair in Lilley and Skinners . . ." the girl was saying. She raised an eyebrow but said not one word, while Evelyn appeared to consider something. "Here, Lil," the kid said after a moment, "why don't you give me a couple of your mum's points?"

She hated the way the girl called her 'Lil'.

"You're joking, aren't you?"

"I'll pay you for them." Evelyn's plump, pretty face was puckered into a fawning smile.

What with? The kid hadn't had a job for months.

"You know, if you didn't keep turning them over like that they'd do you for years."

"I'll give you a quid for five of your mum's coupons."

"Where are you going to get a pound from?"

"I'll put your mum on the po every day for a month, and put the talc on her bedsores."

Evelyn hated seeing to the bedsores more than she hated anything else.

"Evelyn, I am not giving you any of my mother's coupons."

Beneath her blonde sausage-roll curls the kid was scowling at her. People were staring. She hoped there wouldn't be a scene. She hated any sort of scene.

She smiled tightly.

"You're making a terrific spectacle, you know. It's too hot, Evelyn, and I'm exhausted. I've been on my feet all morning tramping about the place, enduring the rudeness of Saturday boys and greengrocers and bakers and goodness knows who else."

She continued along the Holloway Road, leaving the girl behind her on the street. A nice lettuce would be just the ticket. She was imagining Evelyn standing there; it would probably take five minutes before some fellow spotted her and asked her if she was alright. He'd compliment her and suggest that they go and have a cup of tea somewhere and the silly girl would let him run his hands up her leg beneath the table while she asked him if he had any clothing coupons.

Oh for goodness sake! You're not her mother, she told herself. But it was no good. She stopped and turned round, relieved to see Evelyn a few feet from where she had just left her, looking at the furs in a shop window.

"Evvie." The girl looked up at her, expectant. "Why don't we go and get a cup of tea somewhere? I could do with a nice sit down. I'm all in."

The girl gripped her arm and they walked the rest of the way to Nag's Head and turned down Seven Sisters Road. The café was a few yards ahead of them on the other side of the road, opposite Woolworths, and when she saw it she realised that she hadn't had anything to eat or drink since first thing. It was no wonder she was feeling so queer. A cup of tea; a teacake or a roll and butter: she'd feel better then. They crossed the street. A Number 43 bus passed along the top of the road on its way to somewhere better, and she thought: maybe this time Evelyn will do as she is told. Maybe it would all be alright. Maybe the ninepenny lettuces would be green and crisp and the size of a football; like they used to be.

CHAPTER
TWELVE

It didn't matter that it was a Sunday. By definition, crime is no observer of propriety, and observance is for respectable people, living decent lives, and there's never anything decent about a police station, no matter what day of the week it is. The front desk at "N" Division HQ in Stoke Newington was its usual hive of suspicion, recrimination, skulking and general deplorability. The desk sergeant, stood behind the ledger desk, barely had the opportunity to salute the guv'nor as he walked in at the front door: two telephones were jumping off their cradles in front of him, and a third was clamped to his ear. They exchanged a nod as Cooper made his way through the huddle of local characters, some emitting silent menaces, some greeting him with a rueful shrug, the hall ringing with various sides of numerous convoluted stories, wheedling, insinuating, carping, ingratiating, imploring. Beat coppers sidled past him, some of them looking as shifty as the crooks they were escorting. Everyone was guilty of something; it was contagious. A stout middle-aged woman in a dress that was a couple of sizes too small for her was negotiating with a harassed flatfoot, assuring him that none of it was down to her and it would be a mercy if those who were to blame were held to account.

Cooper avoided eye contact. He knew a good deal more about most of the villains in that corridor than was proper. He knew where that one bought his paper; which brand of cigs that one favoured; how many sugars the chap in the checked cap had in his tea and the chemist where he bought his indigestion remedy. He knew that Johnny Bristow called on the girl of that one over there whenever the fellow was out of town, and he was certain that one day he would run across that fellow and that piece of information would prove very valuable indeed. The criminal underworld was a sort of village; despite being presently flooded with deserters and demobees with nothing better to do than cause trouble, it was still a close-knit community and information had a habit of leaking like water from a sieve.

"Mr Cooper, Mr Cooper!"

He carried on walking as a weasel-faced Irishman pursued him along the corridor, plucking at the sleeve of his jacket. Like all narks, Short-time Jackie was a fount of information on any crime that didn't involve him.

"I'm afraid it'll have to wait, Jackie, whatever it is," he said. "I'm busy."

Short-time Jackie carried on walking, looking about him, nodding at a couple of prick-the-garter merchants who, slinking down even further on the bench they were sitting on, sneered in response. Jackie tapped the side of his pickled nose with his finger.

"I might have something for you, Mr Cooper, sir," he said in a whisper. "A certain someone has had a tickle, if you follow my meaning." He looked over one shoulder and then the other, and when he spoke again his voice had dropped even further into his boots. "A nice tickle, I should say."

Cooper stopped walking and absent-mindedly slipped the nark five bob. Jackie winked a rheumy eye.

"O'Leary's up at Archway," he said. "I'll be there any night you care to drop by, Mr Cooper, sir. They got gin. On tap."

"I'll see what I can do, Jackie, but I'm busy."

"You're a true gent, Mr Cooper, sir; one of the best." Cooper continued along the corridor with the encomium ringing at his back. "No. I tell a lie: the very best. You're on the level, sir, God bless you, and that's the truth."

Crumpled detectives littered the main incident room; men like him: badly shaved, balding, dressed in ill-fitting, indistinct blue suits, and crammed into a smoky room the colour of putty. They were making telephone calls, drinking tea, smoking, pinning things on to large noticeboards; they were slumped in attitudes of resignation, frustration, dismay, their elbows leaning on desks cluttered with overflowing ashtrays, unfinished cups of cold tea, stacks of reports.

"We've picked up a murder," he told his number two, who sighed dutifully. "Afraid so, old man; some poor tart rather carelessly got herself strangled last night."

"People are so inconsiderate," said the detective inspector.

"Aren't they though."

"Don't they know there's a crime wave?"

Cooper grinned lightly. "Frank Lucas is running things for me, but obviously I shall have to give it some of my attention."

The number two was a paunchy fellow of about thirty-five, but looked older; he had only just returned to the service after four years in the army, years which had intensified a tendency to mask chronic dyspepsia with an unconvincing cheeriness.

"Just tell me what needs doing, chief," he said, suppressing the need to wince from the pain of an incipient ulcer.

Cooper handed over the samples. "These need to go to Hendon."

The detective inspector winced again. "This afternoon? There won't be anyone there, you know. It's Sunday."

"Well, I wanted half an hour alone with this first, in any case," said Cooper. He held up the bag containing the mackintosh. "Any chance of a cuppa?"

Cooper took himself into a small side room and spread out the mackintosh on a large table set beneath trammels of pipes, thick with paint, running along the walls and across the ceiling. He scrutinised every inch of the mackintosh through his glass until he had a crick in his neck, and the garment was covered in careful crayon circles: green for grass stains; yellow for what looked like semen. There was no blood that he could see, which was perhaps odd given the circumstances, but he quickly discovered a short hair, of a different colour to the victim's, stuck to the inside of the collar. There was also a dry-cleaning ticket pinned to one of the seams, and he sighed to himself as he placed the latter in an evidence bag, imagining how Lucas would respond to being told to trace the laundry: the sceptical pout; the sharp draw on the ever-present fag; the economic lift of the eyebrows. And doubtless, Upstairs would be of a like mind.

But then, he told himself, murder is murder.

When he was quite certain that he had exhausted the possibilities of the mackintosh, he handed it over to the DI to be sent to the lab, and went into his office to pass a cursory eye over the deep pile of notebooks belonging to the "N" Division detectives serving under him. He was supposed to read and sign them off each week but he was always behind with his paperwork. Usually he would do anything to avoid catching up, but he needed a distraction — something to occupy his mind so that he didn't keep telephoning Lucas.

The waiting is always the worst part of an investigation. He had men going through the local lists of missing women. They had sent a good description of the victim to Scotland Yard to be circulated by teleprinter to every police station in the country. There were photographs for the Police Gazette. They were conducting house-to-house inquiries in the area around the murder site, and a search of every front garden and dustbin between it and the nearest main road. The woman's fingerprints were being checked, and in a day or two, if she was known to the police, they might even have a name. In three or four days, if she was not known to the police, the whole exercise would have been an utter waste of time and manpower. You just never knew. You simply had to wait: knowing that every minute of waiting meant even more distance between you and the murderer.

He knew the theory, had assisted on any number of murder investigations, and led a few on his own account; but all of this experience had taught him only that he lacked the flair, the intuition that separates a first-rate murder investigator from the dull, work-a-day plod. He was tenacious, occasionally given to flashes of insight; but when it came to homicide all he really knew to do was follow procedure.

He sighed and tossed away the last of the notebooks. Detectives, he decided, provide a desultory, barely literate read, with their unavailing tallies of unsatisfactory interviews with pawky snouts. It was depressing to learn of crimes that had yet to be committed; of the lorry loads waiting to be hijacked; the coupons hitherto unstolen; the shops unlooted; the safes uncracked — knowing that there was bally-all that you could do about most of it. And even if there was . . . He was painfully aware of the rest of his life stretching out before him in a long never-ending stream of crime report sheets. After a few moments of thinking like this, he rubbed his eyes back to alertness and removed his feet from the desk. Then he picked up his pen, unscrewed the barrel and recorded a few scant pieces of information: the sort of reassuring twaddle that the detective superintendent liked to see. When he had done this, he took himself down to the cells to see how the interviews with the two crooks they had nabbed last night were going.

If there was ever need of proof just how much CID had suffered since the war, it was writ plain on the boyish, worried face of the junior detective sergeant — a fellow named Quennell. It takes a good long while to train a detective, and a lot of good men weren't coming back for one reason or another, and there had been very little recruitment for the duration. The remainder were not always of the highest calibre. Quennell was still wet behind the ears, smooth-chinned, no more than a few months out of uniform and a good few fathoms out of his depth.

"Have you been playing them off against one another?" Cooper asked. "Telling each of them that the other one has landed him in the — you know what — up to his filthy neck." Quennell blinked back at him, doubtful. Cooper took a slurp of tea. "I don't have time to help you on this, Quennell. We picked up a murder today."

"Oh yes, sir, I heard about that."

Cooper sighed.

"Let me have a word," he said.

He went into the first room. Little Jimmy Dashett was one of those to whom war had given a swagger, a sense of entitlement: nothing more than a cosh-boy, the hooligan sort who is nothing without a knuckleduster in his pocket. Cooper knew instinctively that there was little chance of extracting any worthwhile information from him. To begin with, Jimmy would know nothing about the racket; and it was evident that although the stupid kid had grown up before his time, he still had a lot to learn about how things worked. He told him to take his feet off the table and sit up straight. With a good deal of sneering and ill-graced shifting, the kid complied.

"I'm not interested in you, Jimmy," he said. "You're small fry as far as I'm concerned. I'm after bigger fish. Tell me about Johnny Bristow."

The kid smirked.

"What about him?" he said.

"We know all about his rackets."

"So what do you need me to tell you for then?"

Cooper was always unerringly polite when interrogating prisoners, and had never found it necessary to raise his voice when doing so, no matter how wearing it was hearing the same old lies and excuses over and over again. However, he had to suppress the urge to clip Little Jimmy Dashett round the ear.

"We already know about the eggs, Jimmy," he said. One hundred and eighty thousand of them coming up from the West Country, on their way to a Ministry of Food warehouse. "That's a big operation. A job like that requires money up front; it takes planning. Oh, you'll have your part to play, I don't doubt, but what do you stand to get from it? A pony? A few petrol coupons?"

"You won't get me that way, bogey," said Little Jimmy, who had evidently seen too many gangster pictures.

"I'm not trying to get you, Jimmy; I'm just wondering why you should be looking at six months' stir. A bright boy like you? Why should you break your mother's heart? Spending Christmas sitting on the edge of a hard bunk, staring at the floor, eating cold mashed potato — when all the while the real villain is out there, jitterbugging the night away, probably with your girl?"

Cooper stopped talking and drank his tea. He could see that Jimmy was thinking about it, weighing up his options. Cooper was quite content to sit there in silence as he finished his tea, set the cup and saucer neatly upon the table and sat back in his chair with his arms folded in front of him. He could have waited all afternoon, but not so the young detective sergeant.

"Answer the detective inspector," Quennell said. Little Jimmy Dashett lifted up his head and levelled a huge gob of spit at him. He was smirking triumphantly as the flatfoot standing beside him grabbed him by the shoulders and hauled him to his feet.

"I never come copper on anyone," he was shouting above the kerfuffle of scraping chairs and table legs, "and I ain't starting now."

Cooper handed the boy detective a handkerchief and looked levelly at Little Jimmy Dashett.

"Seems you can't do some people a favour," he said. The kid looked away first. "Charge him with assaulting a police officer. I'm going to see if we can get more sense out of his chum."

The other crook was an old hand at the game of interrogation, well known across north London as Quiet Sid, on account of his being the most garrulous individual in the whole Metropolitan Police area. Quiet Sid made Max Miller look like Helen Keller, and was the sort of villain detectives like: the sort who cannot keep their mouths shut no matter what the stakes; the sort who like to brag to anyone who will listen. Cooper was very good at listening.

"I suppose I'm under starter's orders," Quiet Sid said even before Cooper had had a chance to settle into his chair. Within minutes Sid had come up with a whole scenario in which he knew everyone and everything; every angle of every dodge.

"The front's a barber's shop on Fonthill Road," he was saying, "little four-by-two running the game — goes by the name of Manny Cohen . . ."

"Every policeman in London knows Manny Cohen," sighed Cooper. "Tell me something I don't know."

Sid fingered another crook, a rival of Johnny Bristow for supremacy in north London.

"You would not believe the extent of the operation, Mr Cooper. The other week they shifted a million cigs — foreign import. They took them out of the boxes and sold 'em loose — export, see: foreign — not Turks or Greeks . . ."

After Sid had run on in this way for a good fifteen minutes, Cooper leaned forward and looked at him in earnest.

"Sid, tell me about Johnny Bristow."

Quiet Sid sucked in a draught of breath until he whistled, then he withdrew to his side of the table and shook his head.

"Nah nah," he said. "You won't find his dabs on anything, I'll tell you that for nothing, Mr Cooper."

Cooper rubbed his eyes and settled back in his chair. He was tired and hungry, and it was occurring to him that in some profound sense, he didn't give a damn about black-market eggs and cigarettes and Jew fences. The run-of-the-mill crook, such as Quiet Sid, was an open book to him, in it for the dibs, the readies, and although he had never been motivated by greed, Cooper could understand a man who was; there was no mystery there. He needed to give some time to attempting to understand how a man had come to strangle a woman with his bare hands. He didn't want to, but he had to, and the necessity of the task depressed him. He signalled to the detective sergeant to take over, and leaned across the table to shake Sid's hand.

"Thanks, old man," he said. "I appreciate it."

Cooper had another cup of tea in his office and then walked over to Caledonian Road. The walk helped to clear his head a little, and the clarity lasted until he arrived at the station and discovered that Lucas still had nothing to report. No missing persons report matching the dead woman had turned up; nobody living near the murder scene had heard or witnessed anything untoward; so far the dustbins had failed to yield a handbag.

"Extend the house-to-house," Cooper said.

Lucas drew on his ever-present cigarette. "I'm running this investigation with one detective sergeant and two beat coppers," he said.

"Stupid suggestion," said Cooper. "Stupid, stupid, stupid."

He hovered over the incident room like a spectre; from time to time he and Lucas sat either side of a large table going over the evidence, positing theories.

"Something about this doesn't sit right," Cooper said for the 'umpteenth time. "No sign of any struggle, apart from the bruise on her hand. Looks like she removed her own drawers; they spread a mackintosh out on the ground beneath her."

"Could have been a pimp came across them," said Lucas. "Maybe she was treating a client, or keeping the money back. Pimps don't like that."

Cooper shook his head. "A pimp would have beaten the living daylights out of her. Besides, there was no evidence that more than the two people were there."

Lucas tapped the ash from his cigarette into a large tin ashtray.

"I can pull in Greek Tony, if you like. He runs a lot of the local girls."

"She just doesn't look like a tart to me." Cooper ran his hands across his stubble. "What are we missing, Frank? What's gone on here?"

The DI sighed. "Why don't you go and get yourself something to eat, sir?" he said.

Cooper grinned. "If I didn't know any better, I'd say you were trying to get rid of me."

"Can't have you pegging out on us, guv'nor."

"Oh, no fear of that, old man; no fear of that . . ."

CHAPTER
THIRTEEN

Half an hour later Cooper was emerging from the underground at Piccadilly Circus, and stepping into a stupefying heat. Without the lights, Town was bereft of whatever illusory glamour it might once have possessed; the badly dressed staggered drunkenly past him in clouds of brilliantine, cigarette smoke and cheap scent, and it wasn't long before he was wondering why on earth he had bothered to come.

He headed for a restaurant which he vaguely remembered as one that would be serving dinner on a Sunday night, but it was only as he turned into the street that he recollected it was also the place where he had first met Marjorie. How on earth had he forgotten that? Perhaps it was a good sign — proof that he was finally moving on. Bill had wanted so badly to show her off to him, so they had made up a party. He'd gone there with a girl whose name he had forgotten. The mere fact that he had ever done such things as going out to dinner with friends, with a girl, seemed implausible to him now. Of course, this would have been before the war: '36. '37.

After they'd eaten their main courses, Marjorie and the other girl had gone off to powder their noses and Bill had leaned over and said:

"That's the girl I'm going to marry."

The restaurant was still there, although it had evidently suffered as much as he had in the intervening years and had declined into the sort of place where they tell you the price in shillings so it sounds cheaper. He paid a small fortune for a couple of boiled potatoes swimming in greasy Bisto and a well-grilled chop which he needed his magnifier to locate; pudding was half a tinned pear and a sponge finger steeped in evaporated milk; the slice of bread and margarine which he had with it was by far the best part of the whole meal. It was hardly the Café Royal, but he supposed it was better than enduring the misery of a cup of tea in the all-night Express Dairy. He tried not to look about him at the other sad and lonely men hunched over their bowls of soup; it wasn't just that it was dispiriting: looking around a public place marked you out as a copper as surely as if you had walked in with a blue light on your head.

He walked back to the underground, the tarts stepping out from the shadows invariably retreating as soon as they clapped eyes on him. The tarts could tell at a glance: the way he walked, the Homburg, the battered mackintosh; they could smell it on him, for all he knew. He wondered when the fishnet stockings and little veiled hats of the pre-war era had given way to mottled flesh and cheap headscarves.

"Hello, dearie!"

He doffed his hat and shook his head.

"Not tonight."

"Any time, dearie. I'm always here, I am. It's a nice clean room."

As he walked away he wondered if he would ever be that lonely. He didn't want sex; he wanted something else. He could not bear to contemplate what it was he was missing. Besides, he was too much of a prig, too fastidious. His first experience, as a boy of fifteen, finding himself in the midst of war — not the Hitler War, the other one: the one they still called the Great War — had marked him for life. He had been urged on by the older fellows — they were going over the top at dawn. "You don't want to die a virgin, do you, Jimmy?" He had never had occasion to think about such a profundity before: a few weeks earlier he had worried about nothing more than his batting average in the school first eleven. Death. Sex. The stark absurdity of the juxtaposition had struck him even then; an irony of laughable tragedy, like that of the condemned man eating a hearty breakfast half an hour before the drop. It had seemed to him then, and it did now, to be both the most pointless and the most important thing in the whole world. The woman had smelled of garlic and stale rosewater, and was naked apart from her stockings, which were rolled down to her knees, and a dirty cotton shift. Her breasts had been large and greasy. He hadn't known what to do, was utterly clueless, shocked by the way his body seemed to know more about what was going to happen than he did, and the woman had long since grown weary of educating lines of terrified, stupid boys. He kept thinking about his mother and his sisters. The other men had laughed and jeered when he emerged from the tiny attic room, pale and trembling and feeling slightly sick, less than five minutes after entering it; and the joke only wore off when most of them disappeared over the top the next day.

He, however, did not die: much to his amazement, he had lived to have sex again; to love. He had lived and he had loved. It was at once the most pointless and the most important thing in the whole world.

He snorted with derision at the psychoneurotic cycle he was concocting, like some blasted Freudian; but even so, he was unable to prevent his thoughts coalescing around the memory of Marjorie. It had ended badly, but while it lasted there had been such happiness, he was sure of that. How he despised this sort of introspection. He should never have gone to the restaurant: something had been stirred; and now he was missing her scent, her voice, her warmth, her being. He was missing the person he had been when he was with her. When, he wondered, had he become so dull, so sagging, so tired, so hungry? Were all men like him when they reached their forties? Were they all tired and hungry and more than a little scared?

Marjorie had left him on the day that war broke out: such a small thing in the greater scheme, but not to him. To him it was the biggest thing in the whole world. An atom bomb of the heart. And now here he was and nobody would ever want him again. Well, he supposed, at least he had been spared any more misery; and when he came to think about it, this was probably what he had hankered after all along. A strong desire to avoid the misery of human entanglements was what had led him to choose Marjorie: a woman he knew he could never have had all to himself. His best pal's girl. Never again. He was done with all of that. From now on Mrs Oscar was the only woman he wanted in his life; the thought of his redoubtable charlady restoring to him a degree of mental equilibrium.

Descending into the dust-laden heat of the underground, he chided himself for such maudlin thinking and put it down to the quest he was now engaged in. A sex murder is bound to bring down your spirits. A warm breeze coming from the tunnel riffled through his untidy hair, and as he reached up a hand to smooth it he told himself, for the second time that day, that he really must get a haircut, and realised, with a start, that for the past few moments he had been thinking not of Marjorie, but of Policewoman Tring. Damn the girl, he thought. Damn her freckles and her legs; damn her kindness; damn her seriousness; damn her smile. And why must she be so damned attractive? His thoughts swung between the A4 Branch girl and the murdered woman as he rattled his way back to north London on the Tube. Legs, breasts, waved hair and painted nails: it all swirled before him in his tired imagination. He pondered the paradox of the good-quality man's mackintosh, spread out upon the ground as if by a latter-day Walter Raleigh, and the man who had done that, and whether he was thinking all the while as he did so that he would soon be choking the life out of the woman he was about to seduce. He had seen plenty of times before the proof that desire all

99

too often turns to murder but how this came to be still puzzled him. He wondered about the woman who had neatly stepped out of her drawers. He wondered whether there was terror in her eyes when she did that and whether this had appealed to the killer; whether terror in a woman's eyes could ever appeal to him; whether it secretly appealed to all men. He wondered and he wondered, until he was quite sure that none of it made any sense to him. Then he yawned and closed his eyes for the last two stops, disembarking at Caledonian Road and making his perplexed, weary way to the station, where he spent several hours going through the missing persons lists again and again until Lucas told him, firmly, finally, that he had better face it: nobody was missing her. Nobody. By the time, around about two o'clock in the morning, that Lucas called it a day and despatched everyone homewards, he was feeling about as useful as a bottle of Scotch at a teetotallers' convention. He walked back to Stoke Newington, through dark streets heavy with loneliness, shadowy with the ruins of lives and homes and businesses, past a huge hoarding hanging from the exposed end of a bombed terrace urging him to "Save for Reconstruction".

Back home he drank a glass of Scotch and fiddled with the wireless for several minutes before remembering that the accumulator had run down; then he went and sat in the armchair, put his feet up on the bookshelves, smoked a pipe and listened to a gramophone record of Fischer's performance of Schubert's Impromptus. He was slipping in and out of drowsiness, wondering whether Schubert had known he had only a few months to live, before he died of VD. He listened for intimations of mortality in the rise and fall of the melody, in the silences between each cadence; he pictured the hand hovering above the keys in the delayed moment. At some point in the night he awoke suddenly to the certainty that he was still in the foxhole, up to his balls in freezing shit and mud, with his hands clamped over his head, waiting, praying, praying, waiting for the final chord: for darkness. He was surrounded by the spectres of men struggling for breath in the suffocating swamp, their livid hands clawing against the sky. It took him a few moments to remember that he had crawled out of the foxhole, his heart pounding, his breath coming in short steamy bursts; he had run across the wasteland, with bullets whistling past his ears, explosions shattering the ground. He was not a ghost: he was one of the legions of the undead, dying their slow, silent deaths. He hated it when he thought like this, but sometimes one is just too tired. He let himself slip away, succumbing to the thick impenetrable mud, to the sense of impending doom that had accompanied the moments before sleep every night for the past thirty years.

CHAPTER
FOURTEEN

She had been in the café before — before the war — when it had been a cosy little place, with pretty floral prints on the wall and clean gingham tablecloths. The pictures were still there, but now they were barely discernible beneath a sticky coating of dust and a thick haze of cigarette smoke that made her eyes water. One bare light bulb hung from the centre of the ceiling alongside a strip of fly paper, and the whole place was suffused with post-war staleness: rot, accumulated grime, softened by intermittent bursts of steam emitting from a vast urn that was set upon the counter. The urn was tended by a large unshaven man who was wearing a striped butcher's apron over a singlet, his thick arms covered in tattoos. He was reading the *Sporting Life* and every so often he licked his thumb and forefinger to turn the pages. He was concentrating hard and did not look up when they walked in; the waitress, who was leaning on the front of the counter, audibly sighed when she saw them.

She wanted to leave, but Evelyn had crossed to a table and was already asking for two cups of tea and two buttered teacakes. This was typical of Evelyn, who always did just as she pleased; she had a nerve, ordering tea and buns when she didn't have a penny on her. She went and sat down: at least their table was near to the open door, through which a forgiving breeze cut across the thick moist air.

At the next table a blowsy woman with heavy features was drinking a cup of tea and smiling at them. The woman was thickly powdered and rouged and her eyebrows had been plucked to obscurity and then retraced with heavy black mascara. She was dressed in a short-sleeved brown pin-dot dress from which obtruded plump arms ending in grubby white gloves; a fox-fur collar was draped across her shoulders. She had on a reblocked man's hat that had been dyed mauve and adorned with a little spotted veil that fell shy of one eye. There could be no doubt what sort of woman she was.

"Ooooh, hot, isn't it?" she was saying to Evelyn, plucking at the front of her dress. "I'm in a bath of perspiration, I am."

"They say it's got something to do with the Atom Bomb," Evvie said. "They" was Walter, reacting to something he had heard on the wireless the other day.

"Oooer," said the stout woman. She had a piece of fruit cake, which she held as delicately as she was able in her fat gloved fingers, before pushing it into her mouth. "I was going to the coast this weekend," she said, brushing the crumbs from her hands, "to get away from the heat. I can't abide the heat. I was going with my friend." There was something about the way the stout woman said the word "friend" that made her stomach turn. "But he's had to go back to barracks."

The stout woman leaned conspiratorially towards them, and they were assaulted by a cheap pungency that struggled to overcome the smell of stale perspiration: like Flit sprinkled on a bug-ridden mattress. "I don't suppose you've got a threepenny bit, have you, love?" she said in a hoarse whisper. "Only my suspender's gone, isn't it." The stout woman pulled up the hem of her dress to reveal a fat thigh bulging over the straining top of her stocking.

"I don't have any money on me, but my friend does," Evelyn said, turning to her, "don't you, Lil?"

Glaring at the kid, she rummaged in her pigskin handbag for her purse while the stout woman watched closely. She was careful not to bring the purse out, but clicked it open from the depth of her bag, stealthily retrieving a coin and slipping it towards the stout woman, who pushed it underneath the top of the stocking and then stretched the rubber of the suspender over the bulge of her thigh until the two met.

"Much obliged to you, I'm sure," she said, reaching out her hand. "Nesta Jones. Pleased to meet you."

She overcame her revulsion sufficiently to lightly touch the soiled glove that was being held out towards her, suppressing an uneasy feeling that she would live to regret this small gesture of civility.

"I'm Evelyn," said the wretched girl, "and this is my friend Lil — ."

"Mrs Frobisher."

Nesta was eyeing up the string bag of groceries that was lying on the table in a way that made her feel uncomfortable. She held her handbag tight on her knee.

"Did you manage to get any bread?" Nesta was asking. "Only I must have been up and down the Holloway Road half a dozen times and there's not a crust to be had anywhere."

"I had to queue for most of the morning," she said. A sly smile.

"I know where you can get tinned peas," Nesta said, "seeing as how you've done me a good turn, like. I can let you have some for one and threepence."

"You can get them for tenpence at the Co-op."

"If they have any in," said Nesta.

"And you need points as well," chimed in Evelyn. She could have strangled the stupid kid.

Nesta's tongue darted out and licked her lips.

"That's right," she said. "Three points! I ask you! Three points for a tin of peas!" Nesta took a slurp of coffee. "What about tinned soup? Two bob to you."

Evelyn nudged her.

"I'm afraid my husband doesn't really approve of those sort of dealings," she said. In truth, Walter was happy enough to eat a bit of BM ham if it came his way; he just didn't approve of what he called the "slimy types" who supplied it.

"Husbands!" exclaimed Nesta. "Mine was a right bugger. Meaner than ten thousand Scotch Jews rolled together. It was a blessing to me when he died. Take it from me, love," she said to Evelyn, "you're better off without them."

Evelyn laughed.

"Oh, I'm in no hurry," she said. "I'm out to have a good time, me."

"Well, why not?" said Nesta. "You're only young once."

She could feel one of her heads coming on. She groped in her handbag for the packet of phenacetin she knew was in there somewhere. The waitress brought their order of two cups of tea and two teacakes, slapping them down on the table. The kid had a nice figure, but it was a shame about the squint. A squint is such a misfortune to a girl. She swallowed the headache tablet with a mouthful of tea.

"Miss," she called across to the retreating girl, "I wonder, might I have some sugar, please?"

"Sugar's here," said the waitress. She jerked a thumb at a bowl that was sitting on the counter. It was armed with a single spoon that was attached to the tea urn by a grimy piece of string.

"Evelyn," she said, "be a dear and get me some sugar, will you?"

She hadn't noticed the young man sitting in the corner nearest to the counter, but he had noticed her.

"How many d'you want, blondie?"

He was stirring a cup of coffee; his upper lip, wrapped around an unlit cigarette, was turned up in a sort of sneer, but he was not sneering at her: he was sneering at the world, and the thought of such dangerous contempt gave her a queer sort of thrill. He was rather a good-looking fellow, very smartly dressed in a green tweed jacket, nylon shirt and fancy tie. She couldn't remember the last time she'd seen a man so well dressed; certainly not since the war, and probably never in Holloway.

"Oh, thank you," she said, with a faint smile that was calculated to encourage while not appearing to do so. "That's very kind, I'm sure. Two please."

Evelyn kicked her under the table.

"Here," she whispered. "I reckon he likes you."

The young man came across to collect her cup and saucer, and she assumed an air of indifference as she finished off the half of buttered teacake, dabbing genteely at the corners of her mouth with her little finger. She did not want to look like a possible, but at the same time she was flattered. He crossed to the counter and she noticed that his jacket was the swing-back sort and beautifully cut. It was like one she had seen Leslie Howard wearing in some picture before the war. She didn't know you could buy jackets like that any more. Tweed was so scarce. She wondered how many coupons you'd need.

"I reckon he's a spiv," whispered Evelyn. "Here, Lil, you'll be alright there."

"Ssshh, Evvie. They'll hear you."

She glanced at Nesta, who was leaning over the back of her chair.

"Here, Dennis," she called across to the young man, "Paddy's been called back to barracks."

He shrugged and heaped two spoonfuls of sugar into her cup. He stood at the counter with his back to them, stirring methodically.

"Paddy's my friend," confided Nesta. "He's a terribly jealous boy. Isn't that right, Dennis?" Dennis ignored her. "Oh, terrible jealous, he is. Can't bear another man looking at me — especially when he's had a drink. It's the Irish in him, see. Hot-tempered lot they are. Mind you, gives me a bit of a lift, I can tell you." Nesta winked at her and began to cackle.

"That's the Irish for you," said Evelyn, slurping her tea.

The young man brought her cup back to their table and as he set it down she glanced up, briefly, and smiled at him.

He smirked.

"Shut up, Nesta," he said. "Blondie here doesn't want to hear about you and your disgusting habits."

Nesta flung her head back.

"What's the matter with you, Dennis?" she screeched. "It's only natural, isn't it? I'm not doing any harm. She knows what I mean, don't you, love?"

She did not respond. She didn't want to give the young man the wrong impression of herself.

"Here, you alright, love?" Nesta was peering at her. "Only you look a bit peaky."

"I'm perfectly fine, thank you."

"It's the heat," said Evelyn.

"Dripping, I am," said Nesta.

The young man had returned to his table and was leaning back on his chair so that the front legs were lifted clear of the floor; he lit a cigarette and aimed a steady stream of silvery smoke at the ceiling.

"Here," said Evelyn, "have you got a spare cig?"

He shrugged, taking a cigarette from the packet and lighting it for her with the glowing tip of his own.

Evelyn settled back in her chair to smoke, casting her a knowing look.

"I heard they got gin in at the Feathers," said Nesta.

"Good for them," said Dennis.

"There hasn't been any gin in weeks, has there, love?"

"Oh, I wouldn't know," she said, "I'm not really one for drink."

"What do you do in the evenings, then?"

"She likes to go to the pictures, don't you, Lil?" Evelyn said. She stubbed out the last of her cigarette in her saucer. "Or the Empire. Sometimes you go to the Empire on a Saturday night, don't you, Lil?"

She glared at the stupid kid.

"Are you going there tonight, love?"

"I haven't really thought about it, to be honest."

"Oh, you should," said Nesta. "You look like you could do with a good night out. Give yourself a break from that husband of yours." She began to laugh again: a horrible rattle that seemed to come from deep in the back of her throat. "You look all in, if you don't mind me saying." Nesta pressed a handkerchief against her mouth as the cackle subsided in a prolonged bout of wheezing and coughing. She dabbed at her eyes, which were watering. "Isn't that right, Dennis? She looks all in, doesn't she?"

Dennis shrugged.

"Oh, I dunno," he said. He stubbed out his cigarette and reached for another from the packet on the table. "She looks alright to me."

CHAPTER
FIFTEEN

He woke to the familiar sound of Mrs Oscar coming in at the front door. It appeared that he had yet again fallen asleep in his armchair; a cold pipe was lying on his chest where it had fallen from his lips and dottlings of grey ash speckled his vest. His char was used to coming across him like that; she made her customary observation that he ought to take care to put his pipe out before nodding off lest he burn down the entire block.

Cooper washed, shaved hurriedly and painfully; dabbed toothpowder on the worst of the scrapings; put on a clean shirt from the pile Mrs Oscar had just delivered; pulled the day before yesterday's still-knotted tie over his head; grabbed his jacket from the back of the chair, patting the pocket for his pipe and tobacco pouch; remembered that he had left them on the arm of his chair; went back to fetch them; grabbed his hat from the stand; thanked Mrs Oscar (who was complaining about the powdered cheese excrescence on the grill pan) and went out of the door.

He spent the entire Tube journey to Caledonian Road strap-hanging and immersed in nostalgia for fried eggs and bacon: real eggs, not American powdered; two of them, with glossy yolks, the colour of daffodils, and perhaps a few mushrooms on the side. He stopped off at a café on his way to the police station and bought a papery bread roll lined with slippery portions of brawn. It was quite disgusting, but he was so hungry he ate it in two bites, arriving at the murder conference with just enough time to wash away the lingering salt and slime with a cup of tea, which a dowdy, plump A4 Branch woman had set down on the table before him.

The incident room was clogged with the accumulated sweat, tedium, cigarette smoke and flatulence of the previous night. It was hellish hot. The windows hadn't been opened in years. Cooper took a seat at the head of the table. Lucas delivered a summation of the case, smoking lugubriously and constantly, issuing streams of grey dispiriting smoke which cast a pall over the large map which was pinned on the wall behind him, and to which he turned at frequent intervals, jabbing it with a nicotine-stained index finger. Lucas passed around photographs of the body and the murder site; he read from the witness statements. There was a scale drawing that one of the uniforms had prepared, indicating the distance between the body and the road, and the location of the piece of limestone where the woman might have stood with her killer prior to the act of strangulation. The small team absorbed all of this information with wearisome, dutiful interest; occasionally one of them would write down something, his gaze passing from the evidence to the DI and back again.

"Has the handbag turned up yet?" Cooper inquired as the exposition of the case came to a close.

Wordlessly Lucas tipped the contents of an evidence bag on to the table: a cobbler's ticket, a packet of headache tablets, a small hairbrush.

"PC Hawkes here found this lot on top of a hedge up on the main road," Lucas said in between attempts to light another cigarette.

The DI jabbed the map.

"He found it here — about a quarter of a mile from the murder site," he said. Then he cupped his hand over the cigarette and tried the lighter again, successfully this time.

The young uniform perked up, evidently delighted to find he was the object of the guv'nor's undivided attention.

"The house is underneath a street lamp," he said, "located at the exact spot where the street lighting begins heading south-east from the murder site to Holloway Road." He scanned his notebook earnestly. "I checked with the occupant of the house, sir," he continued, "a Mr J Scholes, who assured me that the items mean nothing to him or anyone in his household. And," he added entirely unnecessarily, but in the traditional manner of earnest coppers, "I believe him."

"There's a good chance there's a finger- or thumbprint on some of it," said Cooper. "Have it all sent over to the Yard, and ask them to compare anything they find to the victim's dabs."

Lucas drew on his cigarette, a steady stream of smoke flowing from his nostrils.

"So," he said, "the murderer carries away the victim's handbag until he has left the unlit streets and arrives at

112

the first place where he can examine its contents clearly. He stands beneath a streetlamp and goes through the contents of the handbag, discarding anything on top of the hedge that was of no value to him."

Cooper permitted himself a slurp of tea.

"Anything turn up from missing persons?"

Lucas shook his head.

"And we've definitely gone through all the lists?"

"Yes, sir," said the detective sergeant.

Cooper sighed heavily and drummed his fingers on the table-top.

"I find it exceedingly hard to believe that nobody is missing this particular person," he said.

The DS rubbed his chin sagely. "A lot of people disappear in London, sir," he said, "and I dare say a good many of them are never missed."

Cooper sighed again. "We'll give it one more day and then we'll issue a photograph of the dead woman. How are we getting on with the door-to-door inquiries?"

Lucas clamped his cigarette in the corner of his mouth and leafed through a thick untidy pile of papers on the table in front of him.

"They'll take another day at least to complete, sir," he said, "and that's only the quarter-mile or so around the murder site. I take it you want us to talk to everyone? Only some of those lodging houses are very overcrowded."

Cooper massaged his forehead with his thumb and index finger.

"It's possible," he said, "that the murderer is the only person in a position to notice that this woman has disappeared.

"He might be a fancy man, a ponce — the sort of bastard who goes through a woman's handbag moments after strangling her," said Lucas.

"Perhaps she was keeping some money back," said the detective sergeant. "That's probably why he took the handbag."

"It's possible," said Cooper, suddenly feeling keenly the hopelessness of it all, "although a pimp is more likely to have beaten her up — either before or instead of murdering her. The only sign of any struggle is the bruise on her knuckles."

"Perhaps the fellow she'd gone with got fresh," suggested the detective sergeant. "Maybe she changed her mind at the last minute. Or maybe he asked for something perverted."

"If he was a common pick-up," Lucas said, "he'll be impossible to find."

Cooper nodded circumspectly.

"Keep a note of any not-at-homes," he said. Procedure, he thought. Procedure. "And keep going back until they're there."

Lucas was slowly turning his cigarette between his thumb and forefinger, his mouth forming a shrewd pout around it.

"What about the raincoat, sir?" he asked.

Cooper set down the laundry ticket he had found pinned to a side seam on the table.

"It's a very good-quality gentleman's mackintosh," he said. "I've arranged for photographs and so forth. I dare say we might well be able to identify the store it came from. I shall telephone the manufacturer later on today."

He tapped the ticket with his index finger.

"Start locally."

There was a general shifting in the room, telling glances exchanged between Lucas and the detective sergeant.

"That could take some time, sir," said Lucas. He was giving him the look, the one with the raised eyebrows.

"Yes, I dare say, but we are investigating a murder, Detective Inspector." He paused for effect and in order to finish his tea. "I think we're done here," he said. He stood up to leave. "I'm going to HQ now, and I'll be at the morgue after that. I'll telephone at regular intervals to check on progress."

Lucas was looking at him; he could tell that the DI knew that he was scared: scared he'd make a mistake, scared he'd miss something; scared he wouldn't catch the bastard. He wondered if Lucas was scared.

"I'll have someone drive you back to Stoke Newington, sir?" Lucas said.

"No need for that. I'll take the Tube."

"There's no Tube to Stoke Newington, sir."

"I'm aware of that, Detective Inspector." He put on his hat and slung his raincoat over his arm. "I shall call in at regular intervals," he said.

The journey by public transport from Caledonian Road to Stoke Newington High Street is a bit of a bugger, requiring multiple exchanges of tardy buses, and most sensible people would consider it utter folly to even entertain such an undertaking. Cooper shared the general reservation, but his over-riding concern was that the driver Lucas sent for would turn out to be Policewoman Tring, and it was on this account that he wasted the best part of three-quarters of a precious hour standing at a bus stop in Manor House, before arriving back at the station house and a telephone call from the detective superintendent, wishing to be informed of all that had transpired over the weekend.

"Perhaps we should bring in someone from the Yard while you're on this," the super said on hearing of the murder. The super was not talking about a Murder Squad detective; he was offering the services of the Ghost Squad, so-called undercover detectives who were recognised by every criminal in London, who raced about in an Austin Sixteen taking all the credit for every battle won in the war against crime. Most ordinary detectives despised and envied the Ghost Squad in equal part, and Cooper was no exception.

"That won't be necessary, sir," he said, cursing inwardly.

"Well, if you're sure you can manage . . ."

It was astonishing how quickly the successful recovery of a lorry-load of black-market sugar and the apprehension of two known villains had been forgotten.

"Don't you worry, sir," he lied, "the two blighters we collared on Saturday night have already given us some useful leads."

"No honour among thieves, eh, Jim?" said the super.

"Something like that."

After checking on the cells, where the boy detective looked at least a decade older than he had looked the night before, Cooper returned to a welter of telephone messages (none of them from Lucas), read through some information pertaining to Johnny Bristow which had come by way of an anonymous letter sent by someone purporting to be a "concerned member of the public", and put in a telephone call to the manufacturer of the mackintosh. Then he had a quick look at some surveillance photographs of two crooks in the act of taking possession of what appeared to be a van-load of cauliflowers. Thanks to his sharp eyes and prodigious memory for the faces of north London's criminal underclass, he was able to put a name to one of them, and men were promptly despatched to bring the rascal in. Then he had a cup of tea, and took the call to the mackintosh manufacturer.

"Ah yes, the Westmoreland," said the voice at the other end of the line, "one of our more exclusive lines."

The manufacturer gave Cooper a list of retail outlets, which were, for the most part, the sort of gentleman's outfitters to be found in any provincial town. It would take weeks to contact them all.

"Do you sell any in London?"

"Oh yes," said the manufacturer, sounding more than a little affronted, "Gamages are always most eager to take any we can supply." To hear him the uninitiated would assume that Gamages was akin to the Royal Family.

"Gamages in Holborn?"

"As I said," smarmed the voice on the other end of the line, "it's a garment of distinction."

Cooper thanked the manufacturer for his time, and briefly considered sending someone over to Gamages. It was immediately apparent to him that as the only person whom he could send was himself, and he was due at the morgue, this was a task that would have to wait.

He was feeling pretty bloody by the time he arrived at King's Cross: hunger was largely to blame. After several increasingly frustrating attempts, he eventually succeeded in finding a working telephone and caught up with the office; then he telephoned Caledonian Road, only to be told, infuriatingly, that DI Lucas was "out on inquiries".

He stopped to buy a newspaper and some pipe tobacco, had an ill-tempered exchange with the vendor, who was of the opinion that the bread ration was all on account of the government making a priority of Huns over decent British men and women, went out on to the bomb-splintered street and perused the headlines in the hot glare of the sun.

WOMAN FOUND STRANGLED ON BOMB-SITE.
SCHOOLBOYS' TRAGIC DISCOVERY.

He was not all that surprised to discover that his sex murder had become the subject of several column inches of pure sensationalism. The reporter had succeeded in bringing to the attention of the public all the salient points of the case: the "bomb-shattered terrace", the wilderness used as a "lover's lane", the "silk-stockinged leg", his own bafflement ("the police

118

are clueless"). It was all there, gleaned from interviews with the children who had made the "shocking discovery", and those occupying the houses abutting the murder site. The general consensus was that everything was in decline and London was in the grip of a crime spree. He consoled himself with the thought that as the reporter had included a reasonable description of the woman in the article, it was always possible that someone who knew the victim might see the report and come forward. Knowing full well that the chances of this happening were about as good as his chances of winning the football pools, he considered what he would say when the newspaper reporters eventually ran him to ground. Everything that could possibly be done, he would tell them, in order to bring the killer to justice, is being done. You may be sure of that.

CHAPTER
SIXTEEN

He had never grown accustomed to the chill stink of the morgue; the morbidness of the white tiled walls; the circular drain holes cut into the metal of the operating table between the ankles of the dead; the trays to catch the fluids and the harsh glare of the bare electric bulb buzzing overhead. The formaldehyde induced in him nervous anxiety and incipient nausea, and the crushing awareness that he was not a homicide detective.

The pathologist was bent over the body, utterly absorbed in the task of collecting samples of hair from the dead woman's immaculately coiffed head. The girl assistant of the previous day was nowhere to be seen.

Cooper waited a few moments before coughing discreetly.

"Cooper! You sly dog!" In his leather apron and outsized surgical gloves, the surgeon seemed diminished, even comical. The elegantly suited professional man of the day before had been usurped by an innocent enthusiast, eyes agog behind thick magnifying spectacles.

"Please don't let me hold you up," Cooper said. His eyes passed over the Y-shaped incision extending from the dead woman's navel to her shoulders; when he came to her face, his first thought was that she looked older, more haggard, than he remembered from the day before. The effects of death, he supposed.

The pathologist had finished with the head and had turned his attention to the woman's hands. Cooper noted that her fingernails, and toenails, were painted a deep red, similar to the lipstick-stains on the cigarette end he had found at the murder scene. He had a strong dislike of lipstick on cigarettes; as a matter of fact, he didn't really approve of women smoking.

"Cause of death still strangulation?"

"Rather," said the pathologist without looking up. "The thyroid cartilage has been broken — most likely the result of the neck having been gripped tightly," he said cheerfully. "The thumb of the right hand will have done most of the damage."

Depending on whether or not she is breathing in or out, it takes between fifteen and twenty seconds to strangle a woman to death: marginally quicker if she is screaming at the time. Cooper tried to imagine what it would feel like to press your thumb against a person's throat for that length of time as you squeezed and squeezed the life out of them, watching them struggle for breath, for life. It was a dispiriting and unedifying experiment.

The pathologist had selected a pair of tweezers from a tray of instruments and was using them to retrieve something from underneath one of the woman's nails. Now he was holding up whatever it was that he had found and beckoning Cooper to come in closer.

121

"No skin," he said, meaning that the woman had not scratched her attacker in a desperate fight for life, "but this might prove more useful to you."

The tweezers had captured a single strand of green wool.

The evidence was not as compelling as a fingerprint might have been, but it was certainly better than the samples of hair which the pathologist had doubtless already collected from the woman's thighs and genitals; and better too than the short dark hair that he had found on the collar of the mackintosh. Plenty of men had body hair, but not all of them wore green wool jackets; put it all together and, who knows, maybe you had the missing part to a puzzle you had yet to solve.

He rubbed his chin speculatively.

"That's interesting," he said. The pathologist dropped the fibre into a glass phial. "Any distinguishing marks?"

"Afraid not, old boy. I've arranged for X-ray photographs to be taken of the jaw, and I'll see that they're sent to the *British Dental Journal.* Other than that, all I can tell you with any certainty is that she was five foot four, had potatoes for supper and was in the early stages of kidney disease. Oh, and she's given birth."

Cooper looked at the woman.

"She was a mother," he said.

"Well, she's given birth, at least once. Not necessarily the same thing."

Cooper brooded upon the information as the pathologist turned over the woman's right hand, indicating the bruised knuckles.

"She might not have scratched her assailant," he said, "but whoever was on the receiving end of that fist will have a nice contusion somewhere on his phizog."

Cooper sighed resignedly. It was all so simple. All he had to do was find a dark-haired bastard with a green wool jacket and a bruise on his chin. He was in a damned hole, and could see no way out of it.

"I've kept the stockings for you," the pathologist was saying. "The outside edges are a little bit dirty but not damaged. She evidently spent some time on her back with her legs more or less flat and wide apart."

"That's normally how it goes when a woman is being raped."

The pathologist looked up abruptly, blinking at him behind the huge spectacles.

"Raped?" he said, somewhat astonished. "Why ever do you say that?"

"Well — I had assumed . . ."

"There's no physical evidence of rape, old man; no tearing, no bruising to the vagina or thighs — nothing that I can see." Cooper absorbed the implication of this while the pathologist elucidated. "Judging by the pattern of dirt on the calves of the stockings and the presence of what appears to be seminal fluid and pubic hairs in the vicinity of the upper legs and genitals, it's likely that sexual intercourse took place some time before death — but highly probable that it was consensual."

"So why was she strangled?"

The pathologist was peering at him with those huge magnified eyes.

"You're the detective, old man," he said.

Cooper floundered. His vision of a woman fighting off a fellow who had got fresh with her had dissolved before his eyes; he was groping about in the dark for another scenario — the limits of his imagination reached. Perhaps the murderer was a sadist, he thought, like "Captain" Neville Heath and the Blackout Ripper: the sort of cad who enjoys watching women suffer. He entertained the thought of having someone call around all the local divisions in pursuit of unsolved sex murders: if any sort of a pattern were to emerge he would be able to leave the whole filthy business to the Murder Squad and return to black-market eggs. It was a pleasant enough prospect for the short while he meditated upon it, until he recollected that the dead woman had not been brutalised, the fact of her consent making it all so much worse to his mind as he struggled with the idea of a man strangling a woman to whom he had just made love.

"I had assumed that she'd been beaten, raped and strangled over some argument about money, or for resisting her attacker's advances," he said, "in the common way of these things." He paused for a moment to gather his thoughts. "I don't think I've ever heard of a streetwalker asking for the money after conducting the business . . ."

"I bow to your greater knowledge of these matters, Detective Inspector," said the pathologist.

"She was found in a place known to be a favoured resort of prostitutes," Cooper said. "But then I had wondered about the condition of the clothing. She

124

wasn't beaten up, either, so it seems unlikely that her ponce was responsible. As a matter of fact, the more I look at it, the less like a streetwalker she appears."

The doctor had turned his attention to the woman's left hand.

"Well, I've had a good many prostitutes over the years . . ." he said, pausing for comic effect, just as, Cooper supposed, he must have done countless times before in lecture theatres, waiting for the gales of sycophantic laughter to die down before proceeding to a consideration of the pathology of sex murder. Cooper frowned and a look of irritation creased the doctor's features. "No," he said, bending in closer over the woman's left hand, "she doesn't look like a prostitute."

"So what the blazes was she doing there?"

"Perhaps she didn't want to take him home to meet her husband." The doctor was holding up the woman's left hand. The faint white mark on the third finger was so obvious Cooper could not believe that he had missed it. You damn fool, he thought. He hadn't even looked for a ring because he had assumed that he was investigating the humdrum killing of a common prostitute. How many times had he told the men under his command, never ever assume: let the evidence tell its own story? He ran an appraising, thoughtful thumb over the nap of his Homburg. First, a victim with no identity, and now he had no motive.

"Do you ever read the *News of the World?*" The question took Cooper by surprise. "My driver assures me that hardly an edition goes by without mention of some returning serviceman murdering his errant wife."

The pathologist sighed wearily. "The women of Britain have committed the ultimate betrayal. Not just adultery, but adultery with Yanks, Poles, Canadians, I-ties . . ."

Cooper was feeling slightly queasy. The formaldehyde, the buzz of the electric light bulb, the drain holes in the metal table and the blood-stained implements; they were all conspiring against him, and for a brief moment it was as though everything solid was falling away before him and he thought he might actually pass out.

"I blame the cinema . . ." the pathologist was saying, "it glamorises prostitution . . . It must be almost impossible for a genuine streetwalker to make a living these days, there are so many amateurs about . . . A highly sexed woman, deprived of sexual satisfaction, will quickly be brought to nymphomania . . . It's a disease that has become endemic since the war."

Cooper watched the rest of the post-mortem in a sort of reverie, turning various possibilities over and over in his mind, mentally browsing the murder scene, until he was certain, as certain as anyone can ever be of anything, that he had not missed a single clue: a hair, a cigarette end, a few blades of grass, a good-quality gentleman's mackintosh, a pair of dirty stockings, a shred of green wool. The idea that someone else, other than her lover, might have committed the murder — a jealous husband or boyfriend, perhaps — appealed to him; but try as he might, there was no indication that anyone else had been at the murder site, apart from the victim and her killer.

The heat and turmoil of the streets came as a shock to him after the morgue chill; the blood red of the buses on St Pancras Way startling after the white tiled vacancy. She was leaning against the squad car chatting with some young fellow and smiling so prettily it almost took his breath away. Like a coward he tried to sneak off without her seeing him, chuckling mirthlessly at his own preposterousness.

"Sir, Sir! Oh I say! Sir!" She saluted smartly the instant he turned around. "Golly! I nearly missed you! What a chump I'd have looked!"

He removed his hat and held it limply with the bag of samples from the pathologist.

"Policewoman Tring, isn't it?" he said. "Well, well! What on earth are you doing here?"

She smiled at him and shook her head as if regarding an errant but nevertheless endearing child.

"DI Lucas says we can't possibly have you spending all day going up and down the Northern Line, so he's sent me to take you out to Hendon and anywhere else you need to go."

"Quite unnecessary. Waste of resources . . ."

She put her head to one side and fixed him with a look of such compassion and understanding that he was forced to jut out his chin in order to dam a spontaneous wellspring of feeling.

"It's alright," she said. "I want to help. Please, let me help you."

CHAPTER
SEVENTEEN

It got on her nerves the way Evelyn had to flirt with every man who gave her the time of day. She'd had words with her about it before now: how it looked common, cheap; how no man likes a woman to be too obvious.

The kid was chatting away with the young man in the swing-back jacket and the vulgar woman as if they had known each other all their lives. He looked as if he had come by money in all the ways that had proliferated since the War, and Evelyn was making no attempt to conceal the fact that she was after some of it.

"Oh Dennis," she screeched with laughter, waving her hand at him, "what a thing to say. Isn't he terrible, Lil? Eh, Nesta? Isn't he a one? Oh, don't! Don't!"

She had her long skinny brown legs up on a chair, and kept smoothing her skirt down over her knees in a way calculated to draw attention to them; she threw her head back to laugh at everything he said; she was wafting a cigarette around her, enveloped in hazy blue. Evelyn would do anything for a cigarette.

Dennis had ordered more teas and coffees for them, slices of white bread and margarine, fruit cake. The cross-eyed waitress had almost thrown it at them, before going back to the counter, where she stood huffing and sighing, fanning herself with one of the little card menus. The stout man standing by the urn remained oblivious to it all, engrossed in his sporting paper, pausing only to lick his thumb and forefinger every so often, in order to turn the page, slowly and with immense care.

The heat and the steam, Nesta and Evelyn shrieking with laughter, it all made her feel a little too queasy to "tuck in", as Dennis put it. I must look a state, she thought. It was so hot, and she could feel the damp of her skin, like a layer beneath her clothes.

"Is that the time? I really ought to get going," she said for the umpteenth time, nudging Evelyn. "I need to try and get a lettuce for our supper, dear."

Evelyn and Nesta had brought their chairs in close around the table, and she was boxed into a corner, so it was difficult to leave without drawing attention to herself. And then every now and again Dennis would cast a wolf-whistle look in her direction. He had also taken to rolling his eyes at her whenever Nesta said anything, and she had begun to make little gestures of complicity back towards him: a knowing raise of the eyebrows, a half-smile, a slight shrug of the shoulders. She couldn't deny that she was flattered by his attention — he was young enough to be her son — and it gratified her to think that he preferred her, in some way, to Evelyn, and perhaps the cross-eyed waitress, too, even though she was old enough to be their mother. If I leave, she thought, there's no knowing what will happen. Certainly, Evelyn would not leave — not where there was a nice-looking man handing out free cigarettes; she needed to keep an eye on the kid, who did not have the common sense and experience to deal with a man who was so obviously out to pick up a woman.

"Tuck in, blondie," Dennis was saying. "Get some of that fruit cake down you."

She smiled and patted at the back of her head, wondering what it would be like to find herself upstairs on a bus with him, letting him stroke her leg as far up as she dared, him talking a lot of rot as he made little grabs at her waist and tried to kiss her. Not that she was as bothered with that sort of nonsense as she had once been. Marriage to Wally and then the war had rid her of any traces of sentimentality she might once have had with regard to men; but she still liked the attention. And so she remained in the dreadful café, with Evelyn's legs, and Nesta's cackle, and the plate of bread and marge, all making her feel ill.

"Ooh! Sauce!" shrieked Evelyn. "Are you making suggestions? Is he trying to carry on? Is he?"

Nesta choked on her own laughter.

"We should all go on somewhere," she said, wiping her eyes with a handkerchief.

"Yes," said Evelyn, "we couldn't half do with cheering up, couldn't we, Lil?"

He was looking back at her, his lips wrapped around a cigarette which he was lighting with a good-quality lighter. He lifted his top lip in a sort of half-smile, half-sneer.

130

"I'm not in the habit of going to public houses," she said.

Evelyn looked as if she was about to say something, but then thought better of it.

"We could go to the flicks," she said. "You like the flicks, don't you, Lil?"

"I've already seen the big picture that's on at the Mayfair," she said. "I went on Wednesday. It wasn't very good."

"Empire, then. You often go to the Empire on a Saturday."

She sniffed. "Last time I went the bill was very poor — a plump girl singer with lank hair and a very vulgar comic." This was true, although she omitted to tell them how a man in the row behind her had struck up a conversation when his hat rolled underneath her seat. He had a strong chin and a thin moustache like William Powell's; he was dressed in a suit and co-respondent shoes like Max Miller's. She had taken out her compact several times during the first half, using it to simultaneously conceal and signal her interest in him, watching his reflection watching her. In the interval she had discreetly followed him to the bar (she had fancied a gin but there wasn't any, which was just as well as she never bought her own drinks), but when she saw him chatting to the cigarette girl she had lost her enthusiasm for flirting.

She thought now of taking out her cigarette case, knowing that if Dennis saw her with it he would reach across and light her.

"There's gin at the Feathers," said Nesta.

"Gin," Dennis said. "You and your bloody gin. It's all you think about."

This made Evelyn shriek. "You and your bloody gin! What is he like? I ask you! You ain't half a one, Dennis! In' he a one, Lil!"

He casually removed the cigarette from the corner of his mouth and blew a steady stream of smoke into the air above their heads. He did all of this without taking his eyes off her, and for a moment it was as if everything ran in slow motion, and only the two of them were solid and real. She wondered if he could get nylons and vanishing cream and French girdles without coupons. Perhaps he would take her off somewhere. Dinner and dancing, somewhere smart, like Mirabelle's where the film stars went. Some of these spivs were earning two or three thousand pounds in a single week: he probably had access to all sorts of nice places and preferential treatment. She imagined herself drinking champagne in a nightclub while Dennis lit two cigarettes, one for her and one for him — those Russian ones, with the coloured paper tube to them — like Paul Henreid in *Now Voyager*.

"I haven't seen the picture at the Odeon," she murmured, casting him a sidelong glance. She wasn't sure if he had heard her because Nesta and Evelyn were making such a racket; and maybe it was just as well that he hadn't. She imagined him making love to her, telling her over and over again that he could not believe that she was forty-three and the mother of a seventeen-year-old son.

CHAPTER
EIGHTEEN

He supposed that the trip to Hendon with Police-woman Tring (he had yet to discover her first name) could have gone a little better, and that it hadn't been entirely down to his being a damn fool. He was naturally a cautious man, but Hendon was almost the countryside; as they sped from the bomb-sites, unrelenting grey succumbed to green fields, trees flitted past the car window; the sky above an unbroken, solid bank of blue. All of this was enough to put even the most circumspect man off his guard. He was the sort of man who demanded more of a relationship than mere bodily stimulation (although it could not be denied that Policewoman Tring was jolly good-looking); and the older he grew the more he hankered after something essentially amiable and decent: a sharing of common interests, mutual respect. She was a good deal younger than he was, but not by so much that they would have nothing whatever in common. By the time she was fifty he would be in his sixties and the gap between them would have been breached fairly satisfactorily. He always found it difficult to think about the future. He closed his eyes for a moment and told himself that there had been enough past.

"Here you are in the middle of a dreadful crime wave," she was saying when he came to. He had dozed off for a moment or two, lulled by the warm air passing through the open window and the hum of the motor. "You have nowhere near enough decent officers to help you, and now you're stuck with this awful murder. And here am I, sir. Now, I don't want to blow my own trumpet, but I'm bright, efficient, hard-working, and I can do a damn sight more than drive a car and make the tea."

"I don't doubt it," he said.

"I was a section leader in the ATS."

"That's very impressive," he replied, realising, too late, that she probably thought he was being condescending. She shifted in her seat as she changed gear with undeniable force, and remained silent for the rest of the journey to Hendon. They walked mutely into the laboratory, carrying the bags of evidence between them.

He reckoned that the chap from the lab was in his early thirties, and rather good-looking in that boyish, eager way that many academic sorts convey. He was lean, with large intelligent eyes and dark hair that flopped across his brow so that he had to keep sweeping it back. Cooper noted the slight smile which passed across the boy's thin lips on being introduced to Policewoman Tring; and he noted the unabashed grin which she proffered in return. The lab rat was Doctor somebody or other: women loved doctors. They made better husbands than policemen.

"I would love a cup of tea," he said to Policewoman Tring. "The journey has left me rather dry." He knew she was angry with him, and he felt a bit of a heel knowing damn well that he was despatching her in part because he didn't want her making eyes at the scientist (the slight look of disappointment that crossed the young man's face had not escaped his attention). However, it was the case that he would always have acted thus given the situation: the sort of conversation he was about to have was not one to which a young woman ought to be party.

"The pathologist," he told the chap from the laboratory, as they pored over the samples, "is of the opinion that this was not a straightforward case of assault."

"Jolly good. I like things to be out of the ordinary."

Cooper bristled openly at the bright and breezy manner in which this was said.

"Yes, well. The pathologist is of the opinion that whereas intimacy almost certainly took place shortly before death, it was evidently consensual."

"Tut tut."

Cooper's expression was set very stern; he was beginning to dislike the young man and could not imagine that Policewoman Tring would care for the cavalier manner in which he approached such a serious business.

"Something that has been puzzling me . . ." he continued, satisfied that he had conveyed his disapproval sufficiently. "She was lying on the mackintosh. It's rather good quality. I'm assuming it belongs to the murderer."

The lab rat inspected the garment cursorily.

"Mmm. It's possible that the semen stains might yield a blood type," he said. "And with a bit of luck it won't be a common one."

Cooper, who had become acutely conscious of Policewoman Tring, who was standing a few feet behind him bearing a cup of tea, nodded abruptly in an effort to move the conversation on from bodily fluids.

"Her clothing had been tampered with, but wasn't torn," he said, "and she appears to have removed her own under things."

The scientist whistled.

"Quite a gal, eh!"

Cooper, who did not appreciate gallows humour and, unusually for a detective, had never shared an unsavoury joke with a pathologist over a dissected corpse, frowned. The horror was there: it was the one sure thing in life. Why try and dissipate it with an off-colour observation? The young man took the hint, shrugging carelessly.

"We'll send the grasses over to Nottingham for analysis," he said. "Should have something back in a week or two, with a bit of luck. We'll look at the brick dust here."

"There's a green fibre," said Cooper. "It looks like tweed or something. It was underneath her fingernails."

The boffin brightened considerably.

"Okey dokey," he said. "Now you're talking!" He winked at Policewoman Tring. "I'm part of a team here engaged upon a taxonomy of woollen materials . . ."

How pleasant, Cooper thought sourly, to deal only with certainties.

"Really?" Policewoman Tring said coolly. "That must be so interesting." He could have kissed her there and then.

Once all the samples had been handed over and signed for, Cooper and Policewoman Tring made their way to the front desk, where he telephoned Lucas, waiting an unconscionably long time for someone to pick up at the other end.

"He's on inquiries, sir," the desk sergeant at Caledonian Road said.

"Of course he is," said Cooper. "Out on inquiries" covered a multitude of sins. "Tell him I'll call back in an hour."

He held open the heavy wooden door for her, thinking, as she passed through, how very graceful she was, even in the ghastly flat black shoes. He permitted his eyes to run over the gentle slopes of her waist and hips: he was only human, after all.

"What a very arrogant fellow he was," she said as they crossed towards the car. "It's hardly a matter for ribaldry, is it? I thought you were very good the way you dealt with him."

"These scientific chaps can be very cavalier — pathologists are the worst." He was relieved that she appeared to have forgiven him for whatever it was he had said or done to annoy her.

"Sir," she asked, "isn't it unusual for a woman to be strangled without being raped?"

He swallowed hard.

"Yes," he said. "But it does happen. Men are brutes."

"Not all men."

"No. Not all men." Just once in a while, he supposed, men and women must get together simply to talk: it didn't always have to lead to the bedroom, or a lonely bomb-site.

They were at the motorcar when someone called him back.

"DDI Cooper?"

"Yes."

"There's a telephone call for you, sir. Caller says it's urgent."

He knew at once that it must be Lucas. He galloped up the steps two at a time and snatched up the receiver from the front desk.

The DI's laconic tones, as usual, gave nothing away.

"Something's turned up, sir."

His first thought was that it was another body, hopefully in another division.

"A bloke's just come into Holloway Road nick with an identity card belonging to a Mrs Lillian Frobisher. Says he found it on the hedge where we found the other items."

Cooper raised a sceptical eyebrow.

"Do you believe him?"

"As a matter of fact I do, sir. I'm not saying his reasons for taking the card were entirely honest, but he says when he read about the murder in the newspaper he realised he might have found something significant."

"Where's the address on the card?"

"Holloway. About half a mile from the murder site. Three streets outside the house-to-house search zone."

"That's unfortunate."

"Yes, sir."

"Have the card checked for fingerprints. Urgently," Cooper said, knowing full well that Lucas would have already done this. "I'm on my way back to HQ. Call me there as soon as you know something."

On the drive back to Stoke Newington she talked a good deal as, beyond the hum and rattle of the motor, the greens of fields and trees and hedgerows bled one into another until everything was indistinct: a smudge of green, with acres of sharp clear blue set above. Had he seen *The Captive Heart*? No? A pity; it was absolutely marvellous and she had thoroughly enjoyed it. He really ought to read *Titus Groan*; she had sat up all night to finish it, that's how good it was. Did he like the ballet? Not really. No. She had thought she was going to die when she saw Fonteyn in *The Sleeping Beauty*. He leaned against the open window. No doubt she thought of him as some ancient Colonel Blimp type, issuing condemnations of trouser-wearing, cigarette-smoking women and all other abominations of modern life from his Turkish bath.

It was difficult, in the warm breeze, to distinguish between contentment and exhaustion.

At Stoke Newington police station they parted company.

"You haven't got rid of me yet, you know!" she said.

"No. I don't suppose I have."

"I shall keep badgering DI Lucas."

"Yes, you do that. We could do with an extra pair of hands. 'Bye then."

"Goodbye, sir."

She smiled at him, saluting smartly. He stood on the pavement brushing a speck of imaginary dust from his hat and watched her drive away; then he went to his office and lit a pipe and smoked it while summarising twenty interviews with informants. He lit another pipe and drank a cup of tea and turned his attention to a pile of letters from well-meaning members of the public; all rot, of course, but to be responded to, promptly and courteously, nevertheless. He was just considering how pleasant it was to be distracted from an insoluble murder, when the telephone on his desk jangled into life. It was Lucas.

"It's her. Lillian Frobisher."

"Lillian Frobisher," repeated Cooper.

"What do you want us to do, sir?"

Cooper checked his watch.

"Give it another hour or so," he said. "We'll go in after six o'clock, and see who's at home."

CHAPTER
NINETEEN

Walter Frobisher was the sort of man you would have passed on the street or sat next to on a bus without giving a second glance. He had the unsubstantial, fading quality of a once boyishly good-looking man gone to seed; Cooper disliked him on sight.

"Mr Frobisher? Mr Walter Frobisher?" said Lucas as the battered front door swung open.

"Yes."

"Do you know a Mrs Lillian Frobisher?"

"I should say so," said Frobisher, with the slight note of caution that people customarily display when official-seeming individuals turn up unexpectedly on their doorsteps. "She's my wife." This was followed with a self-deprecating grin that Cooper suspected he had doubtless cultivated over the years, thinking it would endear him to women, but which had acquired a cringing, pathetic quality in middle age. As far as Cooper could deduce, there was no apparent sign of guilt in the way Frobisher responded.

"Do you know where she is?"

Even before Lucas had asked the question Cooper had noted how the fellow had expressed nothing in the way of surprise, concern or relief upon hearing his wife's name. That is to say, he had given no indication whatever that he had been wondering about his wife's whereabouts over the past couple of days. It wasn't until Lucas introduced them as detectives that Frobisher's mien, which up until then had even had something cheery about it, was clouded by perplexity.

"Has Lillian had an accident?" he asked, and the fellow, who had seemed so inconsequential on opening the front door, appeared to diminish even further before their eyes.

Cooper left it to Lucas to break the news about the identity card and the strangled woman; he did this not because he could not do so himself — he had broken countless pieces of bad news in his time — but because the recipients of bad news often betrayed themselves in the way they reacted to said bad news, and he liked to keep himself alert to any tell-tale signs in their comportment, expression, voice. On learning that his wife had quite possibly been strangled on a nearby bomb-site, Frobisher went quite pale; he clasped his own throat with one hand, and clutched at the door-frame with the other. Then he uttered a faint cry. Cooper did not lack compassion, but he was a copper first and foremost and he suspected everyone — especially the close relations of a murder victim. There was something unmanly in the way Frobisher had responded, which made Cooper dislike him even more; but there was nothing to indicate obvious guilt.

"We can't be sure, of course," Lucas was saying. "We shall need a positive identification of the body."

"Yes, of course you will." Frobisher replied in a vacant faraway voice, and as he led the way, slowly, into the house, he certainly appeared to be in shock.

There was an old-fashioned hat-rack in the hallway over-laden with dusty old coats in various stages of decay that they had to push past. The hallway itself smelled of cabbage and dry rot, and was, Cooper noted, lit by gas-light.

"Don't go in there," counselled Frobisher as Lucas made to enter the front parlour. "It isn't safe."

"Bomb damage?"

"The house opposite took a direct hit; knocked out all the windows and the upstairs ceiling."

He led them along a dingy narrow passage into a cramped back parlour which opened on to a tiny scullery overlooking the back garden. Across the scullery window a line had been strung, from which a pair of stockings and little scraps of pink silk dripped into a butler sink. A wireless sat on the window ledge, presumably so it could be heard by someone who was in the yard. It was playing dance music: modern dance music. Frobisher didn't seem the sort to listen to modern dance music. The parlour itself was stuffy and overstuffed: too much furniture, too many things. A line of cream-and-blue tin canisters was ranged along the shelf of a dresser which dominated one side. Salt. Sugar. Flour. Tea. Coffee. To the right of the fireplace there was a shabby armchair, with a drab antimacassar draped over its back. A heavily ticking clock stood on the mantelpiece which was cluttered with photographs and dusty ornaments. An empty fruit-bowl atop a lace doily was set in the middle of a half-folded drop-leaf table, which stood square in the centre of the room.

Frobisher had slumped in the armchair in an attitude of abject misery, but he did not forget his manners. He possessed a feeble sort of gentility, which he mustered now, gesturing to them to sit down on the chairs packed tightly around the table. Then he ran his hand over his sandy hair which was, like the rest of him, slowly fading from view.

"Got any brandy in the house, sir?" asked Lucas.

Frobisher shook his head. He reached across and took down a pipe from the mantelpiece, knocking it out against the surround. Lucas took out a cigarette and shared a match with him. Smoke mazed across the room.

"What happened?" Frobisher asked.

"That's what we're trying to find out, sir," said Lucas. "When did you last see your wife?"

Frobisher fumbled with the bowl of his pipe and Cooper tried to assess whether he was buying himself some time.

"Saturday."

"What time?"

"About six o'clock. Half past. It might have been a little later. No, it was after the news. After half past six." There was a little hesitation in the course of which Frobisher appeared to scrutinise the pattern in the lino. "Oh God," he said in a small absent voice. Then: "Oh no! Oh no! Oh God! Lillian! Oh God!" He clasped his hands together in front of him as if in prayer, and lay

144

his indistinct head upon them. "Oh God! Poor old girl! Poor old girl!"

Lucas and Cooper exchanged a brief look.

"Why don't I make you a cup of tea, sir?" said Lucas. He stood up and went through to the scullery. It was a good opportunity to find out who was listening to the wireless in the garden.

"So you haven't seen your wife since Saturday early evening . . ." Cooper asked.

"No."

"Weren't you concerned when she didn't come home?"

Frobisher gave his sad little smile; meant to ingratiate, it had the opposite effect.

"We had a bit of a row," he said. "You know how it is. She said she was going to her sister's in Jaywick Sands."

"Has she done that before?"

"She's gone off . . ."

"To Jaywick?"

"She stayed there during the war . . ."

"I see." Cooper peered hard at the fellow. It was all a bit queer, no doubt about it, but he wasn't sure that Frobisher was lying to him. Not yet.

"Can you think of any reason why anyone should have wished to harm your wife?"

Frobisher blinked at the detective and shook his head. It was clear that the idea had never occurred to him.

"Apart from visiting her sister in Jaywick, is there anywhere else she liked to go — anywhere nearer to home, as it were?"

"She likes the pictures. She goes every Saturday — pictures or the Empire. She likes . . ." Frobisher stopped and swallowed hard. "She read all those papers about film stars. She knew them all. And she was very clever with her hands. Made all her own clothes. She always looks very smart . . ." His voice trailed off and he began to cry again.

Cooper regarded him now with embarrassment. He tapped his forefinger on the table impatiently and waited for Frobisher to compose himself.

"Did she take a lot with her?" he asked with a trace of annoyance when he could wait no longer. "Only we didn't find anything — not even a handbag, as a matter of fact . . ."

Frobisher sighed heavily.

"We had a row," he said. "She went off in a bit of a huff . . ."

"Did she take a suitcase or vanity case or anything of that sort, as far as you know?"

"Oh, God!" exclaimed Frobisher, "I've been a bloody fool . . ."

"Haven't we all."

There was a photograph on the mantelpiece: a fellow in uniform smiling broadly, sergeant's stripes proudly displayed. Cooper took out his own pipe from his jacket pocket and pointed the stem at the picture.

"Been away at the front, eh?" he said.

Frobisher nodded.

"Bloody nightmare, I shouldn't wonder."

"You know how it is . . ." Frobisher's voice trailed off and he lay his forehead once again upon his clasped

146

hands as if imploring for mercy. Cooper was feeling a twinge of pity; he tried to imagine how it would feel to go through all of that only to return to this: a couple of damp rooms in a half-bombed house. He wondered if disappointment was enough to lead a man to murder.

"I remember coming back from the last lot," he said. "Everything seemed so different somehow." Frobisher had removed a large white handkerchief from his trouser pocket and was wiping his face with it. "Makes you wonder what you came through it all for." It was always awkward, acknowledging one's battle experiences with another man, beyond the raising of eyebrows over a pint, or some other subtle display of common feeling. With Frobisher, however, the effect was quite different: he seemed momentarily to swell. Blowing his nose determinedly with the handkerchief, he assumed a sort of military air.

"Doesn't it, though," he said, pulling his shoulders back. He had been perfectly well spoken before, but now he sounded like the King, or Neville Chamberlain. "We've reached a situation where the ordinary law-abiding citizen no longer feels safe in his own home. People have lost sight of the difference between right and wrong." His bland features were twisted with an ill-suppressed fury, and he gripped his pipe tightly, jabbing at the air about him with the stem. "Hooliganism is ruining this country!" he declared. "Spivs, wide boys . . . I fought in a war — twice — for this country. And look where it's got me!"

Cooper let him have his say. It was the least he could do, or rather it was all he could do; but he was taken aback by the sudden outburst, and the possibility that this cringing pathetic little man was capable of rage, perhaps even violence, made an impression upon him.

"Do you know?" Frobisher continued. He was calmer now, less splenetic; clearly something, some deep measure of frustration, had been relieved. He was brooding upon the empty grate. "I've applied for thirty-two jobs. Thirty-two. I was in insurance before the war, but that's all Freemasonry. Thirty-two letters and only two replies. After fighting and winning a war — two wars — the best this country can offer me is forty-five bob a week National Assistance."

"That really is too bad, old man," said Cooper. "I hope you find something soon." It was a stupid thing to say to a man who had just been widowed in terrible circumstances.

"I've never had to ask for a hand-out in my life!" Frobisher spluttered.

"No. No. Of course not," Cooper said, putting out his hand in a gesture of appeasement. Once again he noted the sudden rage. "I apologise. Mind me asking what it is you do now?"

The fellow stiffened again in the cod military fashion.

"I'm a commissionaire," he said, though from the manner in which he said it, one might be forgiven for assuming commissionaire was a synonym for prime minister.

"A commissionaire?" Cooper tried to sound impressed as this was clearly what was required.

"At Gamages." Again, the tone of ineffable overestimation, which struck Cooper before the full significance of what Frobisher had just told him sunk in.

"Gamages? You mean the store?" He tried to keep the surprise from his voice.

"Yes, you know, up in Holborn."

Cooper swallowed hard.

"Tell me about the quarrel with your wife," he said.

Frobisher retreated back into his diminishment; he was once again the pathetic little man upon whom self-pity sat rather heavily.

"Lillian suffers with her nerves," he said, drawing thoughtfully on his pipe. "It isn't easy being with a woman like that . . ."

"No, I can imagine . . ."

"There's madness in her family, you know. She's very highly strung. Her sister is an hysteric. And the mother is completely senile." Frobisher stopped abruptly and buried his head in his hands. "Oh God! Poor old girl," he cried, and then over and over again, "Poor old girl. Poor old girl . . ."

Cooper asked himself whether he was witnessing grief, remorse, or guilt.

Lucas came back into the parlour and selected the canisters marked Tea and Sugar from the dresser shelf, making a little nod in the direction of the scullery window. Cooper waited for the wild sobs emanating from Frobisher to subside into something more like a hiccup, and then asked him if there was anyone else in the house.

"Why yes," he said, looking up in surprise. "Miss Wilkes is in the back garden."

"Miss Wilkes?"

"Yes ... my wife's cousin ..." Cooper noted a telling hesitation. "But she doesn't have anything to ... She helps Lillian with her mother. She rents the attic from us." Frobisher seemed unaccountably uncomfortable recounting these seemingly innocuous details, and Cooper had the strongest impression that, in between bouts of apparent grief, the victim's husband was displaying the unmistakeable impression of guilt. But as to the derivation of that guilt, he could not be certain.

"Was Miss Wilkes here on Saturday evening?"

Frobisher nodded, his red-rimmed eyes turned on Cooper now had something rather desperate to them; something pleading.

"And would it be possible to have a word with her?"

Frobisher hesitated for a moment, before standing up and moving towards the scullery as if he were made of lead.

"Evelyn!" he called. "Evelyn, come here — something's happened to Lillian." His voice cracked. "Something awful."

A young woman came clacking into the parlour, her heels catching in the torn linoleum. She stood in the scullery doorway, limned by the early-evening light, hands on hips.

"What's going on?" she demanded. She was looking about the parlour with experienced, mascaraed eyes, a wartime product, about twenty-two, twenty-three; blonde; pretty, in an obvious, rather cheap way. She was dressed in sandals and a wide-brimmed sunhat and the scantiest bathing suit Cooper had seen in a long while.

She pouted her full mouth, giving her face a somewhat puckered, spoilt impression. She was certainly very common, and, Cooper thought, shiftless.

"Perhaps you'd like to put something on, miss," said Lucas. He set down a cup of tea in front of Frobisher, who looked helplessly at it as he addressed the girl.

"Evelyn," he said, "these gentlemen are police officers. They say that a woman was found on a bomb-site on Sunday morning. They think it's Lillian."

"What was Lil doing on a bomb-site?"

He could not be sure, but Cooper thought he caught Evelyn suppress a smirk. This was not necessarily significant in itself — he had seen plenty of people laugh outright upon receiving bad news; shock took everyone differently — but there was something about the circumstances in which they all found themselves that aroused his suspicions.

"What's your full name, miss?" asked Lucas, taking out his notebook.

"Evelyn Wilkes," said Frobisher. "She's Lillian's cousin."

A look of undeniable complicity passed between the two of them. It didn't necessarily mean that they had murdered Lillian Frobisher, but it did mean something.

"Lil went off on Saturday," said Evelyn.

"What time?"

"About half past six, quarter to seven."

"Did she say where she was going?"

"Down to her sister's in Jaywick. She's left us with her poor old mum, she has. Very nice, I must say." She had been absent-mindedly patting her bathing costume all the while, as if expecting to find a packet of cigarettes there. She turned on Lucas, smiling expertly, eyes lighting upon the cigarette he had in his hand. "Oooh, I don't suppose you have a spare cig, do you? I'm gasping for one, I am."

Lucas obliged.

"Why did she go off?" he asked.

"Queuing for bread," said Evelyn — very quickly. Frobisher had been about to say something at the same time, but now he sat down heavily and cradled the cup of tea in his hands. "She said she was done in and she'd been standing in queues all day and her whole life was rotten. That's what she said. Rotten. And we could all go to hell. Even her poor old mum."

"And neither of you were concerned when she failed to return home, or make any sort of contact?"

Evelyn shrugged, concentrating on the cigarette.

"We're not on the telephone," said Frobisher. "I assumed we'd have a postcard in a couple of days. Or that she'd come back when she'd calmed down."

"I dunno," said the girl. "She always seemed a bit mental to me." She blew smoke at the ceiling, and wafted her hand about her head. Her nails were painted the same shade as the victim's.

"Did she take any suitcase, clothes, with her?"

Frobisher put his head in his hands and groaned lightly.

"She was always flying off the handle."

"Had she ever disappeared before?"

Evelyn plucked a piece of tobacco from her bottom lip.

152

"She's left me to take care of her mother, that's what she's done," she said.

"And did she say how long you'd have to look after your aunt for?"

A look of confusion crossed the girl's brow.

Lucas persisted in his grave, flat voice.

"Mrs Frobisher's mum — sorry — I thought you said you were a cousin."

"No I never. I'm Lil's friend."

"I see."

"Sorry. I must have been mistaken." Frobisher had retreated into his cup of tea, all innocence, distraction. "Where were we? Did Mrs Frobisher take any luggage with her?"

Evelyn folded her arms across her exposed middle and smoked more thoughtfully.

"I dunno," she said. "I don't think so."

"What about a handbag?" said Lucas.

"Oh, she never goes anywhere without her handbag," said Frobisher. "It's got all our papers in it. She keeps it with her all the time."

"It's very good quality. Pigskin," said Evelyn. "She liked everything to be nice. She looked after herself . . ."

"Her wedding ring was missing," said Lucas.

Frobisher paled slightly.

"She threw it at me," he said in a hoarse whisper. "During the row. I think it rolled under the bed."

Cooper made a mental note to have Lucas find the wedding ring, while Frobisher started to moan like a wounded animal. Remorse was taking hold of him, but remorse is not evidence of guilt. What married man

153

would not feel remorse on learning of the sudden death of his wife — even one guilty of her death?

"She was always threatening to sling her hook," Evelyn was saying. "I've heard her say it a thousand times."

"But it's not something she'd ever done before?" persisted Lucas.

Frobisher thumped the arm of his chair with a clenched fist.

"No! No!" he said.

Evelyn looked at him with dull surprise.

"It's like I said, she was a bit mental." She ground out her cigarette on the edge of the fruit-bowl, and stood there pouting. Cooper couldn't be sure, but he'd lay odds to evens the stub was tinged with the same shade of lipstick as the one they had found at the murder site.

"Husbands don't seem to matter much these days," Frobisher was saying. "Women have been encouraged to, you know, go their own way . . ."

The sound of the front door opening, a shout up the stairs, stopped him in his reverie.

"Oh my God," he said, covering the top of his head with his hands. "Douglas. Oh God, it's Douglas." He looked up, blinking helplessly at Cooper. "What am I to say? What am I to tell him?" He was beseeching now. "I can't — oh, I can't do it." His voice dropped to a whisper. "I simply can't do it," he said; and then: "Oh God. Oh God!"

154

CHAPTER
TWENTY

There were times when it seemed to him as if it hadn't happened, not in the way he remembered it. Memories came to him in improbable shards, distinct but unreal; the act of remembrance was inescapable, relentless. At other times it seemed to him that it was the only thing in his whole life that was real, such that he wondered if it was still going on somewhere outside of his head. Was this, he wondered, the missing part of him, the part that had been blasted out of him? How would he know when he could not remember how he had felt before, only that it was different from how he felt now? When he thought like this he worried that he was going round the twist. In dreams, men screamed at him from beneath the frozen sea, pleading for his help. He tried not to think about them when he had had a good night out, but he had no control over his thoughts, which seemed to come and go as they wished: whenever, wherever. He hadn't had a good night out in a long while.

He hung up the green tweed swingback jacket in the wardrobe, admiring it hanging there. It was easily the best thing he had ever owned: no Burton's ready-mades for him. You never knew what you'd find in the suitcases. That's what made it such a good line. He lay down on the bed and stared up at the light bulb hanging from the dingy brown ceiling. He didn't feel up to King's Cross and suitcases today. On the way home he had considered going into Finsbury Park Station, boarding a train somewhere, anywhere, and climbing out of the compartment. Just to get a thrill. He'd done that. But today the smell of the diesel on the Seven Sisters Road had made him panic, and the crowds hanging about the entrance to the park had depressed him. Pasty-faced kids; drab bints in unmade-up faces and horrible clothes. What the hell had happened to this country anyway? As he had crossed over the road towards his lodgings he had wondered what it would be like to be hit by a bus.

He remembered flying. He had looked down at the debris of the ship and all the body parts scattered on the surface of the sea, the sea which was all lit up like Christmas and Bonfire Night: a great sheet of flame. His eyes were burning inside his head. When the smoke cleared he could see the whole aft section of the ship silhouetted against the orange sky. He didn't remember hitting the water, but he remembered being in the water. It was oily and filled with the remnants of men. Screams drifted on the icy air. He was clutching a hatch-cover and struggling to keep ahead of the flames as bodies drifted past him. He had no idea how long he had floated like that before he had felt the nudge of a Carley float. He had hauled himself into it, sodden, half frozen, and lain in the bottom waiting to die.

He was shivering now in spite of the heat of the day. As a matter of fact, he didn't feel too good. He swallowed hard against the sourness that was building in the back of his throat. He needed to sleep but he was afraid now, so he reckoned he would just lie there on the bed until it was time for the pubs to open, then he would go — and be well and truly lit up; just watch him. There was a pair of shoes he had yet to try which had come out of the same suitcase as the swingback jacket. They were a size too big for him, but he reckoned they'd do. On Monday he would take a few of the other things — a travelling clock, some cufflinks he didn't care for — to a Jew fence on the Stroud Green Road that Nesta knew all about. He didn't need the Resettlement Board. There were plenty of opportunities. He had floated on a burning sea for days. He'd get by. He would let Nesta take him to the fence but he wouldn't give her anything. The dirty whore had made him feel sick in the café, with her throaty cackle and her stink, and the threepenny-bit ruse, just so's she could look in the woman's handbag.

He kicked off his shoes and let them fall on to the floor, and thought some more about the woman in the café. She had been alright. Lillian. A showy little piece: old, but then he always reckoned that the older bints didn't give you any trouble, not like the younger ones. The older bints knew what a man wanted and were grateful for the attention: most of their husbands had been past it for years. And they don't go with men just for what they can get out of them like the younger good-looking ones do; the ones who are after a meal-ticket, who'll take all they can get. What was more, it was obvious that Lillian took care of herself; she was a looker. He reckoned she could have been a pin-up when she was younger. Not many women looked like the pin-ups, but she would've come close. He wouldn't mind running into Lillian again.

He lay there and let images of girls dressed in nothing but little lacy knickers, with peachy thighs and rouged nipples, entertain him for a while. Afterwards he closed his eyes against the tears, letting them run down his face: this happened sometimes; he could not control it. In the dark he could sense the periscopes from the wolf packs of U-boats that were lying just beneath the surface of the water all around him. The water was pitchy, fog-bound, covered in ice. He lay there and waited, hardly daring to breathe. One time, please God, he would fall asleep and not wake up again.

CHAPTER
TWENTY-ONE

Their dark baggy suits, dark ties and Homburgs made them instantly apparent to every villain in any pub they entered; as did their customary habit of glancing around the bar as they paused for a moment in the doorway before entering. Once a detective, always a detective: there was nothing you could do to conceal it. On this occasion neither of them recognised anyone, and no faces turned around to look them up and down.

"I'll get these, Frank," he said, as they approached the bar.

"Thank you very much, sir," said Lucas. The DI went and sat at a table in a dingy corner of the saloon bar and lit a cigarette. Cooper stood at the counter, his eyes still roaming about the place. It was a habit he could not break.

The landlord broke off a conversation with another customer and jerked his head at Cooper without any pretence of civility.

"I'll have two Johnnies, please."

"You'll be lucky."

"White Horse?"

The landlord laughed.

"I've got gin or Bass," he said. "Take your pick."

Cooper opted for two Bass. He carried them through to Lucas and set them down on the table in the smoke-suffused corner.

"Apparently, it's all there is. Sorry."

Lucas lifted his glass up as if appreciating the way the light played upon the amber liquid, before raising it to his eyebrows in a salute.

"Cheers, sir."

"Oh, Jim, please. We're off duty."

"Are we?"

"After a fashion."

Lucas considered this for a moment before lifting his glass again.

"Cheers anyway," he said, and he took a long draught.

"I see there's a fight at Finsbury Park on Saturday," Cooper said. "A couple of very talented coloured boys. Thought I might pop along."

They both knew that this was unlikely to happen, but Lucas nodded encouragingly.

"I like a good fight," he said, loyally.

"They're taking on all comers."

Lucas lit another cigarette, blew smoke at the ceiling. Cooper sighed and sipped his beer. Neither of them said anything for a few moments.

"There's something about this case that I just can't put my finger on, old man," Cooper said, breaking the contemplative silence. "I find it hard to accept all that rot about the victim going to visit her sister in Jaywick Sands. And don't — for god's sake — don't say that much is sticking out like Brighton Pier."

Lucas set the glass down upon the table, and regarded it morosely.

"What does it matter?" he said.

"The victim's sister is coming into HQ tomorrow morning. She's coming down to make arrangements for the old lady. And that's another oddity. Why do you suppose Wilkes and Frobisher didn't telephone Jaywick? They might not have been concerned about the victim, but surely they would have wanted to know what arrangements were being made for the mother." Lucas smoked impassively. Cooper sipped his beer. "Has the description of the handbag gone into the newspapers?" he asked after a short silence had elapsed. "Jolly good. Miss Wilkes had an uncommon acquaintance with its contents, didn't she?" Cooper took another sip of his beer. "I don't suppose we'll see the three books of clothing coupons again, will we?"

Lucas stabbed the ashtray with the end of his cigarette and lit up another.

"Thought we were off duty," he said, "sir."

Cooper laughed lightly.

"Quite right, old man. Quite right." They sat drinking. "So, what do you think of Arsenal's chances next season?" Cooper asked when the silence had become awkward.

"Reckon that boy Bartram will be one to watch," Lucas said, brightening considerably. The Arsenal first eleven was his abiding passion. "Good boy, Bartram — best of the current crop of goalies by far. Well, he's the only one who punches the ball away, isn't he? It's all catches and kicks these days."

Cooper murmured assent. He wasn't really a follower of football — cricket was his game — but he had learned over the years that a passing knowledge was essential if you were to maintain any sort of relationship with the men you served alongside.

"The war put paid to good goalkeeping," offered Cooper. This was something he was not qualified to comment upon, but he had heard Lucas say as much many times throughout the last season.

Lucas jabbed the table emphatically. "You've hit the nail on the head there, sir," he said.

They let the conversation settle, finishing their beers.

"Obviously," Cooper said after a while, "there's been some domestic trouble. Some ill-feeling all around . . ."

Lucas turned his empty glass slowly.

"That's not evidence," he said. "That's just marriage."

"Caring for the old lady, day in day out — can't have been much fun. The house is virtually a hovel. Looked at like that, it's entirely understandable that she would want to run away — if that's what she did. Then again, both he and Wilkes were keen to depict her as a neurotic, which goes some way to explaining why her disappearance didn't concern them. Does Frobisher strike you as a drinker or a gambler? He claims never to have been out of a situation, yet he's living as little more than a lodger in a bomb-site owned by his mother-in-law."

"Sexually frustrated," said Lucas.

"Sorry?"

"The victim. Sexually frustrated."

Cooper nodded circumspectly. He tilted his empty glass towards the DI.

"Fancy another?" he said.

It was busier in the bar now: red-faced and sweating men, laughing, shouting, swilling, heaped on top of one another beneath a pall of cigarette smoke that was saturated with beery sourness and the mournful odour of gin; the sawdust at their feet was depleted in drink-sodden patches. While he waited to attract the barmaid's attention, he thought some more about Frobisher, and the visit, earlier that evening, to the morgue so that the formal identification of the victim could be made. The trip supplied a first-rate opportunity to scrutinise at close quarters the reaction of his only suspect when confronted with his dead wife's body. Cooper, like all detectives, proceeded on the assumption that he would know guilt the instant he glimpsed it: the truth was, sometimes you did and sometimes you didn't; but you invariably convinced yourself either way that you had some sort of infallible ability to detect culpability: something telling in a stance, a gesture, a certain look, a change in the pattern of breathing.

Frobisher had cut a slight, shuffling figure in the gleam of the cold store, shrivelling before Cooper's eyes in his customary way, until all that was left was the merest impression of a man diminished by the solid weight of grief. Embarrassed by yet another outpouring, Cooper had felt obliged to step aside and leave the wretched fellow to his lamentation while he examined the blank space of the tiled floor, despising himself as he assessed the sobs and imprecations. There can be no room for sentiment in a detective; as any one of them will tell you, the most innocent-seeming has often turned out to be the most blameworthy. Or was that something detectives tell one another in an attempt to assuage their consciences? And even if he had detected guilt, what did that really tell him? He had witnessed many times how the close relations of murder victims often appear to betray a guilty conscience: reproaching themselves for not having prevented the death of their loved one; feeling keenly the reprehensibility of a less than satisfactory final encounter. Regret was so closely aligned to guilt that it was often difficult even for the most seasoned detective to tell the difference between the two. He thought of the guilt he had felt at his own father's passing; the self-censure that he had conducted on a daily basis since Marjorie had left him. She was not dead — she was merely with her people in Bristol, as far as he knew — but she had passed out of his life as surely as if she were dead, without ever knowing that he would love her until the end of time; and he would never forgive himself for that.

"Bass or gin?" asked the barmaid. She was a blonde, large-breasted, and was smiling at him.

"Two Bass, please."

"Haven't seen you in here before," she said as she opened the bottles.

"I'm here with someone I work with. It's his local."

"What do you do, then?"

"We're detectives."

He could tell that she was impressed: as she poured the beers she was smiling even more at him. She wasn't his type, naturally, but then she wasn't obvious in the way of most barmaids. As a matter of fact, she seemed to him to be a very nice sort of girl.

"Like Humphrey Bogart in *The Maltese Falcon?*" she said.

"Not really . . ."

"I love Humphrey Bogart."

"Actually, it's quite dull most of the time."

He had succeeded in disappointing yet another woman. She was still smiling at him as she handed over the beers and took his money, but now she was smiling in that professional way of barmaids everywhere, such that only a fool or a drunkard would be taken in. He returned her smile with a forced little effort of his own and retreated as fast as he could.

"Do you think the husband did it?" he said as he set down the beers.

Lucas drew fiercely on his cigarette.

"What, that thin streak of piss?" he said.

"There's untapped frustration and fury there," Cooper said, sipping on his beer. He wasn't entirely convinced by his argument, but it is quite true that you are far more likely to be murdered by someone close to you than by a stranger. And it would certainly make things a lot simpler. "Crippen was a very softly spoken gent," he said.

Lucas laughed.

"What about the girl?"

"Not a chance," said the DI. "Women never strangle. They don't have the strength."

"She was wearing the same colour lipstick and nail varnish as the victim."

"Nah . . . she's his fancy woman, that's all," said Lucas.

"She's half his age . . ."

"It's the times we live in, sir. What can I say . . . ?" Lucas drank half of his beer in one slow steady draught, wiping his mouth with the back of his hand when he was done. "Fact is, either you know who done it, or you don't," he said. "If you do, then the job's simple: prove it. If you don't, well . . . The thing of it is, guv, we don't know."

"Come on, old man. Nil desperandum. This morning we had no idea who the victim was . . ."

Lucas drank the rest of his beer and finished his cigarette. He stood up and began to put on his raincoat.

"I have to be getting home," he said, "if the wife hasn't locked me out. I was supposed to help her put up some curtains in the back bedroom. She's been waiting for me to do it since we took down the blackout." He sighed. "You did the right thing never marrying, sir."

Cooper took another sip of his beer.

"The lady wouldn't have me," he said.

Lucas picked up his hat from the table and ran his thumb along the soft edge of the brim; he was looking down at Cooper with a slight frown. "Do me a favour, sir," he said. "Try and get some kip. You look bloody awful, if you don't mind me saying."

"Thanks."

Lucas set his hat on his head and tipped it back with two fingers in a sort of salute.

"Goodnight, sir."

"Goodnight, old man."

Cooper let the last few drops of beer trickle down the back of his throat and then made his way out on to the street.

He walked over to the Frobisher house and leaned against a wall on the opposite corner and filled a pipe. It was still just about light, a crepuscular glow shimmering around the house skeletons; in the distance a train shrieked and groaned. He did not know what he was expecting, but some instinct had brought him there and sometimes instinct is all you have to go on and there is little point in ignoring it. He decided to stay until satisfied one way or another: it did not take long. He recognised them as soon as they turned on to the street. She was ginned up and laughing, her head flung back, dressed in a little veiled hat and a dress which, although understated, was too small for her, and clung to her hips and breasts lasciviously. He was making clumsy grabs at her waist and shoulders, pathetic, drink-retarded expressions of lust, which she deflected half-heartedly, laughing all the while. Cooper smoked his pipe and watched them make their way up the front path and in at the front door. It didn't tell him anything he did not already suspect, but at least now he knew for sure.

Back at the flat, Mrs Oscar had restored everything to order. There was a neatly folded pile of clean shirts and collars; there was tea, milk and bread; his butter ration sat on the pantry shelf. On the shelf beneath the bathroom mirror there was a packet of razor blades. He could have wept with gratitude, but instead he made himself a piece of toast by way of celebration.

It was too late for music. He considered listening to the Egmont Overture, something exhilarating, life-affirming, but it would only have aroused something in him and he did not want to think or feel. He poured a whisky, tasted a bit, let it scald his throat, then topped up the glass with water. He swallowed the whole lot in one gulp and went and lay down on his bed in the darkened room. After a few moments of stillness he kicked off his shoes, pulled his tie over his head and tried to sleep.

CHAPTER
TWENTY-TWO

The next morning, the Tuesday, in the absence of anyone else from CID, he was called to a tobacconist's on St Ann's Road which had had its cashbox rifled and all its cigarettes taken. Kids, the shopkeeper reckoned; like everyone else, he didn't know what the world was coming to. Wearily, Cooper took an inventory of everything that had gone and gave instructions to the fingerprint chap; then he walked back to "N" Division HQ and went in search of a cup of tea.

Walter Frobisher and Evelyn Wilkes were going to give their statements later on that day, but he reckoned that the chances of learning anything new were about as good as a bloke's chances of finding himself handcuffed to Madeleine Carroll. He assumed that the same logic could be applied to the interview he was now having with the victim's son, Douglas, but it was worth conducting all the same. The kid had his father's pale lashes and hair; the same blue eyes, but his were more substantial, as Walter Frobisher's must once have been. Douglas was also twice the man his father was: no blubbing for him. A couple of times it seemed that he might be in danger of giving way to his feelings, but the stout lad held on to them pretty tightly.

Cooper always found such stoicism unaccountably moving; generous outpourings of emotions always left him feeling slightly nauseated.

"We had tea at about half past five," Douglas was telling him. He spoke in a pleasant well-modulated voice: the product of a reasonable grammar school, Cooper reckoned. He assumed that grandparents had secured the same for him, since there was little evidence that Frobisher had the wherewithal. "I wanted to go out, so Mother got tea ready a bit earlier than normal, and when we'd done, she asked me to go out and telephone the Odeon to find out what the big picture was. It was *Gaiety George,* with Richard Greene and Ann Todd. The evening screenings were at 6.20 and 7.45."

"Approximately how long did that take you?"

"I was probably gone about fifteen, twenty minutes — I stopped off to buy a newspaper."

"So you were out of the house for a short period somewhere between six and six thirty?"

"Yes, something like that . . . I think I was probably back before six thirty."

"When you returned to the house, were you aware of anything unusual?"

"No. Mother said she quite fancied the picture, but she was feeling tired so wasn't sure if she'd go or not."

"She was feeling tired?"

"Yes, but she often says that. She's tired a lot of the time, I suppose."

"After you told your mother about the film, what happened then?"

"I cycled over to Tufnell Park to meet up with a pal and some girls we know."

"What time did you get back?"

"About half past eleven."

"And did you notice that your mother was out?"

"Dad told me the next morning that she'd gone down to see Auntie Mavis in Jaywick."

"Is that something your mother does quite often?"

"She's done things like it, though not since Father came back. During the war, she'd sometimes get stuck in town in the blackout and stay in a hotel or something. It wasn't especially unusual . . . It didn't strike me as all that odd, especially because Father didn't seem concerned. I wondered if Mother had walked out — she's always saying she will one day."

"Is she?"

"She gets a notion, sometimes. Says she can't stand being in the house with Dad, and if it wasn't Grandma's house she'd go somewhere else. She'd say other things too, like she'd put her head in the gas oven — that sort of thing."

"All of that must have been somewhat difficult for you . . ."

The boy shrugged and for a brief moment Cooper thought he might give way to feeling; he was relieved to see the boy was striving manfully for composure.

"I knew she didn't mean it," he said, "about the gas oven, I mean. I don't suppose I'd have been all that surprised if she did leave. But that's only thinking about it now. At the time I really didn't think about it very much at all. I just expected her to come home

171

when she was ready . . ." He fell silent for a moment. "I might have supposed Dad had made it up," he said, "about Mother going to Jaywick — so I wouldn't worry, you know, when she didn't come back the next day . . ."

"Why do you suppose he would have done that?"

"I don't know — maybe because he knew she had gone into town or something and it didn't seem — you know — respectable." The boy sighed deeply. "You will find who did this, won't you?" he asked, his pale-blue eyes searching Cooper's. "Sometimes I can't believe it's happened, and then other times all I want to do is beat the man who did it to a bloody pulp."

"Of course you do. I'd feel the same if it was my mother." Cooper had one more question he needed to ask. "Did your mother have any friends — anyone she might have stayed with?"

The boy thought for a few moments, before shaking his head.

"I don't know of anyone she'd be friendly with," he said, "outside of the family."

Cooper spent the rest of the morning being availed of the north London black market — a welcome respite from the doings of the Frobisher household, the gloom and dinginess of which had settled upon him like a layer of thick dust, and bouts of sheer despair. He did not want to see Walter Frobisher dangle at the end of a rope — he did not wish to see anyone dangle at the end of a rope, come to that — but it could not be denied that the wretched fellow had a motive; and add to that the fact, highly suspicious in itself, that the fellow had not reported his wife's disappearance, that his only alibi was the word of a shiftless girl who it appeared was also his mistress, and the curious matter of the mackintosh, which quite possibly had been bought in the same shop where Frobisher happened to be employed as a doorman, and it would not have required Sherlock Holmes to draw things to a conclusion. He was sorry for the boy, naturally, who, if he were to follow this line of inquiry, might well be deprived of two parents; but there was the distinct possibility that Frobisher, as a returning serviceman, would attract a degree of leniency, though you couldn't rely on that: juries and judges had an unpleasant knack of disappointing your expectations. He thought some more about it, before coming to the realisation that what really prevented him from pursuing the matter was the knowledge that he despised Frobisher, and you really can't condemn a man because of his weak features, weak character and weak morals. He rubbed his brow, lit a pipe and wondered how much longer he ought to give it before calling a halt to the investigation. Upstairs were applying the thumbscrews in regard to the black-market eggs, and Lucas had already instructed the murder team, such as it was, to give priority to numerous other urgent matters over the investigation into Lillian Frobisher's death. For all intents and purposes the investigation was being conducted by the two of them alone, and Cooper knew that he would not be able to depend upon the undivided attention of his adjunct indefinitely.

★ ★ ★

Mrs Mavis Jackson of Jaywick Sands was a stouter and more affluent version of her dead sister. She had come up to London in order to attend to her mother, but before she did so there were a few things she reckoned that the police ought to know concerning Lillian Frobisher. Cooper took her into one of the interview rooms where she settled herself into a chair with a studied, self-conscious poise that nevertheless belied her bulk. She joined together her plump, immaculately white-gloved hands and set them purposefully upon the table.

"This has come as a great shock to me, Inspector," she began. She had overcome her north London vowels with a thin veneer of respectability.

Cooper ran through the usual stuff, expressing sympathy, gratitude, reassurance that everything possible was being done, before coming to the point.

"Do you know of anybody who would wish your sister ill?"

Mrs Jackson pressed her lips tightly together with all the disapproval she could muster. "Lillian and I have never been close, Inspector," she said. "And you may rest assured that I know nothing of her cavortings since she came back to Holloway."

"Cavortings . . . ?"

Mrs Jackson drew a deep breath, and moistened her lips delicately.

"It is not my custom and habit to speak ill of the dead, Inspector," she said, before continuing to do just that with an undue haste, "but it has to be said — my sister has not led a blameless life."

Cooper had the curious sensation he occasionally experienced in an investigation: the inkling that he was about to learn something of immense significance.

Once she had started to speak ill of her sibling, Mrs Jackson was unable to stop.

"She's always been flighty, Inspector, but I had no idea how low she could sink until she came to stay with me in Jaywick during the war. The way she carried on . . . well . . . it was shocking. Truly shocking. Running about with all sorts; out till all hours — when she troubled to come back at all, that is. I warned her time and again that she was taking risks and would come to a bad end if she didn't take more care, and I made it quite clear that I did not approve of her carrying on — not while she was under my roof — but she refused to listen. It was as if something had been unleashed within her, Inspector, some animal force . . ."

"When you say 'carrying on', you mean with other men?"

"She was off every night, leaving me to take care of Mother and Douglas." Mrs Jackson leaned in closer across the table and whispered: "Yanks."

"I see."

"She made no secret of it. They'd come to the house to take her off in their motor cars. No shame . . . It was disgusting, Inspector. It was Joe this, and Jerry that, going on about how they took her to dinner and into public houses, and for spins in the countryside. They'd give her things as well."

"What sort of things?"

"You know — lipsticks, perfume, stockings . . . She never went without, Inspector, not like decent women had to do . . ."

"A lot of married women went off the rails during the war," he said. He was mildly surprised to discern a certain reluctance to fully embrace the notion; he found it distasteful. And he could not suppress the thought that a lot of men must have gone off the rails too. War was inimical to family life, after all. "Do you happen to know if she continued with this way of life after she returned to London?"

Mrs Jackson considered for a moment or two.

"It wouldn't surprise me, Inspector, but I'm afraid I really couldn't say for sure. She came back to Holloway in March 1944, so there would have been plenty of opportunity before Walter came back from the army." She was unable to resist a slight sneer at the mention of her sister's husband.

"Indeed. I wonder, do you remember anything specific about any of these men?"

He was thinking that it ought to be a simple enough task to identify the nearest GI base to Jaywick, but nigh on impossible to trace any individual GI — most of whom would have gone back to America in any case.

"I tried to turn a blind eye, Inspector. There were so many of them . . ."

Cooper sighed.

"And this was something," he pursued, "that started during the war — as far as you know . . ."

"Well, Lillian could never settle to anything — she suffered with her nerves, you know . . ."

"So I gather . . ."

"But I think the war definitely made her worse — what with Walter being away and all that. I certainly don't remember her ever going into public houses before: she didn't even drink, as far as I know. But it must be said, she was never very dependable. She relied on Mother and Father for everything."

"What I'm driving at is: do you think it's possible that her husband knew about any of this?"

Mrs Jackson evidently reserved a special degree of scorn for Walter Frobisher. She pressed her lips together very tightly as if damming a great wave of abuse.

"He never heard it from me," she said, tersely.

"What about friends, neighbours?"

"There was no opportunity for people in Jaywick to gossip to Walter, if that's what you mean." She reached into her handbag and retrieved a dainty lace-edged handkerchief and dabbed at her eyes with it. There was something comically insufficient about the handkerchief in her fat hands. Mrs Jackson sighed deeply. "She never tired of telling me what a burden Mother was to her," she said. "I'm afraid to go into that house. I dare say the poor dear's in a shocking state . . ."

"Your mother seemed comfortable enough when I saw her yesterday. Miss Wilkes has been keeping an eye on her the past couple of days."

Mrs Jackson raised a solitary pencilled eyebrow.

"Miss Wilkes? Do you mean Evelyn? That nasty common girl: I never understood why Lillian brought her into the house. Hardly the sort of influence any normal mother would want around an impressionable boy . . ."

Up until then it had not occurred to him that it was the victim who had taken up with Evelyn Wilkes: he had assumed that she was living in the house at the behest of the husband.

"How long has Miss Wilkes been lodging with your sister?"

"I believe that they met at a dance not long after Lillian came back to Holloway. She told me she felt sorry for the girl."

"I see. So that would be, what, 1944? A couple of years . . . ?"

Mrs Jackson nodded.

"Lillian said she was company for her while Walter was away. Someone to gad about with, more likely." She tuttutted. "Evelyn's a very knowing sort of girl, Inspector. Very knowing . . ."

"Can you think of any reason why Mr Frobisher would introduce Miss Wilkes as your sister's cousin?"

A sly smile crept across her face.

"You had better ask him that," she said.

"I intend to. Tell me a little more about Mr Frobisher — would you say that he and your sister were happily married?"

Again, the little moue of distaste.

"I won't lie to you, Inspector: I've never cared for Walter."

"Why's that?"

"I never understood why Lillian took up with him. They've spent most of their married life living in awful little flats, and I've lost count of the number of times they've come to me with their begging caps — and to Father when he was alive. I dare say the War was the first time in his life Walter Frobisher has ever done anything worthwhile — if you can call pushing papers about while other men were dying at the front worthwhile."

"He didn't go into combat?" Cooper was not surprised, just irritated that the snivelling little wretch had succeeded in convincing him otherwise.

"Walter? Combat?" Mrs Jackson laughed humourlessly. She really was a terrible bitch. Cooper almost felt sorry for Walter Frobisher. "He was in the Service Corps."

"Still did his bit," Cooper said.

"The man's a complete failure, Inspector. He worked for years in insurance, but never made anything of himself. To be quite honest, we've often wondered if he was all there."

"Was your sister happy with Mr Frobisher?"

"Oh, she used to say how he got on her nerves, but then everything got on Lillian's nerves. She was very highly strung. They rubbed along, I suppose. His people were quite respectable — his father was a bank manager on Canvey Island. They paid for Walter to go to school. She used to put on airs and graces, swank about the place — make out that they were better than the rest of us. But I tell you, Inspector, they never had two ha'pennies to rub together."

"As far as you know, was Mr Frobisher ever violent towards your sister?"

Mrs Jackson's eyes stretched at the implication of what he was driving at.

"Walter? He wouldn't say boo to a goose," she said. She thought for a moment. "But I dare say worms do turn . . ."

Cooper went to his office and telephoned Lucas. He reckoned he was looking at a blank wall: back with a random, apparently motiveless killing.

"Funny," said the DI, "I was just about to telephone you, guv."

"Please say something's turned up."

"Two things, as a matter of fact."

"Thank God."

"A bloke's just walked in with the handbag. Says he came by it on Sunday morning — found it behind a wall close to the house where the identity card was found. He took it home with him, but when he saw the description in the newspaper this morning he thought better of it. And before you ask — it's empty."

"There's a surprise . . ."

"I've sent it off to have it checked for fingerprints, but I'll lay odds to evens the only ones we'll turn up'll belong to the bloke who found it."

"And what do you make of him?"

"He's telling the truth, if that's what you mean. And he has an alibi. He spent the whole of Saturday evening in a drinking club in Camden Town. Dozens of witnesses."

"And the other thing?"

"A fellow says he saw a couple on Saturday evening, about half past ten, standing on the pavement beside the murder site. Obviously because there's no street lighting there the chances of him making any sort of positive identification are slim, to say the least; but he says they were both quite short: the man maybe not much more than five seven or eight."

"Did he say anything about how they appeared?"

"Well, they weren't quarrelling or anything like that ... As a matter of fact, he assumed they were a courting couple, though he says he didn't really pay them much attention. And it was dark."

"How tall would you say Frobisher is?"

"About five seven."

Cooper rubbed his brow.

"What time have we asked him and Miss Wilkes to come in to give their statements?"

"Half past four. By the way, I've found someone else to help with the investigation,"

"Oh?"

"Policewoman Tring — the girlie who's been driving you around."

Cooper was surprised by the sudden burst of life in the region of his heart.

"Yes, I know who she is."

"She's very keen. Apparently she was in the WAAFS and seems to have done alright."

"It was the ATS, actually."

Lucas digested this fact.

"I know she's only a slip of a girl," he said, "but beggars can't be choosers. I've cleared it with A4 Branch."

Cooper had a Spam sandwich and a cup of tea and considered doing something reckless; not that he had any real desire to do so: his appetite for such things had long since been abated, and it disturbed him that this was the case — pained him, as a matter of fact. He thought of the time with Marjorie, when an afternoon of lovemaking had been a matter of such consequence he would have pursued the possibility at all costs: risking the disapprobation of his superior officers, jeopardising entire investigations and never thinking of the misery he might cause to Bill, his pal; to Marjorie; to himself. Well, he was paying for it now. He was suffering, had been suffering since 1939. He very much doubted that Policewoman Tring would be able to put an end to his suffering, even if he could persuade her to entertain the possibility, and he knew that he would not be able to summon the energy for that. He was long out of practice with women, could not for the life of him remember what you did or said; and then, of course, it was most likely that any beautiful young woman of sense would take one look at him and run a thousand miles in the opposite direction. The stark truth of it was: he had not the energy to redeem himself; he was exhausted, starving; hungry for love and devilled kidneys; tired of waiting for someone to come along and fill up the emptiness at the core of his being. He washed down the dregs of the sandwich with the last of the tea and decided that he could not bear to see her every day; that he would have to think of endless excuses not to go to Caledonian Road. And then he berated himself for being such a fool. Put it out of your mind, old man, he thought. Put it out of your mind. You're done with all of that. It's over. Over.

As it turned out, the reckless thing he did was take himself off to Holborn — to Gamages — to do the one thing he knew that he was good at: old-fashioned detective work. Frobisher was, naturally, on compassionate leave, but his fellow doorman spoke well enough of a shabby little failure of a man who didn't seem to make much of an impression on anyone. In the gents' department the manager knew all about the Westmoreland, and raised his eyebrows when Cooper asked whether any members of staff had purchased one recently.

"The Westmoreland is a very expensive garment, Inspector," he said.

Cooper regrouped.

"So I gather. I wonder: is there any way of identifying any of the gentlemen who may have purchased one, say, in the past year or so?"

It took a little above an hour to go through the accounts books and extract just over a dozen names. It was a long shot, but the mackintosh was the only piece of material evidence he had. He took the list back to the station with him, resolving to have Policewoman Tring make some telephone calls until she found someone on the list who had owned a Westmoreland that they were not prepared to present at their local police station. You see, he told himself: you see how I am doing everything that can possibly be done. Everything.

CHAPTER
TWENTY-THREE

Evelyn Wilkes, Lucas decided, was definitely too stupid to have had a hand in plotting a murder. She was certainly scheming, and it was obvious that she would have done just about anything for a few clothing coupons, but to cover up a killing required a certain amount of cool calculation, a facility Evelyn Wilkes definitely lacked. He and Cooper had spent an hour in her company, and as far as he was concerned they had not learned anything of any note which had not already been supposed: the Frobishers had quarrelled a great deal since Walter returned from the army; the victim wasn't all there . . .

"One time she flung a cup of tea in his face and told him he was a selfish bloody pig," she told them. Cooper, judging by the sudden flexing of his jaw, had evidently seen something of significance in this revelation, but Lucas thought it was exactly the sort of thing a wife said and did from time to time. "She used to say he got on her nerves." Again, there was no real surprise there. "If you ask me, I don't think she wanted him to come back from the army."

"Why do you think that?" Cooper had asked.

Evelyn shrugged.

"She told me she felt like he was suffocating her. We had a bit of fun during the war: she let her hair down. We'd go dancing and she nearly always got off with someone. She told me that she'd been with a coloured fellow when she was down in Jaywick. And one time she picked up a man in a café."

"Did Mr Frobisher know about her carrying on?" Lucas asked.

The girl shrugged again.

"Why did Mr Frobisher introduce you as his wife's cousin?"

"Did he?" Evelyn laughed. "He ain't half old-fashioned . . ." Cooper frowned.

"How long have you been seeing each other?" he asked. She picked a shred of tobacco from her bottom lip.

"Not long."

"And did Mrs Frobisher know?"

Evelyn's eyes narrowed as she considered her response.

"She found out on Saturday."

"I see. And how did she take that?"

"What do you think?"

"Is that why she went off?"

Evelyn shrugged again.

"She was always threatening to sling her hook. I didn't think much of it. It wasn't as if she cared all that much for Walter . . ."

Cooper and Lucas had a brief exchange in the corridor before going on to interview Frobisher.

"What if she riled him?" Cooper averred. "You know, made him feel unmanly — persistently mocking him until it all became too much and he snapped."

"She was a woman of easy virtue, guv, and you know as well as I do, they invariably end up dead."

"There have been quite a few cases where returning servicemen have assaulted, and even killed their wives when they've discovered infidelity . . ."

"Did these fellows take their wives to a bomb-site for a spot of how's your father before doing them in?"

"I've been thinking about that: what if she was murdered in the house and the body was moved to the bomb-site?"

Lucas did not discount the possibility, and, Lord knows, he was close to agreeing to any scenario, however ludicrous, if it meant drawing a line under the case; but the fact of the matter was, when he looked at Frobisher he did not feel the fellow's guilt in his bones, and he had learned to trust his bones over the years. Rather, there was something about Frobisher that invited pity, and the DI believed wholeheartedly that if the wretched fellow had strangled his wife with his bare hands, he, Lucas, would not be feeling sorry for him . . .

"Let's keep an open mind and see what he tells us, guv," he counselled. But he had already decided that Lillian Frobisher had been the architect of her own demise. It was a sad fact that women like her had a habit of ending up throttled, and their killers invariably got away with it — most often because the more you went into the matter, the more likely suspects you turned up. There had been a case a couple of years back where a tart had been found dead in her bed-sitting room. The place had been full of fingerprints, which were easily traced to a nearby Yank base, and the matter should have been easily resolved, were it not for the fact that the fingerprints in question belonged to half a dozen GIs. One of them was almost certainly the killer, but it was nigh on impossible to prove which of them had been the last to see the victim alive. Of course, that had been during the war, when trained servicemen carried more value than a common prostitute, so nobody pushed too hard for a hanging. He had to admit that the murder of Lillian Frobisher was of a different order, even if it was a hopeless case.

"You know, Inspector," Frobisher said. His pale eyes were disturbingly large, darting about the place insanely. "I've been thinking about something. Lillian always carried a police whistle in her handbag. Don't you think it's a bit odd — I mean, why didn't she use it?"

"Perhaps she didn't have the opportunity; or she didn't think there was any need until it was too late."

Frobisher considered this for a few moments.

"Do you think it's possible that she might have known the person who — who did this to her . . . ?"

"That's one possibility we're considering, Mr Frobisher."

Frobisher's eyes grew even larger before returning to their pallid cast, contemplating that desktop. Cooper sighed; he and Lucas exchanged a look.

"We know about you and Miss Wilkes," the DI said.

The fellow's face crumpled.

"I've been a bloody fool," he sobbed.

"How long has it been going on?"

"Not long." He sighed deeply, the breath shuddering out of him. "A couple of weeks . . ."

"And when did Mrs Frobisher find out?"

"Saturday," said Frobisher, his voice reduced to a croak.

"And is that why you quarrelled?"

Frobisher blinked back tears. "The truth is, Inspector," he said, turning his eyes beseechingly upon them, "Lillian and I have not got on for some time. I thought that when I came back from the army things might be different, but she made it very clear to me from the off that she didn't want that."

"But you decided to stay by her in any case . . ." Cooper said.

Frobisher surprised him with the force of his response.

"I stuck by the old girl — what else was I supposed to do!" he cried. "Divorce — sneaking off to Brighton with a prostitute — is not for people like us, Inspector. Do you think I like living in her mother's house?" He ran his hands through his thinning hair. When he spoke again he was less agitated. "We both thought it was better to keep up appearances," he said. "For the boy's sake. Try and make a go of things."

Cooper sighed heavily. The whole matter depressed him.

"You must see, Mr Frobisher," he said, mildly, "that this does not look very good for you."

From his shocked expression it was immediately apparent that Frobisher had not seen this.

"Oh God," he said in a hoarse whisper, as the implication of what Cooper had just said dawned on him. "But I could never harm a hair on her head. Oh, she could be very difficult, but I wouldn't do a thing to hurt her! You must see that. You must!"

Cooper was implacable.

"Why didn't you report her missing?"

"I've told you: she said she was going to her sister's in Jaywick Sands."

"And you didn't think it strange that she didn't take anything with her?"

"She'd stayed there before — in the war. I just supposed she had things there . . . I don't know . . ." He looked helpless and small. "Oh God, I don't know . . . I — I didn't really think much about it . . ."

"Your situation is very serious, Mr Frobisher," said Lucas. "I would urge you to be completely honest with us. For your own good."

Frobisher let out a long sob-racked sigh.

"I've told you all I know! You must believe me!" he said. He was a man in deep, deep pain. "You must . . ."

"It's not in your interest to defend anyone, you know," said Cooper.

"I'm not defending anyone — I've told you everything I can . . . I don't know any more."

"Did you know that your wife consorted with other men?"

Frobisher was crying now.

"Yes," he groaned. "Yes . . . I knew . . . I knew . . ."

"Do you know the names of any of the men she might have gone with?" asked Lucas.

Frobisher did not appear to have heard him. He fell silent for a moment or two, staring at the desktop.

"Will it go into the newspapers?" he asked in a horrified whisper. "Only . . . Douglas, you see . . . I couldn't bear for him . . ."

Cooper assured him that there was no need for the newspapers to know anything at this stage. Frobisher asked for a glass of water. He sipped from it slowly, his eyes still fixed on the desk. When he spoke again it was as if he was in a daze.

"When we hadn't heard from Lillian on the Monday, I was a bit concerned. I said to Evelyn, I know she's angry and wants to punish me, but I'd have expected a wire or something regarding arrangements for her mother. At the very least I'd have expected word from Mavis, her sister. Mavis is a terrible bitch. She'd have been cock-a-hoop, and to be quite honest, I was surprised that she hadn't turned up on the doorstep to turn me out of the house. I wanted to go out and telephone, but Evelyn told me that Lillian had met some fellow in a café. A spiv . . ."

Cooper felt his heart quicken.

"A spiv?"

"Yes. Evelyn said he'd taken a shine to her, and she reckoned Lillian had gone off with him, as she put it. She said he was very well appointed and Lillian wouldn't want for anything. He'd give her the world . . . All the things I couldn't . . ."

"Do you know his name, this spiv?" asked Lucas.

Frobisher, overcome with grief, shame, humiliation, had evidently lost the power of speech. He shook his head before subsiding into another flood of tears. Then he took out a handkerchief from his trouser pocket and blew his nose.

"Evelyn said Lillian often went off with men while I was away," he said. "It wasn't unusual for her to stay out all night . . ."

"Why the dickens didn't you say all this before?" thundered Cooper.

"I — I couldn't . . . You must see. The shame . . . Oh God . . . Will it be in the newspapers? There's Douglas, you see. I don't want Douglas to know . . ."

When they questioned her again, Evelyn Wilkes told them that all she knew about the spiv was that he was a good-looking boy, very well dressed, and his name was Dennis. She would know him if she was to see him again. She had no idea how tall he was. They'd met him in a café on the Seven Sisters Road — the one opposite Woolworths. He'd been in company with a woman called Nesta who knew how to come by things: there had been talk of tinned soup, peas . . . She had invited them to go to the Feathers public house that evening with her and Dennis. Dennis had been giving Lillian the eye all the while and it wouldn't have surprised her if that's where Lillian had gone.

"Didn't it occur to you to tell us all of this at the beginning?" asked Cooper.

The kid shrugged.

"You never asked," she said.

CHAPTER
TWENTY-FOUR

Evelyn was sitting at the kitchen table rolling a cigarette with enormous concentration, shreds of tobacco straggling from either end. Lillian watched her with distaste.

"Must you do that at the table, dear?" It was pointless to say anything: the kid just did whatever she wanted without any regard for anyone else. "It's not very ladylike, is it? Looks like the sort of thing a navvy would do."

"It's cheaper than cigarettes, ain't it?" She lifted the half-built cigarette to her lips and licked the edge of the paper. "Loads of girls have taken it up." She looked at the result of her labour with pride. " 'Ere, you'll never guess what," she said.

"What now?"

"Mr Newman offered me a quarter-pound box of Cadbury's Tray under the counter."

"I hope you took it."

Evelyn brushed the pieces of tobacco from the table and pinched them back into the packet. "I don't care for chocs," she was saying. "I need to watch my figure. That's why I smoke."

192

"You could have taken the chocs for Mother, or Douglas. You're not the only person living in this house." Evelyn looked genuinely surprised, as if this had not occurred to her; which of course it hadn't. "It would have been a nice gesture — seeing as you haven't paid a penny in rent since heaven knows when."

"Oh, please don't start on that again, Lil. You know I've been trying ever so hard to find something. Anyway, Walter told me not to worry about the rent . . ."

"Did he? Well, it isn't Walter's house. It's Mother's, and he has no right to decide who gets to do what under this roof." She was taken aback by the fury of her reaction: her face was blazing with indignation, with the damn cheek of it. Either that or it was the Change.

Evelyn had returned her attention to her cigarette.

"You shouldn't talk like that, Lil," she said. "Men don't like being made to feel small."

It was on the tip of her tongue to ask what was meant by that, but there was no point in eliciting what would no doubt be a lengthy explanation, chiefly drawn from things that Evelyn had read in the women's pages. She did not have the energy to listen, much less enter into an earnest rebuttal. A weary sigh followed by an awkward silence was the best reaction — awkward for her, that is, since Evelyn was incapable of picking up on any sort of atmosphere — an awkward silence laden with a long-suppressed urge to scream or to drink bleach — to make some sort of gesture — agitating her nerves beyond endurance.

It often occurred to her that there was something so mean and slighting about the situation she found herself in, that it was almost comical. And it was easy to imagine that somewhere somebody was indeed having a good laugh at her expense. She glowered at the array of groceries spread out on the table with a deep-seated resentment, and wondered how on earth she was supposed to make a meal for four of them with such ridiculous ingredients. And then do the same tomorrow, and the next day, and the next. But it was not the utter hopelessness of it all that was funny, so much as the sad fact that she still had hopes that somehow things would change for the better; that in some curious, as yet imperceptible way she would know joy, wealth, luxuries: all the things to which she had, surely by now, entitlement. It pained her to think back to that brief period of happiness, when she had gone out with the gang, possessed of an authentic undeniable attraction which had enabled her to take part in another sort of life altogether. It seemed impossible to her that those days really were gone.

"I'll bet that Julian Huxley can get his hands on anything he wants," she said, "and then he has the nerve to come on the wireless and tell the rest of us we never had a healthier diet." Evelyn struck a match and for a moment was obscured behind a dense choking cloud of smoke. "Oh, those things smell awful, Evvie." She grimaced. "I don't know how you can smoke them. You must be desperate is all I can say." She was waving her hand about in front of her face in an exaggerated fashion. "What did he want for them?"

"Who?"

"Mr Newman — what did he want for the Cadbury Tray?"

"Ooh Lil! 'Ere — whaddya take me for?" Evelyn laughed. "What would you have done for a box of chocs then, eh, Lil?"

"That's for me to know and you to wonder about," she said breezily, though her heart was not in it. She felt herself soften, the urge to do something significant subsiding. "Evvie, will you help me with my hair later? Just the back of it . . ."

"Course. Going to meet your fancy man, are you? I tell you, he didn't half like you, that spiv. He weren't bad-looking neither."

"Shut up, Evelyn!" she cried. The girl was looking at her, wide-eyed, open-mouthed; shocked. She wondered why she had done that. "If you must know," she said, "I was thinking of going to the Odeon tonight." In truth this had only just occurred to her, and now that it had been uttered she felt a distinct flutter of anticipation in the pit of her stomach: a thrill. It was only the pictures, she told herself. Nothing will come of it. He probably won't even be there.

"I thought you said you'd seen the big picture and it weren't any good," said Evelyn.

"I only said that to get rid of that awful woman — besides, that was the Mayfair. I'm going to the Odeon . . . maybe . . . It depends on how I'm feeling later on. I'm done in right now . . ."

She was concocting menus in her head. Cooked-meat sandwiches. Macaroni in sauce made from the tinned milk — she had a bit of flour somewhere and their butter ration, and some of that Canadian powdered cheese which was alright mixed up in something. Or she could make them potatoes in their jackets with a little bit of the butter and a spoonful each of the powdered cheese. All the proper food went to the Germans, she thought. She used to believe that there must be some good Germans, that they couldn't all be Nazis, that some of them must have been ordinary women like her — housewives and mothers, just getting by. But after the horror camps she wasn't so sure.

"I thought that Nesta was alright," said Evelyn. She was relighting her cigarette again, a small pile of spent matches at her elbow. "A bit of a laugh . . ."

"She was very common. Not the sort of person you should be consorting with, Evvie."

"She knew where to get things an' all. 'Ere, I wouldn't mind going to that pub they were talking about. The Feathers. How about it, Lil? Go on . . . Make a change . . ."

"You go on your own, Evelyn, if that's what you want. Maybe the spiv'll give you twenty cigs, if you play your cards right . . ."

"Oooh, Lil, what are you like? You are awful, no, really you are."

This time she did not join in the kid's joking. It was time to look in on Mother. The thought wearied her. She'd make up a little bit of bread and milk to take up to her.

"There's a pile of linen on the floor in Mother's room," she said. "I'll give you half a crown . . ."

The kid was lighting her cigarette again, the dense smoke making her cough.

"I'll go up now if you like," she said cheerfully.

"Would you, Evvie? You're a pal."

She cut a thin slice of the loaf, poured a bit of the tinned milk over it and sprinkled a spoonful of sugar on the top. "Try her with this, though I don't suppose you'll get very far . . ."

Evelyn balanced the half-smoked cigarette — which had once more gone out of its own accord — on the edge of the ashtray, intending to return to it later. Lillian could hear her humming as she went upstairs. A dance tune. She went to the dresser and took a knife from the drawer, sat down at the table and began to peel the potatoes. Mash and luncheon meat, with the runner beans: that would have to do them. She'd like to see Julian Huxley do better. They ought to give housewives a medal.

CHAPTER
TWENTY-FIVE

Policewoman Tring was bright-eyed, smooth cheeks flushed with a sense of achievement; she was starched and crisp and clean-limbed. The crumpled men in the incident room were looking upon her as if she was some fabulous creature which had suddenly, magically, appeared in their midst; manifesting out of the cigarette pall, among the dirty teacups and the greasy telephones, the untidy piles of papers and the chewed pencils. Cooper was as dumbstruck as the rest of them; even Lucas had permitted the corner of his mouth to turn up ever so slightly in wonder.

She had done everything Cooper had requested in a matter of a few hours. She had telephoned the gentlemen account-holders on the list from Gamages; she had been to the Odeon with the victim's photograph. And this assiduity had garnered two pieces of essential information which she was now recounting to the rest of the team, sorely depleted since the detective sergeant had been despatched to an attempted jewellery theft.

"Mr Vickers had a suitcase stolen from King's Cross a week before the murder," she was telling them. "I've checked the crime report and it tallies with everything he told me on the telephone. The suitcase was being

198

forwarded to Edinburgh where he was going on business. It contained a number of items of gentleman's clothing — quality items, valued at £163.14/6d. Apart from the mackintosh, there was a pair of shoes, three shirts, some underclothing, a pair of pyjamas, a travel clock, a pair of cufflinks — and a green tweed swingback jacket." She beamed at Cooper. "A green tweed jacket," she repeated. "Green tweed — like the strand of wool retrieved from the victim . . ."

"Good work, Tring." He wanted to sound as if he was conceding a point, but grudgingly. She really was very lovely, that much was obvious even to a blind fool, but on no account could he risk letting her know that he thought as much; risk her putting him off. He was, he assumed, almost certainly in love with her; he supposed that to acknowledge this had the benefit of giving him something with which to occupy himself, another dimension to a life that had become arid and flat. It was a cherished secret. Other people had secrets, so why not him?

"How did you get on at the picture-house?" he inquired, not looking at her, pretending to peruse some papers he had been carrying around all morning. He was punishing himself; not her. She could not have cared less; had no thought of him.

"She's done very well there too, guv," said Lucas. Cooper had never heard his DI utter a single word of encouragement before. He was astonished. "We've brought in the cinema manager and he's made a positive sighting of the victim. Says he saw her enter the cinema at about five and twenty past seven on the Saturday. He recognised her, knew her slightly to say hello to. She told him she was done in. He said she looked tired, but not at all agitated. He's pretty certain that she left at half past ten along with everyone else. He says there was nobody in the cinema after that time apart from himself."

"Did he notice whether she was with anyone?" asked Cooper.

"No," said Policewoman Tring, darting a look at Lucas, concerned that she might be speaking out of turn, but too eager to prevent herself from doing just that. Lucas nodded slight acquiescence and brushed cigarette ash from his lapel. "But then he didn't actually see her leave," the girl continued. "It's just that he would have noticed if she'd left earlier than that — I mean before the picture ended — or if she was still in the cinema when he prepared to close it."

Cooper considered the implications of this.

"So," he said, "either Wilkes and Frobisher are lying when they told us that the victim said she was going to her sister's in Jaywick, or she told them that for some reason of her own. The visit to the picture-house certainly ties in with the son's statement, and he has no apparent reason to lie to us about his mother's intentions. He also hinted that his father may have invented the whole Jaywick Sands story in order to put up some sort of front of respectability — understandable, perhaps, in the circumstances, and not in itself an indication of guilt or complicity . . ."

"She was intending all the time to go to the picture. She'd planned to meet up with her fancy man," said Lucas flatly.

200

"Or," said Cooper, "is the whole story about this spiv — this Dennis — a concoction of Wilkes and Frobisher? I don't recollect any Dennises coming up before now, do you? And between us I think we must know every spiv in north London."

Lucas shook his head and sighed.

"But the green tweed jacket," said Policewoman Tring. A host of bloodshot eyes turned to her in dull amazement. "And the mackintosh . . ." she faltered, suddenly self-conscious. "Unless . . ." she looked perplexed. "Are you saying that the victim's husband is the person who stole the suitcase?"

Lucas lit a cigarette, his hands cupped around it as if he were in a wind.

"Whoever pinched the suitcase," he said, "had access to the raincoat and a green tweed jacket. So, either he's the killer, or someone he knows is."

"I want this Dennis found," said Cooper.

"He's a spiv in Holloway." Lucas turned his palms up in an uncharacteristically expansive gesture. "If he exists we'll turn him up." It was the first time so far on the case that Cooper had heard him say anything positive. And he was further astonished to see that Lucas was actually smiling at Policewoman Tring: as a matter of fact, DI Frank Lucas was beaming, for what was quite possibly the first time in his life.

The café was a hell of steam, grease and cigarette smoke, through which could be glimpsed a large, heavily tattooed fellow. He was standing behind the counter, studying the racing tips beside a large belching tea-urn. He failed to respond with alacrity to Cooper's request for information.

"This is a murder investigation," Cooper prompted.

The large fellow shrugged as if to say it was nothing to do with him. He returned his attention to the sporting pages, effectively dismissing Cooper from his premises. Cooper glanced at Policewoman Tring and rolled his eyes, which made her smile. He was so pleased that she had asked to come with him. He had hoped that she might, and nerved himself to agree to the request; not that he had any intention of pursuing anything, naturally; not unless she showed her hand first and gave him some impression of what she thought about him. He was already making a fool of himself, but so far only in his own eyes.

"Does anyone called Dennis come in here?" he asked the café proprietor.

"Can't say he does," the fellow said without looking up.

"Think back to last Saturday afternoon."

The café proprietor made an unconvincing show of doing just that, stroking his chin in mock contemplation.

"A lot of people come in here," he said at last, the pantomime having run its course, and returned to his paper.

Cooper leaned on the counter. There was a basket containing a few very small eggs next to the urn. He pointed casually at it.

"Where do you get your supplies?"

"Now you look here," said the proprietor, drawing himself up to his full height. "I keep myself to myself, see, and I expect my customers to do the same. Most of them just sit there and make a cup of tea last till Kingdom Come. I don't speak to them and they don't speak to me. And I don't care who they are or what they are. As long as they have the readies and don't cause any trouble, they can do what they bloody well like."

"What about a woman called Nesta?"

"I don't check their flamin' identity cards."

Cooper inspected his nails.

"Was there anyone else in here on Saturday afternoon," he asked, "who might be able to assist us?"

The fellow licked his thumb and forefinger with studied deliberation and slowly turned a page of his newspaper. Cooper regarded him with an implacable air. He wanted to grab the bastard by the scruff of his neck and haul him over the counter, but he knew that to do so would have yielded only partial success.

"You know, I can wait here all day," he said.

The café proprietor tried to ignore him for a few more moments, but he knew when a copper had the better of him.

"Joyce!" he called, without looking up. "Come out here will you. There's a nosy bogey asking questions."

A young girl emerged from behind a filthy curtain drawn across a doorway at the back of the counter. She wiped her shiny brow with her hands, smearing them down the front of her grubby apron.

"What is it?" she whined. "I'm trying to get those rolls buttered before the lunchtime rush." Cooper glanced over at Policewoman Tring with a sardonic raise of his eyebrows, which made her grin. It was hard to imagine anything approaching a rush in that godforsaken place.

"I'm so sorry to interrupt your duties, miss," he said with just a trace of irony. "We have a couple of questions. It shouldn't take long, and then you can get back to your bread and butter."

The girl lifted a damp curl from her forehead, which enabled him to see that she was frowning. She was a brunette, about eighteen, nineteen, he reckoned with his detective's unerring instinct for such things, and in point of fact, pretty well made despite the squint.

The café proprietor was tracing the runners in the 2.30 at Newmarket with his forefinger.

"Says it's a murder investigation," he grunted.

"Murder?" The waitress glanced nervously at her employer, though it was clear that her interest had been aroused.

"We're looking for a fellow called Dennis who was in here on Saturday afternoon."

"Is he the murderer?"

"He might be able to help us with our inquiries."

"So he hasn't murdered anyone then?"

Cooper sighed.

"He's in his early twenties," he said, "slim build, fair hair. He was in here on Saturday afternoon with a stout middle-aged woman who goes by the name of Nesta, and two others. Ring any bells?"

It was difficult to be sure with the squint, but Joyce appeared to have developed a fascination with Policewoman Tring; that is to say, she was running her eyes up and down someone or something with a resentful air.

"Are you a policewoman?" she asked, ignoring Cooper.

"Yes," said Tring.

"What's that like then?"

"It's jolly interesting."

Cooper cleared his throat.

"Saturday afternoon . . ." he prompted.

Tring handed her the artist's impression of Dennis that Evelyn Wilkes had supplied.

"Yeah," said Joyce, keeping at least one of her eyes on Tring, "he was in here with three women. He comes in quite a bit — I haven't seen him the past couple of days, though. And I don't know his name. He's a flashy type. Keen on himself. Looks like a spiv."

Tring touched Cooper lightly on the shoulder, which made him startle. He nodded at her to say whatever it was she wanted to say.

"Can you remember what he was wearing?" she asked. Joyce looked at her as if she were a dog on a bicycle playing the cymbals. "You said he was dressed like a spiv," Tring persisted. "Can you remember what he was wearing?"

"Can't say as I paid him much attention," Joyce said. "Like I said, he isn't really my type."

"Well, if you do happen to remember," Cooper said, picking up the reins of his investigation, "or if he puts in an appearance in the meantime, perhaps you'd be so kind as to let us know."

Tring handed the waitress a card with the station numbers on it. The girl inspected it with interest.

"That Nesta was in yesterday," she said. "She was with a soldier."

"A soldier?"

"He's Irish. I think it's disgusting. She's old enough to be his mother."

"What does he look like?"

Joyce thought for a moment before giving Cooper a reasonable description, which Tring took down. He didn't sound much like Dennis: very tall, red hair, florid complexion.

"Thank you very much," Cooper said while Tring took down her name and address. "You've been most helpful. We'll be in touch about you coming down to the station to give a statement."

"She ain't doing that in my time," the proprietor said without looking up from the *Sporting Life*.

"The police station?" The waitress had perked up noticeably at the idea of a visit to the police station, and seeing her reaction, Cooper reckoned that the café was in good hands: there was no hope of Joyce being considered for the A4 Branch, not with that squint — no matter how many men the Met were short — but it didn't hurt the investigation to have her think that she might be in with a chance.

"I can't believe people like that dreadful man don't want to help the police," Tring was saying as they made their way to the Feathers.

"We're jolly lucky he didn't throw us out on to the street," Cooper said.

"I thought you dealt with him very well, sir."

"Most people will relent if you hang about long enough, just to get rid of you."

They walked a little further along the baking street. A newspaper wrapped itself around his feet. She laughed at his clumsy efforts to detach it.

"Sir," she said after they had walked a few hundred yards more, "I'm thinking of applying to 'C' Department." She had half turned towards him and was smiling as his heart broke into a hundred thousand pieces. They passed a wood yard, a watchmaker, one of those hardware shops that smell of polish and paraffin and clutter the pavement with a paraphernalia of buckets and broom handles: the bleak scenery of his disappointment, destined to be imprinted on his memory for as long as the grey enduring ghastliness of his life stretched out before him.

"Don't do it," he said, managing, just, to keep from begging. He was thinking how there was nothing for it now but to run away. He had not run away from Marjorie, but that was only because she had taken herself off.

"Why ever do you say that?" she asked. She sounded genuinely surprised.

Because, he wanted to say, I love you.

"It's an awful, sordid business," he said, "dirty and depressing at worst; dull as ditchwater at best."

"Well, I can't think of anything I'd rather do," she countered.

"Modern police work isn't like a Harriet Vane novel, you know," he said. Harriet Vane! Good God! That dated him. Why not bring in *The Perils of Pauline* and *Mutt and Jeff* while you're at it, old man, he thought. He really was an ass. "Besides, it's man's work." He knew that these were feeble objections; the dying clutches of a drowning man, and she, quite rightly, snorted in derision.

"Man's work?" she exclaimed. "With respect, sir, this is 1946. I suppose you think I ought to be living in the suburbs with a nice doctor husband and a couple of children." As a matter of fact he did, but with him instead of some dull provincial GP. "You sound like my mother!" She laughed; she had a very jolly sort of laugh. "You know I was in Nairobi with the ATS."

"So you've told me."

"I was a motorcycle despatch rider. I know ju-jitsu." She drew her bottom lip over her top lip and he wondered if she was about to cry. "I just want to do my bit, sir," she said, "like I did in the war."

He had one last stab at putting her off.

"What does your father think about you wanting to spend your time parading about the streets dressed like a prostitute, or acting as a decoy for a sexual maniac?" It was a low blow; unworthy of him, and he despised himself for dealing it.

"My father died when I was twelve," she said, simply, unaffectedly. "He was gassed in the Great War and never really recovered."

He might have told her that he knew how that must have been — the gassing, that is, but his generation hardly ever talked about such things; of course, she was not his generation, and it would have been entirely the wrong way to go about making amends. His heart was sinking fast as they walked along. Why did she have to be so very lovely? Why did he have to want so very badly for her to like him? He was lonely: that was the whole matter. He was lonely and in danger of making a fool of himself with a lovely girl half his age who had not the slightest interest in him.

They walked along the Seven Sisters Road in a desultory silence, steeped, on his part, in embarrassment. He was fervently praying that they could both forget that the conversation had ever taken place when they passed another café, even dirtier than the one they had just left, and his attention was taken by a familiar face hunched in the farthest, dingiest corner and slurping tea from a saucer.

"Hello," he said. He tapped on the window and exchanged a brief telling look with the man. "It's safe to talk," he told Tring, and they both entered the café.

"Will he know anything?" she asked. He was relieved that they appeared to be back on speaking terms.

"He knows everything."

The price of information, swiftly negotiated, was a plate of watery dried eggs served up on a round of milk toast. Cheaper than the customary ten-bob note, but times were hard.

"I'm looking for someone called Dennis," Cooper began, once the eggs had been declared satisfactory. He rattled off the description, and Tring handed the nark the artist's impression. It met with a blank stare and was handed back with a brief shake of the head.

"What about a woman called Nesta? Deals in an under-the-counter sort of way."

"I know her," said the nark, shovelling a fork of the egg mixture into his mouth. "I ain't seen her for a few days, but she drinks in the Feathers. She goes with an Irish fellah and I heard they'd come into a bit of luck and he'd taken her off to Brighton. He's called Jimmy."

"Jimmy what?"

"Jimmy," the nark repeated.

"You're sure it's Jimmy. Not Dennis . . ."

"Jimmy. He's Irish."

Cooper sat back and sighed. If he was a man who worried he'd be worried: every corner they turned, they seemed to run into a blasted brick wall.

The landlord of the Feathers was well known to Cooper. He had a look of Stanley Holloway about him, that air of common, salt-of-the-earth decency that everybody finds reassuring. Publicans, Cooper told Tring as they prepared to enter the saloon bar, are in general more forthcoming than other sorts of witnesses: they had a good deal to lose, and it paid them to keep in with the police. She seemed to respond positively to being told things of this nature, and he had begun to harbour a hope that, by showing willing to train her up in the ways of detection, she might favour him. There was no indication that she had forgiven him, but neither did she appear to be holding him to account; and in this way he reassured himself, all the while

210

knowing that the reality was far worse than either of those possibilities. He was too good a detective to be capable of much self-delusion: the fact was, she had no feelings for him whatsoever, and he could bear anything except indifference.

The Feathers was, unusually, open for an hour or two at lunchtime, but he didn't recognise any of the faces which turned, with palpable lack of interest, to look him up and down over the top of their half-pints of stout. The tables, which probably passed muster in the smoke-laden gloom of the evening, in daylight were scarred terribly with cigarette burns and beer mug rings; the whole place was suffused with the bitterness of stale beer and gaspers.

The publican's cheerfulness was at odds with the surroundings. He was keen to help, but in practice had very little to tell them. It had been exceedingly busy on Saturday night, quite the busiest night they'd had for a long time. The warm weather was good for business; as was the word, somehow got out, that a supply of gin had come in.

"We ran out of bitter fairly early on, but the gin kept people going until closing time," he was saying. They'd been rushed off their feet from the moment they had opened at eight o'clock, until last orders were shouted at half past ten. "This Dennis," the landlord had told them, handing back the artist's impression, "he's not one of the regulars, not as I recollect, anyway."

The barmaid said the same.

Cooper was not about to give up.

"What about a stout, middle-aged woman, name of Nesta?"

The landlord chuckled.

"Oh yes, we know Nesta," he said. "You can't miss Nesta. She's the life and soul when she's had a few drinks — nothing troublesome, you understand. Is she mixed up in all of this, then? I can assure you, Mr Cooper, if she came in here trying to sell BM tins or anything of that sort I'd have seen her off. You can bet your life on that. It's more than my life's worth to encourage that sort of carry-on."

Cooper reassured him, but made a mental note about the BM tins.

"Was Nesta in here on Saturday night, as far as you know?"

"Try and keep Nesta away when there's gin in! She seems to know before I do when there's any in town." The landlord laughed again.

"Was she with anyone as far as you remember?"

"She was with an Irish guardsman she walks out with when he's on weekend leave. Nice enough fellow — young enough to be her son, though, but then that's Nesta all over. They spent some of the evening with a gang of Irish boys who were spending pretty freely."

"Irish boys, eh?" said Cooper. "Can you remember what any of them looked like?"

The landlord scratched his bald head and thought for a moment.

"They're mostly working men," he said. "Navvies, you know."

"Well dressed for a night out?"

212

"Not so's you'd notice."

He already knew from Joyce, the café waitress, that the guardsman and Dennis were two different people, so there was no point in pursuing that line.

Tring handed the publican another of the cards with the Caledonian Road station number on it, and he assured her that he would telephone right away should Nesta, or any of the Irish boys she liked to spend time with, come in.

CHAPTER
TWENTY-SIX

When he finally came round he could remember very little, and what he did remember came to him in nightmarish splinters for the most part. He had the vaguest recollection of being in the back of some shop with a seedy Jew, selling or buying something. He had the idea that he was with someone for some of the time, but couldn't for the life of him think who it could be. He had a sour feeling that didn't sit right: he'd probably been sick at some point, at least once, but that was not it. It was the vaguest memory of something momentous; something horrible. His head was pounding as he drew forth the image of himself in the Feathers drinking with that dirty bitch, Nesta, and some Irish boys; he remembered that the Feathers was a dump, but it had gin in, so you had to go. No bitter. Just gin. He remembered that it had cost an arm and a leg to get drunk enough not to care how much it was costing you. He remembered that it was rough stuff, too; like downing a glass of paraffin. And then he remembered (or thought he did) leaving the Feathers and going into another pub. After that, nothing more apart from another blank and a few reminiscences in which the world appeared to be swimming all around him. Somehow he must have found his way back to his lodgings, but he couldn't for the life of him remember how. Perhaps Nesta had helped him home, but he could not be sure of that. Fact was, he could not be sure of anything.

He wondered how long he had been under this time. It might have been for days for all he knew. Since the crack on the head he had suffered the blanks when he'd had too much to drink. It went with his condition: the missing part. The first few times it happened it had scared him shitless, so much so he had even thought about giving up the booze altogether; but over time he had grown accustomed to it for the most part, and usually his first thought on coming to was of a drink and a smoke. He was thinking of that now. He wondered what time it was. He lifted his head from the pillow. It hurt like fuck. He had fallen asleep, or been put to bed, in his clothes. When he moved the stink of drink and fags coming off him made him retch. The fawn-coloured slacks were covered in stains; the nylon shirt was stuck to him in places. His shoes, lying on the floor at the foot of the bed where he must have kicked them off, looked like they'd been marched through a ploughed field. With a start he remembered the green tweed swingback jacket: he was relieved to see it on the other side of the room, draped across the back of a chair. It was only later that he remembered the mackintosh, gone for good. Someone most likely pinched it from one of the pubs. That's what happened when you let yourself get into a state. When he went to check the time he was dismayed to see that his watch was also missing.

His head was splitting in two. His eyes were bleary and hard to focus. He sat on the edge of the bed and tried to accustom himself to solid ground, walls, ceiling. It took a few minutes before he felt confident enough to stand up and grope his way across the room to the table where his fags were. He went to shake one out of the box but they were all gone, so there was nothing for it but to go outside and buy some more. The thought made him want to go back to bed, but his need for nicotine proved stronger than any other impulse and so it was that a few minutes later he found himself slouching along a morning street — which morning he had no idea — dazzled by sunlight.

The tobacconist looked at him with ill-concealed distaste.

"You alright, Dennis?" he asked. "Only you don't half look rough."

"What time is it?"

"Half past eight. Up early? Or ain't you been to bed yet?"

"What day is it?"

"Cor blimey — you're in a right old two and eight, ain't yer? It's Tuesday, innit."

Tuesday. Christ, he had lost two whole days. No wonder he was feeling so queer, mouth like the underside of a doormat.

"Usual is it?" He was a good customer. Under the counter. The tobacconist brought out a packet of twenty cigs. "Only Kensitas this time," he was saying. "That'll be two and fourpence."

He reached into his trouser pocket and pulled out the empty lining. The same on the other side. He patted his shirt, but he knew that he wouldn't find anything there. The thought came to him slowly, swirling into his consciousness. Some bastard must have pinched his money along with the mackintosh and his watch. He had a vague idea who, an' all. The filthy whore . . . He'd see to her alright. Then he had another blank, talking himself out of it, refusing to drop. "Can I have a glass of water, mister?"

The tobacconist called up the stairs at the back of the shop.

"Edie! Edie! Bring Dennis a glass of water. Quick. He's come over all queer."

The next thing he remembered was the budgie tweeting in its cage, then the back of the armchair holding up his head which was still splitting, and finally, as he was gradually restored to reality, the comfortable outline of the tobacconist's wife against the net-curtained window. She was looking down at him with a concerned expression.

"Would you like a cup of tea, dear?" she was asking. "Fancy letting yourself get into a state like that. And you always so nicely turned out."

CHAPTER
TWENTY-SEVEN

Douglas was a good boy. It was a blessed relief to her that he had turned out so well, since, gracious, it had not been easy raising a child single-handed, with a husband in the army, and all through a war as well, with all the worry that ensues. He had dried the dishes for her, before going out for the evening. He was the only one who thought of her. Evelyn had gone up to her room to listen to dance music on her wireless as soon as she'd finished her tea; and Walter had gone and sat in his armchair with a pipe without saying a word. Only Douglas had commented on the food that had taken her all morning to gather; and it would never have occurred to either of them that she might want a little help after having been on her feet all day. Douglas, however, didn't have to be asked. He was a good son to her. She had no doubt but that he would make something of himself: certainly, he would not be a failure like his father.

He was putting on his bicycle clips.

"I'm off now, Mum," he said. He smiled at her. They weren't one of those families that hugged, or in other ways made a spectacle of themselves. "Have a good time at the flicks."

"I still haven't decided," she said. She put a hand to her brow as if she had one of her headaches coming on, but in truth she was feeling a twinge of guilt thinking about her motive for going to the pictures, even though there was only an outside chance that the spiv would be there. He probably hadn't even heard her say about the Odeon; besides, he probably had scores of young girls hanging about him. It was more likely he was going drinking with that awful woman. The Feathers. She knew where that was, but she could never have gone into a public house by herself, and there was no way that she was going to give Evelyn the satisfaction of witnessing her disappointment; for she was certain that she was destined to be disappointed.

With Douglas gone, she was alone in the kitchen with Walter. She hated finding herself alone with Walter. It agitated her. He was smoking a pipe and arguing with the wireless about the youth of today. The wireless was saying that the youth of today were essentially decent and hardworking and would help to build a better Britain; what was more they had grown up in the egalitarian atmosphere of the war, where everyone, regardless of their family connections, had pulled together, side by side. Walter had never heard such absolute tosh in all his born days, and although she would have died sooner than admit it, she agreed with him. Not because there was going to be a communist revolution, as Walter was declaring, but because there had never been and never would be a time when everyone pulled together. There were lucky people and there were unlucky people and that was all there was to it.

"Oh do shut up, Walter."

It did not make her feel any better when he did just that, but then she hadn't expected it to.

He took his pipe out of his mouth and turned to look at her.

"When are you off out, old girl?" he asked.

"I haven't decided whether I'm going or not."

"Not like you to stay in on a Saturday night."

It got on her nerves the way he claimed parts of her, owning the right to tell her what she did and what she didn't do; his entitlement to comment on her every move, as if he knew her.

"I don't have to go out," she said. "There's no law says I have to."

"No, no," he murmured, drawing back into himself, "of course not . . ."

He puffed away on his pipe with an irritating modicum of contentment and that sad stupid grin on his face, and she toyed with staying in just to spite him, to show him that she could do whatever she liked and he did not know her or own her or control her; but the only thing she had to look forward to was Saturday night and the pictures. It would have been like cutting off her nose to spite her face.

"I'm going to look in on Mother before I go out," she said.

"You do that, wifey. You do that."

Mother was sleeping. Evelyn had emptied the commode, and put the towel and the nightdress from

220

the morning into a bucket of disinfectant to soak; the saucer of milk and digestive biscuit had been cleared away. That was two bob well spent, she supposed, although why Evelyn couldn't just do these things was beyond her. As long as things got done and she didn't have to do them, what did it matter? But it rankled, that she had to think like this, make excuses.

She went into her bedroom to get ready. She sat on the edge of the bed and changed her stockings, an action she performed with enormous care. She had only these two pairs left. She'd had them off a spiv who was selling them from a suitcase outside the North London Stores on Holloway Road. She would rather die than go out in bare legs. She fixed the back of the left stocking to her girdle gingerly because the suspender was hanging on by a thread, and she had sewn it back on so many times that there was now little of the fabric left. The whole girdle was on its last legs, but there was as much chance of replacing it as there was of being taken out to dinner by Franchot Tone. She was wondering whether she ought to put on a different costume, but after she had looked at her reflection in the mirror she decided just to change her blouse, which was not looking at all fresh.

She crossed to the tallboy and poured a bit of water into the washing bowl, washed her face and applied a damp flannel to her underarms and between her legs. This simple action made her feel much better. Then she rinsed the stockings she had taken off and draped them over the dressing-table mirror to dry. She could feel herself beginning to wake from apathy, from hopelessness. Thank goodness for the pictures, she thought; whatever would I do without my Saturday nights? She did not allow herself to think about the spiv; instead she lit her Saturday evening cigarette and inspected her face in the mirror through the softening smoke. A little bit of powder; mascara; rouge: a slick of Damson Delight to match her nails. All that was required was for Evelyn to see to the back of her hair and she would do. She stubbed out the cigarette and went out on to the landing.

"Evelyn," she called out, "Evelyn, will you see to the back of my hair?"

Evelyn had a very small room in the attic. It contained little more than a small bed, washing stand and chest of drawers, on top of which sat Evelyn's wireless. She could hear the wireless as she climbed the stairs. Dance music. Benny Goodman. And as she reached the door, she could hear something else too: a sigh emanating, slight and brief, but enough to prompt an inexplicable pang of jealousy, so suffused was it with satisfaction; deep relief. She could not remember the last time she had been capable of emitting such a sigh, but it awakened all kinds of sensations, too powerful to bear.

"Evelyn," she repeated, "can you fix the back of my hair for me?" She tapped lightly on the door before opening it and entering the room.

At first she wasn't sure what she was looking at, but gradually the spectacle of Walter, perched on the edge of the bed with his trousers around his ankles, stroking

222

Evelyn's head, which was nestling in his lap, swum into focus. Walter was blinking at her, as if dazed; after a few moments Evelyn lifted her head with immense languor, and leaned back on her heels.

Her first impulse was to laugh. Walter looked so ridiculous, and the whole situation seemed so ludicrous, so comical. Then she began to feel an implacable fury. She unleashed a torrent of abuse, forged in every slight, every abuse of her good nature, every frustration she had ever experienced. It was all directed at Walter, who sat there on the edge of the bed, blinking at her but not saying a word. The humiliation of the situation reeled around in her head, blinding her, deafening her to her own voice, to any objections that either of them might raise, to Benny Goodman, to life itself. When she had exhausted her stock of vile names and terrible threats, she pulled off her wedding ring and flung it at him in a triumphant gesture. It struck the bed-rail, rolled across the floor, and Walter raised that awful, sad smile.

"I'm so sorry, Lillian," he said mildly. "Please say you forgive me."

For some reason his cringing, pathetic manner made her even angrier.

"What do you mean by that?" she demanded. "Do you seriously expect me to forgive you after what you've done? What sort of fool do you take me for?"

Evelyn had been standing next to the bed all the while, her stupid mouth hanging open.

"It just happened, Lil," the kid said, shrugging.

"And if you call me Lil one more time," she said, "you're going to wish you had never been born!"

Walter buried his face in his hands and rocked himself backwards and forwards on the edge of the bed, in his braces and shirt sleeves with his trousers around his ankles, weeping. For one brief moment she felt a softening towards him, but then the sense of her own humiliation, her endless frustration, was intensified by the pitiful spectacle before her, rallying her once more.

"You can both go to hell!" she cried. "I'm done with this rotten life! I'm going and I hope to God I never have to see either of you again!" She turned on her heels and stalked out of the room, slamming the door behind her. Outside on the landing she took a deep breath or two. Her heart was pounding, but she felt alive for the first time in an age. She could hear Walter sobbing, and the dance music, which made it all seem as if it had happened in a film; she could hear Evelyn complaining, her indignant tone, though she could not hear what the kid was saying. She gathered her breathing: she had relished the drama of the situation, but it was more than that. Walter had betrayed her with a common little slut and in doing so he had provided her with the perfect justification for whatever it was she intended to do next.

She went into the bedroom and grabbed her handbag, running down the stairs to the front door. I really am out of control now, she thought; and the thought at once appalled and thrilled her. And as she stepped on to the broken street she knew that there was to be no going back: whatever had gone before, it was done with, over.

224

CHAPTER
TWENTY-EIGHT

The morning that war broke out he had been sitting at his table eating a plate of bacon and fried bread. This, of course, was back in the days when he had Sunday mornings to himself, to be spent at leisure, with the prospect of a pleasant day before him — smoking his pipe while taking a stroll in the park, perhaps; listening to his gramophone records. If he could ever have been said to have experienced contentment that was certainly the last time he had known it. As Chamberlain's weary intonation gave way to the siren yearn, he had put down his knife and fork and crossed to the window. The street below looked just the same as it had done an hour before, but everything had changed irrevocably. You blasted fools, he thought; meaning himself as much as anyone. You blasted, blasted fools. A few people had come out of their homes, and were peering up and down the road, then up at the sky, evidently murmuring to one another, unsure what to do next, what to expect; and seeing them he had felt a mild rage like a distant rumble of thunder. How could this be happening again? Lessons unlearned, his own culpability in permitting peace to come to an end for the second occasion in his lifetime: all those times he had looked at the newspapers with dismay before turning the page. When the telephone rang he had known it would be something bad. Marjorie's voice on the other end of the line was agitated, distraught.

"I'm so sorry, my darling," she was saying. "I'm so sorry. Please, please don't hate me." He had stopped listening after a moment or two; the terrible words "it's over, it's over" resounding in his head, breaking his heart. "Please try to understand. I can't leave Bill. Not now. And I can't go on as we have been. He might not be coming back. You must see that. I'm so sorry, my darling. So very, very sorry."

It was over. Over. Her wretched voice; the terrible lies she was uttering offering no consolation whatever.

"You know, I will always love you, Jim. Always. Always . . ."

It was just something people said at such times: it meant nothing; but of course he understood; of course he forgave her. He forgave her everything. How could he not? She had made his life so wonderful; he had not known that it was possible to be so happy. He took to heart all the usual sentimental rubbish you say at such moments; and might even mean, too, at the time. And meanwhile, outside, the world spun crazily towards destruction. What did it matter whether he was happy or unhappy? Whether he lived or died? He had let her go, resolving never to try and look for her; never to see or speak to her again. It was over. Everything was over; and the world was at war for the second time in his life.

It would have been unsurprising if Marjorie had contrived to keep their affair going: a lot of perfectly

226

decent people went haywire in the war, after all. Plenty of married women got a taste for adultery, and what red-blooded man can look at a woman whose husband is away without thinking he could give it a go. It was just his luck, he supposed, to fall in love with the exception to the rule. The idea of sacrifice, of duty, made her even more wonderful in his eyes; made him love her even more deeply.

Which was not to say that he had a low opinion of the Lillian Frobishers of the world: he was suspicious of moral judgment, and besides, what did it matter what she had done when she had harmed nobody? Others would say that she was not a victim but an active participant in her own demise: an amateur prostitute, as the vulgar, DI Lucas, the pathologist, the yellow press, would have it. Well, he saw a more profound force at work. He had no interest in why one might be provoked to crime, but he had a compassion for the victims of crime; and that included those who left their doors or windows open, who went into low pubs or on to racetracks, who walked the dark streets late at night. There had been a slow, groggy return to normality once the war had ended, like waking from a hangover; and the return to normal life, or to what had passed for it before September 1939, had not been a simple matter for more people than cared to admit it. Lillian Frobisher was evidently among them. A highly sexed woman deprived of sexual satisfaction is quickly brought to the verge of nymphomania. It is not admirable; but nor is it entirely blameworthy. A woman can be as tormented by her desires as any man: perhaps more so; for her emotional life is an all or nothing business. No, he could not condemn Lillian Frobisher any more than he could condemn Marjorie. He had no idea whether the victim had suffered the pangs of remorse as his lover had done, and perhaps it didn't matter: she had risked everything for love, for sex, and she had paid the ultimate price.

He was no less determined to find her killer. And now that he had expunged every last vestige of suspicion in regard to Walter Frobisher, he found himself drawn towards the vortex of grief established by the wretch who had strangled a woman, after first making love to her, and then run off with her handbag. He thought not so much of Lillian Frobisher, of her terror, her surrender — though he did think of that at various points in the day — but of the boy Douglas, striving so manfully to deal with loss, and, yes, of Frobisher too: his pale, red-rimmed eyes and sad, cringing smile. In his desire to avenge the needless death of a woman who, if not blameless, was certainly undeserving, in his eyes at least, he had seen to it that the word had gone out among north London's criminal underworld. It was a village in which everyone knew everyone else, yet nobody knew of a good-looking young spiv named Dennis. Of course, it was entirely possible that Dennis might be the bastard's alias, but the artist's impressions supplied by Evelyn Wilkes had been met with blank expressions from all the usual suspects. Indeed, if it hadn't been for the testimony of the waitress, Cooper might have supposed that Dennis was nothing more than a phantom conjured up for the convenience of Evelyn Wilkes; but unless there was some conspiracy between the pair of them, the reason for which had thus far eluded him, that seemed unlikely. Somebody had strangled Lillian Frobisher, and as things stood at the moment, the mysterious Dennis was the chief suspect. In short, he knew who had dunnit, and now all he had to do was find him and make it stick. It was a waiting game: it was nearly always a waiting game. Wait until the fellow walked into the café or the Feathers; wait until he came to the remembrance of some nark or other; wait until he made a mistake.

He had gone home after working late at divisional HQ and was trying to sleep when the case began to break, though the beginning of the end did not come in the way he had expected. He had woken twice in the couple of hours since nodding off, after finding himself up to the waist in the quagmire with the whizz bangs flying overhead, a thick blanket of mist enveloping him. When will it end? he asked himself on the second occasion, a question he rarely asked any more, having decided long ago that it never would. He tried to switch his dreary thoughts to more pleasing ones of Policewoman Tring, arriving at a momentous decision: he would let her know, by dint of some romantic gesture, what he thought of her. A romantic gesture being entirely at odds with his character, he had no idea what form it would take, eventually, in the course of a two-hour fractious meditation, working it down from something vague involving roses to an invitation to share a sandwich and a coffee somewhere away from the station canteen. And having set upon this as a suitable course of action, he was trying to sleep once more, on the grounds that no good ever came from lying in bed thinking about a woman, when the telephone rang.

It was one of those telephone calls that begin with "Mr Cooper, I have something for you . . ." or words to that effect; the sort of call that he had taken countless times, as has every detective in the world. This particular one led him, a mere forty-five minutes later, to a bombed-out building behind a packaging factory in Tottenham Hale: paneless windows, their relinquished glass crunching underfoot; stairs gone for a Burton; floors suspended flying-buttress-like from debilitated walls. Against one such, rolls and rolls of fabric and boxes and boxes of nylons and silk undies, worth thousands, were stacked ten feet high, twenty feet wide.

He had just had the measure of the haul in the wavering beam of his torch before three villains rushed at him and the uniform who had accompanied him. He managed to land a punch in the face of one of them, a satisfying, pulpy crack greeting his fist; he could hear the panting and scuffling of the struggle between the flatfoot and one of the other villains, who was knocked backwards, colliding with him. He punched him hard on the side of his head, this time hearing the sickening crack of his own knuckles, and the fellow fell to his knees. In the meanwhile he had dropped his torch, which rolled across the floor, illuminating, in intermittent swathes of light, the third crook in the act of attempting to escape. The uniform lunged at him, grabbing him in a rugby tackle and pulling him to the ground. Cooper seized him by the lapels and secured him in this manner while he was cuffed. The first crook was groaning on the floor, holding his battered face as he rolled back and forth; the second was already on his knees as they prepared to put on the bracelets, his hand up, imploring for mercy.

Cooper's collar was flapping, his hair hanging over his eye. He sucked the blood from his knuckles, as the back-up squad hauled the villains into the back of a motor and took them to the station. He knew them, of course: they were old hands at thieving, blacketeering, and doubtless working for Johnny Bristow; if so, they'd be better off in custody. Johnny wouldn't be pleased with them: they had allowed themselves to be caught with the goods, taken entirely by surprise, with no weapons on them. Johnny would draw the conclusion that one of them might well have supplied the tip-off; it was a possibility that Cooper himself was considering. In the space that the Johnny Bristows of the world inhabited there was no such thing as loyalty; it was all treachery and suspicion, which is all you can expect if you hang about with men who would sell their own grandmothers for a ten-bob note.

When he went to see him in the interview room, the oldest of the crooks, the one who had begged, entertained him with the usual whine.

"You know me, Mr Cooper: I want to go straight, honest, but it's hard without the dibs."

"Shut up." Cooper was in no mood for it. "I've had a long day, and I'm tired of listening to rubbish. Just tell me who's behind it. You haven't the brains to pull a stunt like this, or the readies." You need capital to buy vans, bribe dockers and employ idiots; you need brains to plan a job; you need buyers lined up. "How much has he paid you? A pony? Fifty? A hundred? Whatever it was, it isn't enough. You're looking at a long stretch this time." Cooper's fist was aching, so was his head. He leaned across the table. "I want names," he said.

In point of fact, he wanted one name in particular: one snitch was all it would take to bring him in. The crook appealed to his better nature, mutely, with a sort of sad, broken expression.

"I can't tell you that, Mr Cooper. You know how it is," he said. "I got a family." The crook had a long scar down one side of his face which he was fingering now. "I got responsibilities."

"This could be your chance to get out. You're too old for all this."

The crook shook his head, slowly, almost regretfully.

"It's going to go badly for you," Cooper warned. "Assaulting police officers, resisting arrest — and that's before we move on to the receiving stolen property charge . . ."

There was a brief flicker in the fellow's eyes, and catching it, Cooper leaned back in his chair and waited. Afterwards he reckoned that he had been on the brink of hearing the name "Johnny Bristow" fall from a villain's lips, when the wretched desk sergeant appeared at the door of the interview room.

"Damn and blast to hell," Cooper muttered under his breath. "What the blazes is it now?"

232

It was only the serious expression on the desk sergeant's face which prevented Cooper from telling him to go away in far from polite terms.

"I think you had better come and see this, sir," said the sergeant, and Cooper could tell at once that he really had to do as he was bid.

The contents of the pockets of all three villains were in the process of being locked away, their owners having signed the inventories. The desk sergeant pointed at a clothing coupon book that was nestling among the detritus.

"It was only as I was putting it away that I looked at it more closely. I should have done it at the time, only I thought it was his, you see."

Cooper turned the book towards him. It was written there quite clearly. A blind idiot could have seen it. On the front of the book where it said "Name" was written in a perfectly legible hand: Douglas Frobisher; and in the space following the word "Address" was the last-known residence of the strangled woman.

CHAPTER
TWENTY-NINE

It was almost half past seven the next morning by the time he had finished in the interview rooms. The day had broken in a haze of fierce, shimmering light, but he had no idea about that as he went in search of breakfast. Douglas Frobisher's clothing coupons had come to the villain by way of Manny Cohen, a fence who operated from out of the back of a barber shop over on Fonthill Road. They would take Manny Cohen by surprise in a couple of hours' time, just as he opened for business. It was unlikely that he had had anything to do with the murder of Lillian Frobisher, but he had taken possession of her son's coupon book from someone, and that someone could very likely lead them directly to the strangler.

As he entered the station canteen, Cooper was feeling none of the excitement that a detective on the verge of his biggest break in a murder case might be expected to feel. Far from it: he was feeling more battered and crumpled than ever. He thought of himself, cutting a sad figure, as he plodded hopelessly from one interview to the next — it came to all detectives sooner or later, the awareness that this was their sorry lot in life — and even though he always felt better about himself after a well-deserved bashing, he was presently too tired to feel anything other than exhaustion. Policewoman Tring was sitting at a table with DS Quennell, the young idiot who had been spat at by Little Jimmy Dashett on Sunday night, which seemed an eternity away. Quennell had lost his boyish demeanour in the presence of the policewoman: he had turned his chair around and sprawled his legs either side of it; he was smoking a cigarette and holding forth about something or other. It was gratifying to see that Tring was regarding the whelp with something like amused detachment — not that this deterred Quennell, who was too young, too inexperienced, too cocksure of his powers of attraction, and not yet a good enough detective to notice.

Cooper hoped to pay for his cup of tea and cheese roll before retreating back to his office without her seeing him, but she must have sensed that she was being looked at, and glanced in his direction; and before he could look away and pretend he hadn't seen her, she was smiling and waving at him, Quennell evidently signalling his dismay, as Cooper saw her pull a face and shake her head discouragingly at the young DS before standing up and inviting him to join them.

"My goodness, sir, whatever happened to you?" Her lovely face was creased with concern, and the sight of it made him suffer pangs of embarrassment on account of his appearance, and desire.

"Rough night was it, sir?" observed Quennell in an offhand way.

"Rather."

"You poor thing — you look as if you need a good night's sleep."

He grinned sheepishly at her and set his roll and tea upon the table.

"Never more so."

"And look at your poor hand!" The blood that had seeped through the handkerchief he had tied around his busted knuckles had dried in ragged-edged rusty circles. "And, goodness, your eye!"

Quennell knocked the ash from his cigarette into his saucer and looked sourly in his guv'nor's direction. He was young and relatively good-looking, but he knew when he was beaten.

"What time are you supposed to be on duty, Quennell?" inquired Cooper mildly, checking his watch. He was enjoying himself. It was good to be the object of her pity: at any rate, it was better than nothing.

Quennell took the hint. He stubbed out his cigarette on the saucer and picked up his hat from the table. "Let me know about later on," he said to Policewoman Tring.

"I'll have to see — it depends on how busy it gets today," she said. She cast the briefest of glances in the boy detective's direction before returning all of her attention to Cooper. "Why don't I drive you back to your flat, sir, so you can have a wash and brush-up? It will make you feel so much better. You can't work through the rest of the day in that state."

Quennell lingered for a moment and Cooper almost felt sorry for him. He knew how it felt to yearn.

"Cheerio then," the kid was saying.

"Cheerio," she said, without looking at him.

"Cheerio," said Cooper. He slurped his tea and chomped contentedly on the roll as Quennell lurched off, disappointment dogging every step. "Actually," he said to Tring, "that's not a bad idea — provided DI Lucas doesn't need you for anything." He was suppressing all thoughts of effecting a seduction in the confines of his bachelor rooms.

"Oh, I'm not supposed to be here for another two hours. I came in early to get going on the paperwork; I can easily catch up. It's much more important that we have the guv'nor in good working order!"

"My char will be there," he said.

She looked at him curiously, and he worried that he might have seemed presumptuous. "Oh," she said, "that's good."

On the drive to Stoke Newington he told her all about the call in the middle of the night, the silk, the fight, the interviews, the clothing coupons, and the impending visit to Manny Cohen's.

"You were jolly lucky that they weren't armed."

"They weren't expecting us. It was a tip-off. Someone like Johnny Bristow makes a lot of enemies. Other crooks who don't care for him queering their patch. They like to slash each other with razors, or snitch to the police."

"Horrid," she shuddered. "Weren't you worried you'd be attacked?"

In all truth, he never thought about the danger when finding himself in these situations, as he did with tedious regularity. One day, he supposed, his luck would run out; but in general, when faced with a gun or ducking a cut-throat razor, he rarely felt a shred of fear. This, he reasoned, had less to do with courage than determined world-weariness.

"No, not really," he said.

It was bliss to be driven by her, to have the opportunity to listen to her prattle on about how much she was learning and how she had had no idea how much there was to learn and how grateful she was to him for giving her the opportunity, which she was determined not to waste, by the way; how she was more set on a career in CID than ever before. He received all of this in what he supposed was a glow of paternalistic indulgence.

"Of course, it's early days, I know that," she was saying. "But I can already tell I'm going to love it. It's wonderful to be part of something so — so essential. I haven't felt this excited about anything since I was in Nairobi with the ATS."

"I do hope that the men are behaving themselves," he said. "You mustn't stand for any nonsense, you know."

She laughed.

"Oh, I won't, don't you worry about that!"

"You're to let me know if any of them try and take liberties."

"That's very kind of you, sir; but I can take care of myself."

"It's just that I couldn't help but notice young Quennell there in the canteen . . ."

"He's alright; quite amusing, really. I came up against much worse in the services."

"I don't doubt it."

"I'm not without experience . . ."

He shifted in his seat. The conversation was taking an inappropriate turn. He looked out of the dusty window, feeling uncomfortable, yet, at the same time, wanting her to continue with the revelation, the intimacy.

"I suppose you could say I'm a sadder but wiser girl," she said in a wistful tone which he found irresistible. She laughed lightly, swinging the car expertly into his street.

"There was this chap when I was in the ATS, but . . . well, you know how it is . . . War time and all that . . ."

"I'm so sorry . . ."

She laughed again.

"Oh golly, no — I didn't mean — that is — he made it through, and went home to his wife . . . Not that I knew he was married, of course . . ." Cooper swallowed hard and frowned at the rubble-strewn scene beyond the window. Stoke Newington had never before held such a fascination for him. "Oh, but I'm embarrassing you!" she exclaimed. "I am sorry, sir; it's just that you're so easy to talk to — such a good listener. Most men only want to talk about themselves. Oh, there I go again!"

"This is me," he said, as they pulled up in front of his building. She parked the car and pulled on the handbrake. "You needn't wait. I can make my own way back." He clutched his hat and raincoat to his chest as he opened the door and prepared to step on to the road.

"Oh no," she protested. "I'll come up with you. You need someone to dress your hand."

"There's really no need . . ." He sounded feeble. "My char is there . . ."

He was feeling slightly on edge as she followed him up the stairs to his flat; he made sure that he called out to Mrs Oscar as he unlocked the door. Tring followed him inside.

"Whatever happened to you?" said Mrs Oscar, who was dusting the gramophone. "You look as if you've spent the night on the tiles." She looked Tring up and down as Cooper introduced them to one another, sniffing dismissively before returning to her polish. Tring grinned at him.

"As ever, Mrs Oscar," he said, "you're quite right about everything." He was trying to untie the makeshift bandage with his teeth.

"Let me do that, sir," said Tring. Mrs Oscar sniffed again. "You need to clean it, otherwise it will turn septic."

"You'll find a tin of Germolene in the bathroom cabinet," said the char.

He had a quick wash and a shave and changed into a clean shirt, and then settled down to let Tring smear his busted knuckles with the antiseptic lotion. Then she expertly bandaged his hand with clean strips of an old pillowslip supplied by Mrs Oscar.

"Terrible waste of a good piece of linen," the char grumbled. "Would have done for dusters."

He didn't dare look up at Tring while she saw to his injuries; he kept his eyes resolutely on the back of his hand and contented himself with marking her breathing and the clean fresh scent of her hair.

"You should have been a nurse," he mumbled shyly.

"It's a shame steak is so hard to come by," she remarked briskly. "We could have seen to that shiner as well."

He was feeling light-headed with tiredness, but somehow more at ease with the world. There was a faint warming, something uplifting about his heart. Let's not go back to work, he wanted to say to her; let's spend the day together, get to know one another. Tell me your first name. We could have lunch somewhere decent; go to the pictures; a walk in the park. Anything: only don't leave; please don't leave. It was all madness, of course. He was brought to his senses by the telephone, jangling on its table in the hall. Mrs Oscar put down the empty fruit-bowl that she was dusting and shuffled off to answer it.

"Are you here?" she cried. "Only Inspector Lucas wants to know."

Oh hell, he thought, the dismal reality of his life returning to him. All colour, all warmth was draining from his soul. What the blazes is it now?

And hearing the DI's flat affectless tones on the other end of the line, he was aware of a slow flush spreading across his cheeks; was seized with an irrational anxiety that somehow the entire division would be able to tell that Policewoman Tring was here, in his flat, with him. He told himself not to be such an ass, thanking God that Mrs Oscar had answered the telephone.

"Do you need me to go down to Manny Cohen's, sir?" Lucas was saying, "Only something has come up here. I can send someone else, but thought I'd better check with you first."

"No, no, I'll take it," Cooper said, "I'm on my way there now."

He put down the telephone. It was an opportunity, he supposed; a little longer in her company. He knew that he would do nothing whatever with the opportunity, but he could always kid himself that he might, if it made him happy.

"We need to get going," he told her. "Duty calls."

She had been chatting to Mrs Oscar about the gramophone collection; now she turned around to face him, and she was smiling.

CHAPTER
THIRTY

Within a few moments of leaving the house, it had occurred to her that she had no idea what she was going to do. She couldn't go back there, not for a few hours at any rate; that was certain. She wouldn't give them the satisfaction. She pictured herself boarding a Number 43 bus, riding it to Muswell Hill or Friern Barnet, but had no idea what she would she do once she was there. It was too late to look for lodgings, and besides, she didn't have enough money on her to start over. Walter always kept her short, and she'd spent most of the housekeeping money on shopping. She kept walking with her head down while panic began to mount. There's the coupon books, she thought; four of them: Mother's, Douglas's, Walter's and her own. She supposed she could try and sell them. She thought of the spiv, Dennis, and wondered whether she oughtn't to try and find him at the Feathers. Her heart was pounding quite hard, though she couldn't tell whether this was down to the thought of committing a crime or the prospect of seeing the nice-looking young man again. She tried to steady her breathing, which had become a little shallow, making her feel faint. She wasn't sure whether she ought to sell her own, or whether she could bring herself to sell Douglas's, so she attempted to calculate whether Mother's and Walter's would bring in enough to pay the rent on a bed-sitting room for a week or two — just while she looked for a little job in a hat-shop, perhaps, or a nice tearoom; but she had no idea how much coupons went for, so the exercise was futile. Perhaps she should just go to the Feathers now and ask him how much he was prepared to give her, and if it wasn't enough she would just thank him and that would be it. She had never walked into a pub on her own before; she hadn't even been in that many pubs with other people, but as things were, it was hard to see what she had to lose. This is a turning point, she told herself. All she had to do was step through the door of the pub and everything would be changed for ever.

It was relatively early and still light, but cooler now; the heat of the day diminished. She slowed down as the reality of what she was contemplating set in. Walter wouldn't blame her for starting over, not after what he had done. He would see that they were better off without one another. He would probably let her keep the coupons without a second thought: it was the least he could do. She paused, the realisation slowly occurring to her that she would have to tell Mavis to make arrangements for Mother, and Mavis would want to know where Mother's coupons were. Perhaps she could say they'd been stolen. Coupons were always being stolen. The thought of the police coming and asking her questions caused a small tremor of panic to make her heart shudder. What had she done? What was she going to do? A rivulet of sweat trickled between her breasts, and it came to her that the Holloway Road might as well be the Atlantic Ocean, because she was not going to cross it now; nor was she going to walk into the pub and sell the coupons to the spiv. Whatever had she been thinking? She had been utterly ridiculous and now she wanted to cry. One thing was quite clear: she couldn't go home, not now. Perhaps she ought to go down to Liverpool Street and catch a train to Clacton. She probably had enough money on her for a ticket and Mavis would just have to pay for the taxi when she got to Jaywick. This seemed like a good plan, but then she thought of how Mavis would have a field day, with "I told you so" — I told you he was a rotten failure. I told you he's not all there. I told you not to marry him. So did Father. So did we all. On and on and on. She couldn't bear that. She'd be better off dead than putting herself at Mavis's mercy.

No, she'd be better off just going to the Odeon, as she had planned to do all along. Richard Greene and Ann Todd. She felt as if she was being pressed to death by a heavy slab of defeat, disappointment. She told herself that she liked Ann Todd, who'd been very good in *The Seventh Veil*. She had played the piano beautifully. Perhaps she would enjoy the picture, and afterwards she could go back to the house and decide what to do next. Her nerves would be better then. And besides, why should she be the one to leave? It was her mother's house, after all: Walter and Evelyn were only there because of her. She took a few deep breaths to calm herself and considered how she would feel safe in the warmth of the Odeon. Ann Todd had gone mad in *The Seventh Veil*, and after Herbert Lom had helped her she'd gone off with James Mason, who had a wonderful voice and had been her true love all along. She doubted that this picture would be as good as *The Seventh Veil*, but she started to walk towards the cinema in any case, as if in a dream. Maybe, she thought, maybe the spiv would remember that she was going to the Odeon and would come looking for her there. She looked for him in the line waiting to go in. Perhaps it was a turning point after all. A hat-shop. A nice tea-room. She would begin again some place that the war hadn't touched. She would meet nice men for lunches and for cocktails. She would steady their hands as they reached across to light her. She would go somewhere that wasn't broken and covered in dust; somewhere that was not haunted by the ghosts of houses, by the remains of vanquished lives. And everything would be nice again, just like it used to be.

CHAPTER
THIRTY-ONE

Manny Cohen was a dapper little Jew in a pork-pie hat and a bow-tie and a spotlessly clean snowy-white barber's jacket. He was also one of the best fences in London, about whom it was commonly averred that he could fence anything from a cigarette to an elephant. He was that good.

Cooper told the fellow who was having his chin shaved to get out and shoved the coupon book under Manny's nose.

"A little bird told me," he said, "that you sold him this on Sunday morning."

Manny barely glanced at the coupon book before shooting Cooper a wide smile, all crooked brown teeth at odds with his spotless jacket and immaculately trimmed little 'tache.

"I don't know anything about coupon books, Mr Cooper," he said. "You ought to know that."

Cooper sighed heavily and removed his hat and swept his hair back from his forehead.

"You want a little dab of Brylcream, Mr Cooper?" asked the barber.

Cooper shrugged and took a dollop from the proffered jar.

"I'm tired of people lying to me, Manny," he said. "Really, really tired."

The barber nodded sympathetically.

"You know me, Mr Cooper — I don't know anything about coupons. Why do you take the word of some thief over mine? I always thought we got along pretty well."

Cooper wiped the remnants of the Brylcream on to a towel, fighting an irrational impulse to pick up Manny's razor and hold it against the fellow's throat.

"The coupons are implicated in a murder case," he said. He watched Manny pale. "I just need to know where you got them." He waited for a beat or two, before drawing himself up to his full height and bearing down on the little barber. "It's murder, Manny."

The barber stroked his chin nervously. He wasn't smiling now.

"Murder, eh?" he repeated in a quiet voice. "I swear to God, Mr Cooper, I don't know nothing about no murder."

"Where did you get the bloody coupons?"

"I don't want any trouble . . ."

"Listen to me," said Cooper, "I'm not interested in your shabby dealings. I'm trying to solve a murder, and right now your coupon book is my best chance."

Manny pondered his options for a moment or two.

"So there won't be any trouble?" he asked.

"I'm turning a blind eye, Manny, but you're testing my patience."

"The murder — is it — does it have anything to do with Johnny Bristow?"

"I don't know," said Cooper, "but if you're worried it's a matter of some razor battle between two thugs, then I can assure you, it isn't."

The barber swallowed hard. He seemed relieved.

"A woman comes in here from time to time," he said.

"What woman?"

"Her name is Nesta. That's all I know about her, I swear to God. She was in here on Saturday night, about seven o'clock, with a kid. He had a pair of cufflinks he wanted to sell. I still have them out back. You want I should fetch them?"

"That will do for a start."

Manny went away and came back a few moments later with the cufflinks and an expensive-looking travel clock.

"She was back here on Sunday morning, about half past ten, eleven, with the clothing coupons and this." Cooper took the travel clock and the cufflinks. "She said she was leaving London and wanted a quick sale, but she knew how much she wanted for them, alright." Manny sighed. "I swear to God, I don't know anything about a murder," he said.

Cooper waved him aside. The juxtaposition of cufflinks and a travel clock had brought to mind the pinched suitcase — the one that had also contained the green tweed swingback jacket and the mackintosh. He turned to where Tring was standing in the doorway and showed her the two items. She was frowning, the corners of her mouth turned down, as she took them from him.

"I'll contact the owner of the suitcase," she said, "as soon as I'm back at my desk."

Cooper turned back to Manny.

"Where are the other books?" he demanded. "You said there were four of them . . ."

"I don't like dealing in coupons, Mr Cooper. It's not in my line of business. I got rid of them quick the next morning. Took them up to Johnny Bristow's. I sold them to one of his boys for the same as I'd bought them, I swear to God. That's the whole truth. I don't know anything about a murder."

"Can you remember the names on any of the coupon books?"

Manny shook his head.

"I don't want any trouble," he said again.

Cooper reached into his mackintosh pocket and withdrew the artist's impression of Dennis.

"Recognise him?"

Manny smoothed out the creases and stroked his chin as he scrutinised the image.

"It could be," he said. Then nodding, with more certainty: "It looks like the kid with the cufflinks."

Cooper folded up the artist's impression and stuck it back into his pocket.

"Do you know where I can find Nesta?" he asked.

Manny shook his head. "No idea," he said.

Cooper sighed.

"If she comes in again," he said, "you know where to find me."

Tring was waiting outside in the car. He threw his hat on to the back seat and sat for a moment in grim contemplation. She had her hands on the steering wheel, waiting for his instruction.

"It seems odd to my mind," she said, "that everybody knows her, but nobody knows where to find her."

"She probably moves around a lot from one lodging to another. It's the post-war world . . ."

He was thinking that Nesta would doubtless turn up, given enough time, but time was the one thing he didn't have; or rather time was one of a long list of things he didn't have.

"Turn right on to Seven Sisters Road," he said.

She did as she was told, and a couple of minutes later they pulled up outside a half-bombed shop a short distance from Finsbury Park Station. Cooper told her to stay in the car while he went inside. He banged with the flat of his hand on the bomb-splintered door that was patched up with sections of corrugated iron.

"It's DDI Cooper," he called out, and after a moment or two a small weasel-like fellow appeared in the doorway, looking cautiously up and down the street.

"It's alright, Codger, I'm on my own. Is Johnny at home?"

"He won't want to see you, Mr Cooper," said the weasel, but he let him in all the same. Cooper passed down a narrow passageway to a surprisingly large room at the back where a few thugs were hanging about playing pool, or rather they were standing around the table watching Johnny Bristow taking his time to pot a couple of balls. Cooper joined them and waited patiently. When the third failed to roll into the pocket,

Bristow knocked his expensive hat on to the back of his head and squinted at Cooper through the smoke of his cigarette.

"What do you want, copper?"

The spiv was dressed in a nylon shirt and well-cut fawn-coloured trousers. Whenever his hand moved, the large gold signet ring on his little finger glinted.

"A pal of yours was taken last night with some clothing coupons on him."

Johnny shrugged.

"I don't know anything about clothing coupons," he said. "Not worth my while."

"A woman was strangled on Saturday night and the coupons were taken from her handbag, probably by the murderer."

Johnny rubbed chalk on the end of his cue and blew the dust towards Cooper.

"I was tucked up in bed all weekend with a Windmill girl," he said.

A couple of the men began to laugh but stopped when it was clear that Johnny wasn't joking.

"Your pal brought the coupons in here on Sunday. There were four books, but so far only one has turned up." Cooper looked around the room, fixing each of the thugs with a cold stare. "Any ideas where the others are?"

Nobody stepped forward. He hadn't expected them to.

Johnny was leaning on his cue, smoking. He removed the cigarette from his mouth and inspected the glowing tip. "A strangled dame," he said, "is not my type of thing. A little outside of my area of expertise, you might say."

Cooper smiled.

"I'm appealing to your better nature, Johnny," he said. "You do have a better nature, don't you? You can't possibly be bad all the way through. And even if you are, it isn't your fault, is it? Not really. Something happened to you, I dare say, a long time ago."

Johnny drew hard on his cigarette until it was spent; then he threw the butt to the floor, grinding it with his expensive boot heel.

"Why don't you fuck off, bogey," he said.

One of the thugs, a burly fellow with a shock of red hair, stepped forward. He had one hand wrapped menacingly around the knuckles of the other.

"Want me to get rid of him, boss?" he asked.

Cooper wasn't bothered. He had already reckoned, long ago, that he had nothing left to lose.

"Nah," said Johnny. "He ain't worth it."

Cooper nodded slightly, as if in agreement.

"I remember you when you had to stand on tip-toe to pinch an apple from a barrow," he said.

Johnny shrugged. "So what?"

Cooper contemplated his next move. For a brief moment he toyed with giving Johnny the blasted eggs in exchange for Nesta Jones, but instead he pointed at the kid's twisted foot.

"Helped to win the war, didn't you?"

"Nobody won the fucking war," Johnny snarled. "Look around you."

"Still, you were out there, weren't you, fighting the Nazis, when others were at home feathering their nests? A few of them in this room, I dare say."

The red-haired thug stepped forward again.

"Let me deal with the bastard," he said.

"I said leave him," said Johnny. "Don't give him what he wants."

"That's not what I want, Johnny," said Cooper mildly. "I don't give a damn about you or your pathetic little capers. The days of easy money will soon be coming to an end and you and all your sort will find yourselves on Carey Street — that's if you don't end up in prison or dangling from the end of a rope before then. I'm looking for a wicked sod who goes around strangling women for no good reason. A murder, a stolen handbag, it might all be the same to you, but it isn't to me. So, if you come across a woman called Nesta Jones I'd like to think you're going to let me know about it."

A few of the crooks laughed nervously.

"You've gone crazy, Cooper."

"Perhaps," he said. "Perhaps."

CHAPTER
THIRTY-TWO

"Have you gone stark raving mad," asked the DI, incredulous, "sir?"

Cooper held up his palms in mock surrender. "It was the act of a desperate man," he said.

"Now he'll think we're in the market for information." Lucas lit a cigarette and smoked it furiously.

Cooper shrugged. "I thought of that," he said, feeling tired. "We pay crooks for information all the while; we pay them to tell us who's up to what, when the next consignment is coming in, who the buyers are . . . It's really no different."

"But this is Johnny Bristow, not some ten-bob nark. We don't want him thinking we owe him something."

"We're running out of time looking for a killer, Frank."

"You could have been done in," said the DI. He attacked the ashtray with the end of his cigarette.

Cooper shrugged. He was feeling strangely disconnected from the whole matter; as if a great weight had been taken from him and he was floating above it all, careless instead of helpless. It was not a bad feeling, he decided; certainly a chap could grow accustomed to it.

He went and fetched himself a slice of Victoria sponge from the canteen and made his way to the incident room. She was sitting at her desk, on the edge of which was perched Quennell. The boy detective was leaning over in the act of whispering something to her, perilously close to her neck, and seeing this Cooper felt a lurch of disappointment, of sourness, dyspepsia. A large box of chocolates was spread out on the desk in front of her, incongruous amid the tidy piles of paperwork and stationery items, and he watched her reach for one as she chatted gaily to Quennell all the while. He took another bite of cake. His plan was to make his way across the room to a desk over on the other side, as far away as possible, before she noticed him, but the mention of his name made him stop where he was, frozen in anticipation.

"DDI Cooper?" she was saying. His heart beat hard against his ribs. "Oh, I don't think so." She laughed and he thought how her laugh was so warm and melodic. "As a matter of fact," she said, "I had thought he might be queer . . ."

His heart plummeted faster than a falling lift, and the mouthful of sponge he had just taken tasted like sand in his mouth; or maybe it *was* sand: these days food was rarely what it purported to be. In a cold sweat, he tried to scurry away into a dark corner, but Quennell had seen him and was jumping off the edge of the desk and to attention.

"Morning, sir," the boy detective said. Cooper caught him casting a quick look askance at Tring.

256

"What the blazes is going on here?" Cooper bellowed; he was surprised by the power of his own voice, somehow finding its way from the depth of his misery.

She had snapped to it now, and was smiling. If she was shocked or anxious about having been overheard she didn't show it.

"Where did you get those blasted chocolates?" Cooper thundered. "No, don't answer that. Chances are, I don't want to know. Great Scott, we're running a murder investigation here . . ." She was hastily putting the lid on the box, trying to tidy it away out of sight. "If this is what happens when we let women . . ." He didn't finish the sentence He didn't have to. He was gratified to see her flush red all the way up from her neck. She was biting her lip and he wondered if she might be on the brink of tears; he was ashamed at the horrible pleasure he derived from the thought. "Quennell," he barked, "get over to St Ann's Road right away; there's been a break-in at a grocer's." Sod off, you little bastard, was what he wanted to say, but he rarely expressed anger: he was a master of suppressed rage, of suppression in general. Then he turned on her. "And I want that paperwork on my desk in fifteen minutes."

"Yes, sir," she said, "right away, sir."

He was feeling such a cad, but he had to keep up the pretence or else all would be lost. He stalked across the office and sat down heavily, fumbling with his pipe, with a match that wouldn't strike. The crumpled men had lifted their heads to glance at him with mild concern as he passed by their desks, but now they were yawning, stretching, returning their attention to their telephones, their cigarettes, the vast piles of papers in front of them. Oh Christ, he thought, whatever am I going to do? He was descending into despair and for a moment was gripped with a panic that he would not be able to stop falling, not ever. Shut up, you stupid bastard. Get a grip, man. People have been dying in their millions all over the world and you're fretting over some blasted girl. The sheer ludicrousness of the situation made him laugh, abruptly and entirely without any humour. He had finally succeeded in lighting his pipe, and sucking on it, was drawing in the comforting smoke in long, deep breaths.

When he opened his eyes, she was standing in front of him, clutching a sheaf of papers to her shapely bosom.

"Here's all the paperwork, sir," she was saying. He noticed that there was a deep crease of concern between her eyebrows. Of course, he should have known that she was far too efficient to let an idiot like Quennell with his blasted BM toffees hold her back in the pursuit of duty. "I do hope everything's alright." She deposited the forms into his in-tray, but lingered for a moment longer than was necessary. "Would you like me to fetch you a cup of tea and another slice of cake?" The crushed remains of the Victoria sponge were on the desk in front of him.

"That would be very nice," he said. "Thank you."

He felt like a child who had just thrown a tantrum, and instead of punishing him, his parents had reacted with shocked concern. When he met her eyes they were filled with pity.

"I should have thought of it earlier. I suppose that cake's all you've had to eat this morning."

"Please." He couldn't keep the groan from his voice. "Just . . ." He puffed on his pipe, letting the smoke conceal him in his shame. "A sandwich would be simply marvellous," he said.

She smiled kindly at him.

"I'll see what I can do."

She turned to leave, but he called her back.

"I didn't mean it," he said, "about women, I mean. I think you're doing a splendid job."

"Thank you, sir." She was looking very serious. "It matters to me what you think. In fact" — she took a deep breath — "it matters more than anything."

CHAPTER
THIRTY-THREE

It didn't take him long to determine that Nesta had pretty well cleaned him out of everything of any value. The travel clock was gone, so was every penny of his cash, and the cufflinks — though when he came to think about it, he had a vague remembrance of going with her to the Jew fence to sell them; if so, this must have occurred at some point, he was guessing, on Saturday night before they went to the Feathers. He ground his fists into his temples as he tried to drag the memory out of his brain, until he was exhausted. He'd been pretty sick at the tobacconist's, only just making it to the lav in time, and now he was feeling like he was going to spew again, even though he had nothing left to throw up, apart from the few glasses of water the tobacconist's wife had given him. He sat on the edge of the bed with his head in his hands and waited for the feeling to pass. Then, when he was quite sure that the floor wasn't moving, he stood up and went out on to the landing.

"You filthy, rotten whore!" he shouted at the top of his voice. He banged furiously on her door with the heel of his hand. "What have you done with all my stuff, you stinking bitch?" He tried the handle of her door, which was unlocked, and burst into the room. It only took a few moments to realise that she had gone: the room was empty, though the stale smell of her still hung about.

The landlord, a dreary halting old boy, had come up the stairs.

"You can't make that sort of a racket, you know," he was saying. "You can go and find somewhere else to live if you keep that up. This is a respectable house."

"Where's she gone?" he groaned. "She's taken everything."

He was feeling desperate, his head pounding; he had to steady himself against the iron bedstead to stop from fainting.

"Mrs Jones?" the landlord said. "She left on Sunday afternoon. Said she needed to get out of London for a bit. Wasn't sure if she'd be back. I've got someone coming to look at the room in a couple of hours."

He wasn't sure what he was supposed to do. His pal wouldn't be back on leave for another week, and he was too ill to go down to King's Cross and pinch a suitcase.

"I ain't got no money," he said. "She's taken everything. Hasn't even left me with a brass ha'penny."

His legs were shaking as he went back into his room. His eyes wouldn't focus properly. He rummaged desperately through all the pockets of his clothes; he was looking for loose change, but turned up nothing, not one stinking penny. He snatched the green swingback jacket from the back of the chair where he had left it, and patted it all the way down the front. To his amazement, there was something solid in one of the front pockets. He reached in and retrieved a silver cigarette case that he could have sworn blind he had never seen before in his life. He sat down on the bed and inspected it wonderingly, turning it over and over in his hand. There was an inscription on the front of it: it looked like an "L" and "F", and he supposed that it must have been in the suitcase even though he had no memory of it. Why had he put it in his pocket? Perhaps he'd been meaning to sell it along with the cufflinks? Well, that was his only hope now. He reckoned he'd get a few bob for it, though he couldn't risk taking it to a regular pawn shop. He smoked a cigarette and by the time he was done with it, he had sort of worked things out as much as he could and knew what he wanted to do. He was feeling a little bit better as he lay down on the bed clutching the cigarette case to his chest; he racked his brains to see if he could remember whereabouts in Holloway the Jew fence had been. After a few minutes of this effort, he closed his eyes against the pain in his head. A bad feeling was setting in around his heart and guts, very bad, a sort of fear. It had something to do with forcing himself to remember, with the missing part, with whatever it was that had been blasted out of him. It was such a horrible feeling that he thought he ought to give up the remembering for a while.

If I ever see that bloody bitch again, he was thinking, I'll choke the life out of her with my bare hands, so help me God.

CHAPTER
THIRTY-FOUR

He had just finished a bowl of Brown Windsor soup that tasted suspiciously like an Oxo cube dissolved in hot water, when the big break in the case came. He had more or less reached the end of the road. For the most part all a detective has to do is keep an ear cocked, but he had no desire to hear any more. He was done with it. Not just the sex murder, but the whole ruddy lot. He wanted to go away, somewhere, anywhere; as far away as possible from the smell of gas and the dust, from the smuts burning in the back of his throat, from narks and cups of cold tea; from her. He knew that he had nobody but himself to blame for the misery of his life.

All suffering is the result of the careless drift towards blissful numbness, the foolish pursuit of reassurance and peace. There was to be no peace, he understood that now; not for him, not for anyone. If he was a religious man perhaps he might have persuaded himself that there was always something to hope for, but he had lost his taste for redemption in the mud of '17.

He would never have supposed, therefore, that redemption, when it came, would come to him in the form of a nineteen-year-old waitress with a squint. He was mopping up the last of the Brown Windsor soup with a stale roll, when Tring appeared before him with the news that Joyce had telephoned.

"She recognised him at once," she was saying, breathless with the excitement of it all.

He would probably never feel excited about anything ever again, but he did permit himself a slight flicker of anticipation. She was smiling at him and her eyes were bright and shining.

"Dennis?" he said.

Tring frowned slightly.

"No, 'fraid not," she said. "But Nesta Jones's soldier boyfriend has just walked into the café. I've told Joyce to make sure he waits for us."

Cooper grabbed his hat from the table and they both moved quickly to the motor.

"Just imagine," she was saying as she manoeuvred the car on to the main road, "we might have the whole case wrapped up within a few hours." He smiled indulgently. It was unlikely, but you never knew. "It's a great breakthrough, isn't it, sir?" She glanced at him, looking for reassurance.

"It's certainly an exciting development," he conceded. Just because he was dead inside, it didn't entitle him to clamp down on the hopes and dreams of others. "Jolly well done, Joyce and you."

"Me? I didn't do anything!"

"Yes, you did. You made Joyce feel that she was part of the investigation. If I had gone into the café on my own, chances are that she would never have telephoned us. She'd have been more concerned about defying her boss."

264

They pulled up outside the café, and as he stepped on to the pavement and put on his hat, Cooper could see Joyce through the window. She was chatting to a tall young man with close-cropped fair hair. He stood aside to let Tring walk in ahead of him, and the waitress grinned shyly at her in greeting.

"This is Corporal O'Leary," she said. "He's friends with Mrs Jones."

The Irishman tipped a finger at Cooper.

"I was her friend," he said. "We've been down in Brighton over the past few days, but we had a row about her drinking. She's a terrible woman when she's had a drop of gin."

"Whereabouts in Brighton can we find her?" asked Cooper.

"Oh, she's not in Brighton any more — as far as I know."

"Any idea where she is?"

The soldier shook his head.

"She left the hotel we'd been staying in without paying the bill," he said. "I had to fork out the best part of two quid."

Another blasted brick wall, Cooper thought. Tring was hovering beside him, and he wanted to protect her from the disappointment.

"When Mrs Jones was in London," Cooper said, "do you happen to know where she stayed?" He wasn't at all sure if it had been that sort of relationship — the soldier couldn't have been more than twenty-three, twenty-four — but nothing surprised him any more.

"Oh yes," said Corporal O'Leary. "To be sure. I've been there quite a few times. Nesta liked to have little parties." As a matter of fact, he could take them there now; it wasn't very far. They could easily walk there, but he didn't have a problem with going in the motor.

Nesta had been living in the spindly etiolated house for the best part of two years, and the spindly etiolated landlord had been somewhat surprised at the suddenness with which she had departed on the previous Sunday. She had, or so she had told him, come into a bit of luck and fancied taking herself off to the coast. As he led the way up the stairs he told them that he hoped they wouldn't take long as he was expecting somebody who was interested in taking the room. The landlord opened the door and Cooper stepped inside. The room was small, dark and devoid of any of the usual signs of occupation. The brown flocked wallpaper had, he hoped, seen better days; there was a rug, thrown over floorboards that had been painted black, which had had great gouges chewed out of it by moths. There was a lingering stale smell, which had been overlaid with Flit, presumably coming from the mattress as a precaution against bugs. It didn't take Cooper more than a couple of minutes to deduce that there was nothing there worth finding. Tring hung back in the doorway, watching him so closely as he moved about the room he felt obliged to put on a bit of a show, cursorily picking up the edge of the counterpane, opening and closing each of the empty drawers of the dressing table in turn, unlocking the door of the empty wardrobe. When he had exhausted all possibilities he sighed deeply and stood in the middle of the room stroking his chin.

They were just thanking the landlord when another door on the landing creaked open and a young fellow appeared before them, not much more than twenty-two, twenty-three, Cooper reckoned. He was probably quite good-looking, but had gone rather to seed.

The kid was contemplating Policewoman Tring with a sneer, and then he turned on Cooper.

"About bloody time too," he shouted. His speech was slurred and he appeared to be swaying slightly in the doorway.

"Now, now, Dennis," said the landlord. Tring gasped and Cooper's heart lurched into his mouth. "We don't want any trouble, do we?"

"Hope you find the filthy old bag," the fellow continued. It was dark on the landing, but Cooper scrutinised the boy's face until quite certain of a small fading bruise just above his left cheekbone. "When are you going to find my money?"

"What money's that, then?" asked Cooper.

"She stole all my money," the kid was saying. "Every fucking penny."

"Language," said the landlord.

"Something oughter be done. You can't have people going around stealing other people's money." His protest subsided into a fit of coughing. He didn't look at all well and was gripping the door jamb; for a moment he looked as if he might collapse. Tring instinctively reached out and grabbed his arm.

"Help me get him back into his room," she said.

They managed to bring the young man to the edge of his bed, where he sat with his head between his knees, Tring keeping a slight pressure on the back of his neck. She asked the landlord to fetch a glass of water, and looked at Cooper with huge, startled eyes. He could see the rise and fall of her breasts beneath her jacket. He lifted his hand, waving it slightly in a practised gesture of reassurance and quiescence, and she let out a deep sigh of composure.

Cooper grazed the room; it was his custom and what detectives did. He spotted the green tweed jacket almost immediately.

"Is this yours?" he inquired carelessly.

The young man looked up briefly. "Yes," he said.

"Nice jacket. Very good quality. Generous cut." It wasn't enough, of course; he knew that. But there were too many coincidences, and coincidences always made him suspicious. "Where do you find a jacket like that?"

The young man shrugged. "Got it down Petticoat Lane," he said. Cooper knew he was lying.

"Mind if I have a look around? Just in case Mrs Jones has left any evidence . . ."

Cooper didn't wait for permission. He moved skilfully around the room. In the wardrobe there was a neatly pressed sailor's uniform hanging alongside some items of very good-quality clothing; there was a brown leather suitcase that must have cost a bob or two. He picked up a pair of brown brogues that would have set anyone back fifteen guineas.

"Sailor, eh?" he said, familiarly.

"I was. Spent four years on the Atlantic convoys."

"Hard going, I'll bet."

The kid shrugged again.

"I think I'm going to be sick," he said.

Tring took the glass of water from the landlord.

"Drink this," she said. "You'll feel better."

"What's your name, son?"

"What d'you need to know my name for?"

"It's standard procedure when investigating a theft to take down the victim's name."

"Dennis. Dennis Belcher."

Cooper nodded circumspectly. Tring was beseeching him with her eyes, but he wasn't going to rush. His eyes came to rest on the bed where the boy was sitting. It was unmade and the linen was in need of a good laundry. He ran his eyes over it until something caught his eye.

"Looks like Mrs Jones didn't take everything," he said.

Dennis turned to where Cooper was indicating, and picked up the silver cigarette case.

"Funny thing," he said. "I never seen that before today. I thought maybe she'd had it from another room and the ugly thieving bitch left it behind while she was going through my things. It's got an inscription on it."

"Mind if I take a look?"

Dennis handed him the cigarette case with a slight shrug and a sneer. Cooper turned it over in his hand, opening it; closing it. Most of this was done for show: he had made out the "L" and the "F" within a couple of seconds. And he didn't doubt for a moment that

Walter Frobisher would be able to identify it as the property of his late wife.

He looked at the kid while considering his next move. Tring was pretty strong and he could certainly look after himself. The boy, on the other hand, looked like death warmed up and, as far as he could tell, was unlikely to be carrying a weapon.

"Dennis Belcher," he said, "I'm arresting you on suspicion of the murder of Mrs Lillian Frobisher."

The boy was taking a drink of water. He looked up at Cooper with the glass poised halfway towards his lips. As Cooper went through the rest of the formula, he laughed lightly. Then he frowned.

"You gotta be joking," he said.

CHAPTER
THIRTY-FIVE

The picture hadn't been all that good. Maybe it was the heat, which was awful. She was in a bath of perspiration, and found herself wishing it was over long before the end. It had been a very bad idea to go to the pictures on such a warm evening, but then she hadn't had any choice in the matter, had she? As people started to leave, she remained seated. The cinema manager knew her and was friendly enough. She wondered if he might like to go for a coffee with her, but dismissed the notion as fanciful almost as soon as it had come to her.

After a short while she picked up her jacket from the back of the seat, slipped her handbag over her arm and made her way outside. There is no feeling worse than finding yourself alone on a busy street, having left the sheltering fug of a picture-house. She stood on the pavement, looking along the road in the direction of home. Home. That made her laugh. She didn't have a home. She had a bomb-site and a senile mother and a son who had his own life and didn't need her any more. That was it, now that she couldn't any longer say that she had a husband. In spite of the sultry night air, she shuddered, hugged herself and prepared to walk back. She was going to cross the road to catch a bus: it was only a short distance, but there was no street lighting for most of it, and the world was still a dangerous place.

"Hullo, blondie."

She stopped where she was. The thrill, a little burst of triumph, was undeniable. Coo, she thought, what it is to have sex appeal. He was standing a short distance off, lighting a cigarette, his hand cupped over the match. He appeared to be swaying ever so slightly and she guessed he was probably a little bit tipsy, recollecting that they'd had a consignment of gin at the Feathers. It didn't bother her. Perhaps he'd need a bit of Dutch courage.

"What was the picture like?" he asked. "Any good?"

"Not really."

"Thought I'd walk you home."

She paused; there was a moment, a heartbeat, during the course of which she almost said no to him. But it was only a moment and it passed.

"That's very nice of you."

They walked together in silence towards Cally Road.

When they were about to turn the corner into her street, she stopped and placed her hand on his arm.

"Is that it?" she said. And he pulled her towards him and kissed her full on the mouth. He tasted of alcohol and cigarettes, but the kiss was warming, liberating.

"It's been such a long time," she sighed as they broke apart.

What follows is the ending of A Commonplace Killing transcribed from Siân's notebook after her death.

-R.P.

CHAPTER
THIRTY-SIX

He had sobered up quite a bit. The kid was skinny in his underpants; he looked scared and vulnerable against the stark prison walls. Pentonville was the most cheerless place on earth. Cooper noted that there were no bruises, scratches, no signs of violent struggle whatever, anywhere on the boy's body — apart from the tell-tale bruise on his cheek. When they had seen enough, Lucas handed the kid some mismatched clothes taken from his room, and they watched him get dressed.

"Tell me again, Dennis," said Cooper. His tone was avuncular, even kindly. It was a ploy he used, ever the gent. "Where'd you get that bruise?"

The kid shrugged. "Dunno," he said.

"Seems to me," observed Lucas, looking up from the page upon which he was making notes, "you don't know a lot."

"I told you," Dennis said, "I don't remember. Really I don't. I don't remember anything about Saturday or Sunday after going to the pub."

Cooper sighed. "I want to believe you, Dennis," he said, "really I do; but you must see how queer it looks."

The kid sat down in the chair and folded his hands together on the table, resting his head upon them as though he was in prayer. Lucas passed the kid a cigarette, lit it for him and signalled to the uniform to get some tea.

Dennis drew long and hard on the gasper, his eyes levelled on the table-top. Then he looked up at Cooper: "I can see this looks bad," he said, "but you gotta believe me, mister. I really don't remember."

Lucas sighed impatiently, retreating behind a cloud of smoke. He found it hard, sometimes, this taking things slowly: Cooper could tell he thought the kid was guilty as sin.

"The thing is," the kid was saying, "I got a bash on the nut when I was in the convoys and ever since then it's like . . ." He paused, turning the cigarette on the edge of the ashtray. "I dunno, it's like something's not quite right." He tapped the side of his head. "It's like something's fallen out, a part of my brain, or something. It's like something's missing."

He leaned back in the chair and finished the cigarette.

"I'm pretty sure I'd remember if I killed someone," he said after a moment's contemplation. He leaned forward to stub out the fag. "I'm pretty sure I'd remember that."

Cooper could sense Lucas bristle in the chair beside him. The uniform came in with a tray of teas. They all took a few sips.

"Do you know a woman called Lillian Frobisher?" Cooper asked.

The kid appeared to be thinking hard, his brow furrowed in concentration. He put his hand across his forehead, rubbing his temples hard.

"Did she say I know her?"

"She's dead," growled Lucas. "She's the poor cow you choked the life out of on Saturday night."

Dennis groaned. He pushed the teacup away.

"I swear to God, mister, I don't remember anything about Saturday night. You gotta believe me."

Cooper nodded circumspectly. The kid was like most of his generation: aged before his time; an uncomfortable mixture of worldliness and youth — even childishness. A veneer of cynicism masked bewilderment; a practised sneer on full boyish lips that quivered at the slightest provocation.

"Tell me about the convoys, Dennis," Cooper said. "Must have been tough."

The kid shrugged, pulled the teacup towards him, drinking the contents down in one gulp.

"What is there to say?" he said sneerlingly. "The constant racket, the horrible food, the lack of sleep, the lousy clothes, the cold and damp. I was seasick for six weeks. Lay on my bunk wishing I was dead. When you're on a boat in the middle of the ocean there's fuck-all you can do about it. You can't go into town for a beer, can you? I used to try and imagine how it would be — drowning. Never thought I'd make it through. Never give it a second thought. Drowning." He let out a hard, cynical laugh. "Only way out for a matelot."

"War's a terrible thing," murmured Cooper, instantly despising the platitude. Lucas lit another cigarette and rolled one to the kid, along with a box of matches. Dennis was staring at his hands, splayed upon the table-top. "Makes you realise we're all just meat," he said. He seemed lost in thought for a moment or two; then: "Someone shouted torpedo," he was saying, "and I saw this white line cutting through the water, coming towards the ship. I ran to the other side and there was this terrific bang which rocked the whole craft, so I tried to make my way to the boat deck like they tell you to do in training, but another torpedo came at the other side and all I can remember is flying through the air towards this great wall of flame and looking down beneath me and seeing the sea all on fire, and scattered with arms and legs and heads and pieces of the ship. And that's when it must have happened."

"What?"

"I told you. That's when whatever it was was blasted out of me."

Cooper took a sip of tea without taking his eyes off the kid.

"What do you think it was?" he asked.

Dennis shrugged. He sighed, leaning back in his chair until it tipped off its two front legs, his hands folded behind his back.

"Dunno," he said, "but it was some part of me that I needed — same as if it had been an arm or a leg. Only because nobody can see it's gone, nobody gives a shit."

"Did you talk to the navy doctors about any of this?"

"Fucking navy couldn't care less," the kid sneered. "All they do is tell you about VD and how there are plenty worse off than you are. I got two weeks'

276

survivor's leave. The depot they took me to had vermin running up and down the walls. There was one shower for a hundred men."

"So you thought you'd come home and strangle women," said Lucas coolly.

The kid lit the cigarette and blew a smoke ring towards the ceiling.

"I already told you," he said. "I don't fucking remember anything about Saturday night. I was ginned up. And sometimes when I've had too much to drink I lose . . . It's like it's all gone. Gone for good. I don't even remember coming home and going to bed. I didn't even know that fucking bitch was in my room and stealing all my stuff."

"Yes," said Lucas; "all your stuff . . ." He dropped the name of the gentleman who had had his suitcase stolen from King's Cross; the suitcase with the mackintosh and the green swingback jacket and the items Nesta had fenced. "Know him, do you? Did he give you permission to take his bag home with you?"

Dennis, amazed, looked back and forth between Lucas and Cooper.

"What's that gotta do with any of this?" he asked.

Cooper rubbed his chin.

"Never mind that now," he said. "We'll take a short break. Finish your cigarette. Want another cup of tea?" He signalled to Lucas to step outside.

"This is going to take a bloody long time," he said when they were in the corridor.

Lucas pursed his lips around his cigarette.

"A good barrister could make something of that head wound." The DI looked at him quizzically. It would be a miracle if a good barrister were to be found for the five-pound fee paid out under the terms of the Poor Prisoner Defence Act.

Lucas issued a long irritated stream of smoke from his nostrils.

"There's more than enough evidence, sir," he said, "and he's a bad hat alright. I've never seen anyone more likely to end up the subject of a short stop-press in the evening edition in all my born days."

Cooper nodded distractedly.

"Maybe," he said.

"I wouldn't believe him if he told me twelve pennies make a shilling."

"Let's leave him alone for a bit and then show him the victim's photograph. See how he reacts. Meanwhile, ask the lab whether they've cross-checked the fibre with the green jacket. And get the lad something to eat. He's probably starving."

Cooper certainly was and he needed some air. He hated the stale air of Pentonville. He took himself across the Cally Road to the station canteen, mildly afraid that Tring might be there. He ate a plate of fried Spam and mashed potato, washed down with a cup of coffee. Then he lit a pipe.

"Mind if I join you, sir?" she said. She always looked so fresh, no matter what time of day or what had occurred. He shook his head and puffed away, retreating beneath a comfortable shelter of smoke, while she sat down with a cup of tea and a couple of biscuits.

"I just wanted to say, sir," she said, "how absolutely marvellous you were."

He demurred.

"Well, thank you for being so calm and helpful. You must have been jolly nervous."

She grinned. "I've never seen anyone being arrested before, never mind a murderer."

"It went well enough." He lit his pipe again.

"Are they usually so, well, so calm?"

"Not often."

"It was strange how he reacted. Almost as if he knew it couldn't possibly have been him. Telling you his name and everything." She shuddered. "Not a flicker of emotion or guilt or anything."

"He doesn't believe he did it."

She dipped one of her biscuits in her tea and bit into it as she thought about what he'd said.

"But we know he did. He must have done. All the evidence . . ."

"Oh, he did it alright. But he doesn't think he did." Cooper drew on his pipe. "He's brain-damaged. War wound."

"He isn't just saying that?"

Cooper turned down the corners of his mouth.

"Maybe. Lucas thinks so."

"And what do you think?"

"Quite honestly? I don't know. I haven't decided yet. I need to spend a little more time with him. The demeanour of a chap under questioning is the whole matter really," he said. "It's not so much what a suspect tells you as the way he tells it — or not." She nodded thoughtfully.

"He'd have to be jolly clever to pull off a ruse like that," she said.

"Yes. He would."

She cradled her teacup in her hands, blowing the heat off its surface.

"I really admire you, sir. I think you're one of the finest men I've ever known."

"Well . . . hardly . . ."

"No. I really mean it. And the respect most of the men have for you . . ."

He was wondering whether a girl admiring you in the way that she meant could ever be induced to love you. Marry you. He told himself not to be so ridiculous and puffed heavily on his pipe three or four times in rapid succession until she was almost lost to him in the resulting haze.

"I love you," he wanted to say. But he did not. He knew that he never would, the moment having passed for ever.

"I'm very impressed with the manner in which you've conducted yourself the past few days," he told her instead. "I'd be delighted to give you any sort of reference, recommendation . . ."

She beamed at him.

"I suppose," she said, "we've made a pretty good team, haven't we?"

"Yes," he said, feeling his heart break. "Absolutely. A damn fine team."

280

CHAPTER
THIRTY-SEVEN

They stopped on a corner just outside of the lambency of the street lamps. A road stretched out ahead of them, ramshackle, war-scarred. You could just make out the stump of a house in the thin light spilling from the windows of buildings on either side of it. There was a doorway, or the remains of one, stopped up with a piece of rusting corrugated iron, at the bottom of which was a chink the size of a man's boot. He pulled her towards him again and kissed her hard. He slid his hands over her hips. "You naughty boy," she said. "You mustn't do that."

"I really like you, blondie," he murmured into her hair. And for one wild, abandoned moment she thought of taking him back to the house with her, to spite Walter, but she didn't want to upset Douglas.

"Don't you have somewhere we can go?" she said, thinking that a spiv must have a flat or a room somewhere. He didn't respond. As they stood there, a couple emerged, laughing, from behind the corrugated iron. The woman was smoothing her dress; the man was slicking his hair back out of his eyes. The couple stood for a moment in what had been a front garden, lingering, not wanting the moment to end, before moving off, hand in hand, up the road.

The spiv took her by the arm and gently pulled her towards the bombed house.

"C'mon, blondie," he slurred. He pushed the corrugated iron slightly to one side and gestured for her to go through.

"Oh," she said. "I don't want to ruin my stockings."

"You can take them off," he said. "I can help you if you like."

They laughed; he had her by the hand now and was leading her towards a tree. He stumbled. She helped him up. They were laughing a good deal by now, like two kids. She hadn't laughed like that in a long while.

"I'm well and truly lit up," he said. "But I really like you, so it shouldn't be a problem . . ."

It was all a little bit wild, dangerous; she felt heady, like she was drunk too, like she was the sort of woman who did this sort of thing: went with strange men on bomb-sites. The thought of it gave her a thrill that ran through the whole length of her body. She leaned against the tree and with a sudden abandonment of all reason, all sanity, pulled him towards her and kissed him hard, full on the lips. She didn't mind the gin and cigarettes. She didn't care about anything. He wiped off her lipstick with the back of his hand. After a while he took a step back and swaying slightly said:

"C'mon, blondie. You know you want to."

And oh she did. How much she did.

He put his mackintosh, which he had swung over his shoulder, down on the ground, after kicking a few bits of rubble out of the way. She slowly lifted her skirt and pulled down her drawers. Then they both sat down on the mackintosh beneath the tree and started kissing again, feverishly, like a couple of kids. He reached up under her skirt, over the tops of her stockings. She moaned and slid down beneath his weight and let him take her. It was all she wanted at that moment; it was as if it was all she had ever wanted, and she didn't care what happened next. She didn't any longer care about any of it.

CHAPTER
THIRTY-EIGHT

They had left him for a good long while in the bare brown-and-cream painted room, prison sound echoing all around. At least it seemed a good long while. He had no way of knowing for sure, and time had been dragging on, like in a dream, since the detective, the quiet one, the one who was trying to be his pal, had arrested him for the murder of some bint he had never heard of. Now they were back with another cup of tea and a plate of fucking biscuits. If he had any more tea he'd need to take a piss and he wasn't sure they'd let him, especially not the other copper, the arsehole who hated him. The feeling was mutual.

"Had time to think, Dennis?" the quiet one was asking him. If he hadn't known better he might have believed the bastard was actually worried about him. He reminded him of one of the navy chaplains who always had a slightly queasy smile on his fat chops. "Got anything you'd like to tell me?"

"I've been thinking," he said, "and I can't see what evidence you've got to pin this on me. Can't you tell me?"

The detective sighed and turned down the corner of his mouth.

"No," he said. "I'm afraid I can't. Not just yet."

The other detective lit a fag and passed it to him across the table. Then he took a photograph from the pile of papers in front of him and slid it over.

It proper shook him up. He was wondering about all the other times he'd been well and truly lit up — got so weak in the head and lost his place in the world. He looked at the photo for several moments.

"Is that her?" he asked.

"Do you know her?" the friendly detective was looking all concerned.

He needed to think this through. He remembered, vaguely, a woman who looked a bit like this one. If he tried hard, he could, in a flash, see her face upturned towards his and smiling at him through a gin and Bass fog. He thought he could even remember the sweet powdery smell coming off her.

He knew it looked bad. He was afraid of what would happen next. He pushed the photograph away from him, thinking that he might be sick if he looked at it any longer. He drew hard on the cigarette until it made him cough, bringing tears to his eyes.

"The thing is," he said, "I don't remember. Everything's a blur. I'd had rather a lot to drink."

The bastard detective pounded his fist on the table so hard their teacups jumped in the air.

"Do you know her or don't you?" The other detective kept his eyes on him all the while and didn't say a word. "I'm sick of all this tosh about not remembering," said the arsehole. "Tell you what, sunny Jim, you had better start getting your memory back pretty damn quickly."

"I told you before: I got a knock on the head and when I've had a bit to drink I don't always know where I am, what I did, stuff like that."

He swallowed hard. He didn't want to cry in front of them. He pinched the fag hard between his thumb and forefinger until it was all but done with. Then he ground out the stub, stroking it against the side of the ashtray.

Cooper wished on these occasions that he could have the certainty of a man like Lucas, who for the most part occupied a black-and-white world where the line between right and wrong was clearly defined, rigid. On those occasions when he cared at all, which, increasingly, was not often these days, Cooper could not allow himself to be certain about anything. He could not inhabit a stark landscape of Right and Wrong, as all policemen must for the sake of their own souls, where he and all those like him were "good" and men like the prisoner were "bad". He understood that it helped to tell oneself that such men got what they deserved, but he had come to expect no such justice in this out-of-kilter world. He supposed that if he did care he would never sleep at night.

He rubbed his eyes as the boy told them, yet again, that he could not remember anything at all between entering the Castle public house at eight o'clock on Saturday night and waking up in his rooms on Tuesday morning. He let the kid tell him again about the knock on the head, the missing part, the effect drink had on him, and let weariness wash over him; the same weariness he always experienced when crooks went through their patter. Everyone was innocent; nobody was guilty. It was a wonder so much crime was committed. The same weariness when he read the newspaper or listened to the wireless. The drift towards the inevitable: Yanks against Russians; fear of Stalin instead of Hitler; Germany; the Balkans; Nuremberg; the atom bomb; Buchenwald. He sighed and turned his teacup in its saucer. What did it matter, really, if the kid did it, or said he did it, or went on and on about his blasted war wound? Lillian Frobisher was dead and nothing would bring her back. Lucas, beside him, pounded the table in frustration. He believed in guilt, confession, retribution. The kid went on again about how he couldn't remember. He wasn't sneering now. He was scared. He looked as if he might cry, his head wreathed in cigarette smoke; he reached across the table, stroking the end of the gasper in a ruminative gesture against the side of the ashtray. Cooper was aware of him looking straight at him, his skinny face pinched with fear.

"Tell me, mister," he said. "If a fellow went with a woman and they got into a fight or something and she ended up dead, would it still be murder?"

Lucas sat back in his chair smoking absently, flabbergasted, ash falling unnoticed, unimpeded on to his lapels.

Cooper swallowed hard. "Is that what you're saying happened, Dennis?" he asked.

The kid was crying.

CHAPTER
THIRTY-NINE

Policewoman Tring and he went together to the funeral of Lillian Frobisher. It always seemed the least he could do, even when a case remained unsolved. Of course he had succeeded in finding the murderer of the unfortunate woman, so her family and friends were warm and receptive. It embarrassed him. It was nothing, really, he assured them. Routine police work. A team effort. Tring had arranged for a utility wreath of red and pink carnations on behalf of "N" Division. It was the last occasion on which he would see her; although she stayed on at Cally Road to complete the paperwork in connection with the investigation, he had no reason to go there. She was to drop him a line a few weeks after, saying that Hendon was to train police officers and she was going to apply and would he support her application. Of course he would. He had rehearsed what he would say to her, a ludicrous fantasy, should she ever decide to take an interest in him. He was to tell her that he had gone to a place of perpetual gloom and misery and that there was nothing to be done about it. You don't want anything to do with me, he would say; I'm old and battered and I don't any longer see the point of much. He could see her green eyes soften. Let me help you; I want to help. But he didn't want her to. That's just it — he would only end up despising himself even more if he were to trap her in his self-loathing. Upstairs wanted him back at division HQ hunting down black-market toothpowder and rubber heels and knicker elastic. It hadn't taken long for the arrest of Dennis Belcher to recede from the superintendent's attention: a few days. It had, after all, been nothing more than a commonplace killing.

Walter Frobisher, in his hard-worn suit, and clutching his battered bowler, thanked him earnestly, tears streaming down his face, until Evelyn, cheapening one of the victim's smart black costumes, a couple of sizes too small for her, came across and slipped her arm through his, pulling him away. He and Tring thanked Lillian's sister for the kind invitation to join the mourners at the pub for a glass of brown ale, but declined. "Brown ale," the sister had said. "I ask you."

As they prepared to leave, Douglas Frobisher approached them, his face blotchy with grief. He put out his hand and Cooper shook it warmly.

"I'm sorry, old chap."

Douglas thanked him politely.

"One thing," he said as Cooper and Tring turned to leave. "Would mum . . . would she . . . did she . . ." — his face crumpled — "is it a bad way to die? Was there pain? I keep thinking of her alone and frightened." Tears were streaming down the kid's face. Tring stepped forward and put her arm across his shoulder.

"It's over for her, son," said Cooper. "It would have been over for her very quickly. No time to fear anything. No time at all."

The boy nodded, wiping tears away with his fists.

"Thank you, Inspector" he said. "I'm so glad that you caught him and he's going to hang."

CHAPTER
FORTY

The condemned cell at Pentonville; he can hear the maudlin singing coming from the Irish pub across the Cally Road.

Cooper, like most, if not all detectives, if they are being honest, yearned always for a confession. Especially in a hanging matter. They rarely came; not like in the crime novels. He knew that the boy was guilty — the evidence told him that — but he wanted to be certain that the boy knew that he was guilty; that he could remember some part of that evening's events; the moment at which Lillian Frobisher had had the life squeezed out of her.

"Tell me, Dennis, it doesn't matter now, but I'd like to know: did you do it?"

The boy shrugged.

"If they say I did," he said, "then I suppose I must have done."

CHAPTER
FORTY-ONE

They lay back on the stony ground, looking at the stars. He lit two cigarettes and handed one to her and they smoked in silence, the glowing tips dancing against the black unforgiving sky. After a while she heard him snoring beside her. Hardly glamorous, is it, dear? she thought. Hardly cocktails at Quaglino's. The shattered buildings, the bonfire air, the trains shrieking, rattling, shunting down the line a few yards away, the wet and gritty soot catching in the back of your throat, settling on your hair and clothes. Soon, in a minute or two, she would get up, put on her drawers and make her way back through the shabby unlit streets. Normally she would take a bus the short distance from Caledonian Road, but there was nothing to fear now. It would be like the war and not like the war. She would not be making her way through dawn streets to the sound of pavements being swept, the tattered curtains fluttering in front of windows that were no longer there. No siren. No All Clear. No crashing. No splintering. No falling bombs. No Yank airmen with boxes of "candy". No longing sighs and yearning regrets and fond heartfelt goodbyes. So young. So handsome. So brave. Steadying your hand as they lit you. Oh dear, Lillian, she thought, what have you come to? Now she knew for sure that there was nothing else; nothing at all. Just more and more of the same until it all ended.

She felt the spiv stir beside her, moving in the shadows. She would ask him to walk her home. She wondered how much he'd give her for her mother's coupons. Her thighs were stiff and there was a slight chill across her bare breasts. She reckoned she must look a state. She needed to powder her nose. She needed to get on. She groped the ground beside her for the pigskin handbag; it was a few moments before she realised that it was gone, and a few moments more before she realised that the spiv was kneeling on the ground beside her, going through its contents.

"You little bastard," she cried. She got on to her knees and tried to take the bag from him. "You thieving sod!" She sloshed him. He tried to slosh her back, but missed. She tugged at the handbag. "Give me that, you little bugger. You sod. You thieving bastard." They grappled over the bag. "Don't be like that blondie," he was saying.

"Don't you blondie me . . ." He wrenched the bag from her and she toppled backwards with the force. She started screaming. "Thief! Thief!"

"Shuddup, you silly cow," he was saying. "Shuddup. Shuddup. Shuddup."

The last thing she saw was his white face looming over her, his hands coming towards her. Oh, the shame. The shame was all hers.

CHAPTER
FORTY-TWO

He was tired and the night air was muffled with gasometers and traffic and dereliction. The moon was far away and misty. He listened to a few gramophone records and drank a glass of Scotch, but it didn't help him to sleep.

He was thinking of the boy. Usually murderers seemed unreal to him, distant. He could push them away: the wide boys, the cosh-boys. He had dealt with a few in his time and some of them had deserved to hang, whereas others had been victims of circumstance. This boy was different somehow. What he had done was the end result of one long suicide attempt; attempt at self-murder, intended to scratch out the botched part of himself; the part that the war had gouged out of his brain.

Cooper tried not to think of the boy lying awake in the condemned cell on his last night on earth. It would be so hard to die like that, he thought; knowing the precise moment. Nine o'clock tomorrow morning. To have death steal up on you knowingly, expectantly. He imagined that all you can do in such circumstance as that would be to deny that it is going to happen; believe that there will be a reprieve — even up to the last second. He thought of the poor kid, too terrified to sleep, waiting for the final creak of the cell door, the warden asking what he would like to eat. "You can have anything you fancy, son."

That last act of kindness. In an hour you will be dead; a healthy sentient being, dead; with the doctor leaning over you listening for a heartbeat. It was dawn before he fell into a troubled fractured sleep, against the first stirring of the birds over in Clissold Park, with images of a shuddering mortal in the grip of terror populating his brain — just such a one as he had been. Jaws clenched. Shoulders rigid. Tears streaming down his face.

The deep black well of sleep was shattered by the jangle of the telephone. He stumbled through to the hall. It was Lucas. "Just thought you'd like to know Belcher is dead. They need you at Pentonville to identify the body."

The body was quite sound — apart from the marks of suspension. Cooper duly signed the form. The man of whose body I have had the view was Dennis Belcher. He asked the warder if there had been a last-minute confession. There hadn't.

And that was that.

It was a crisp early-autumn morning when Cooper stepped outside the prison; clear blue skies with not a cloud to be seen. He started walking towards Stoke Newington High Street, to division HQ. He had the feeling that he had once done something worthwhile, something good, but he had forgotten whatever it was and now would never remember it. It had been a very long time ago.

The streets were shabby in the bright light; grey and covered in a thin layer of dust. He walked on past hoardings inviting him to buy things he had no need of, but which were impossible to get in any case. *Cadbury means quality. Don't be vague, ask for Haig. Vote Communist.* He thought how tired everybody looked, how drawn and haggard; how threadbare. It was as if the childish hope that it would be alright, somehow, some day, when things were like they used to be, had been extinguished, and they had become conscious that it had not all been a bad dream from which they would all awaken.

He couldn't face the office, so he went to Clissold Park instead. He was looking for affirmation there under the golden brown trees. Little children skipping. Dogs running after sticks. He sat down on a bench and told himself that if there was doubt then there would have to be faith too, in among the mangled steel and splintered wood and dark alleys and greasy cafés. There had to be some reason to keep going. He wondered if it were enough simply to desire faith. There were tears in his eyes as he closed them and tried so hard, to imagine a better future.

Also available in ISIS Large Print:

Brighton Belle

Sara Sheridan

1951, Brighton. With the excitement of the war over and the Nazis brought to justice at Nuremberg, Mirabelle Bevan, ex-Secret Service, moves to the seaside to put the past behind her. She takes a job as a secretary at a debt collection agency run by the charismatic Big Ben McGuigan, but when confronted by the case of Romana Laszlo, a pregnant Hungarian refugee, Mirabelle discovers that her specialist knowledge is vital. With enthusiastic assistance from the pretty insurance clerk down the corridor, Vesta Churchill, Mirabelle follows a mysterious trail of gold sovereigns, betting scams and bodies to a dark corner of Austerity Britain where the forces of evil remain alive and well.

ISBN 978-0-7531-9090-6 (hb)
ISBN 978-0-7531-9091-3 (pb)

Sidney Chambers and the Shadow of Death

James Runcie

Sidney Chambers, the Vicar of Grantchester, is a 32-year-old bachelor. Tall, with eyes the colour of hazelnuts, he is both an unconventional clergyman and a reluctant detective. Working in association with his friend, Inspector Geordie Keating, Sidney is able to go where the Police cannot, eliciting surprise revelations and confessions from his parishioners; whether it involves the apparent suicide of a local solicitor, a scandalous jewellery theft at a New Year's Eve dinner party, or the unexplained death of a jazz promoter's daughter. Alongside his inquiries, Sidney also manages to find time to enjoy cricket, warm beer, hot jazz, and the company of an attractive, lively young woman called Amanda.

ISBN 978-0-7531-9044-9 (hb)
ISBN 978-0-7531-9045-6 (pb)